Elinor Brent-Dyer was born in 1894. To mark the centenary of her birth, Armada are publishing a facsimile edition of her first Chalet School book, *The School at the Chalet*, which was first published in 1925 by W. & R. Chambers Ltd of Edinburgh. Chambers were among the leading publishers of school stories at this time.

The School at the Chalet was not Elinor's first published book (this was *Gerry Goes to School*, which is no longer in print), but it remains the most popular. This new edition is a faithful copy of that produced in 1930 (because no owner was willing to allow their earlier edition to be submitted to the ravages of the printing process!) and the cover has been reproduced from an original jacket, with a little retouching where the old jacket was torn or marked.

First published in Great Britain by
W & R Chambers Ltd 1925
This facsimile edition
first published in Armada 1994
3 5 7 9 10 8 6 4 2

Armada is an imprint of
HarperCollins Children's Books,
a division of HarperCollins Publishers Ltd,
77/85 Fulham Palace Road, Hammersmith,
London W6 8JB

ISBN 0 00 674912-7

Printed and bound in Great Britain by
HarperCollins Manufacturing, Glasgow

The School at the Châlet

BY

ELINOR M. BRENT-DYER

AUTHOR OF
'GERRY GOES TO SCHOOL,' 'THE MAIDS OF LA ROCHELLE
'A HEAD GIRL'S DIFFICULTIES,' ETC.

Illustrated by
NINA K. BRISLEY

LONDON : 38 Soho Square, W. 1
W. & R. CHAMBERS, LIMITED
EDINBURGH : 339 High Street

TO
LILIAN, JEAN, AND FLO
BUT ESPECIALLY TO LILIAN
IN MEMORY OF OUR JOLLY TIME TOGETHER
IN THE TYROL

CONTENTS.

LIST OF ILLUSTRATIONS.

The School at the Châlet.

CHAPTER I.

MADGE DECIDES.

'IF only I knew what to do with you girls!' said Dick in worried tones.

'Oh, you needn't worry about us!' replied Madge.

'Talk sense! I'm the only man there is in the family—except Great-Uncle William; and he's not much use!'

'Jolly well he isn't! Poor dear! He's all gout and crutches.' And Madge threw back her head with a merry laugh.

'Well then! I ask you!'

She got up from her seat on the Chesterfield, and walked across the room to her brother. 'Dear old Dick! You really mustn't worry about Joey and me. We shall be all right!'

He lifted his fair boyish head to look at her. Not pretty in the strict sense of the word, yet Madge Bettany was good to look at. She was slight to the verge of thinness, with a well-poised head covered by a mop of curly dark-brown hair. Her eyes were dark brown

too—the colour of old brown sherry—and were
shaded by long, upcurling, black lashes.
Dark eyes and hair presupposed an olive
complexion, but there, Madge had deserted
the tradition of the Bettany women, and her
skin showed the wonderful Saxon fairness of
her mother's family. Her mouth was wide,
but with well-cut lips, and her slender figure
was as erect as a young poplar. There was
enough likeness between her and Dick, despite
the disparity of colouring, to proclaim them
unmistakably brother and sister. Now she
slipped a hand through his arm as she announced, ' I 've got a plan all ready for us.'

' Let 's hear it,' he commanded.

' Well, the best thing is to go over all the
possibilities.'

' Oh, for Heaven's sake, don't make a long
story of it ! ' he implored.

' All right. But I want you to see my
point, so——'

' That means it 's something you think I
sha'n't approve of,' he said shrewdly. ' Well,
get on and let 's hear the worst.'

' You see,' began his sister, balancing
herself on her toes, ' whatever happens, Joey
and I must keep together. We are all agreed
on that point. But—there 's no money ; or,
at any rate, very little. You can 't keep us
on your pay ; that 's quite out of the question !
So last night, I thought and thought after I
had gone to bed ; and, honestly, I think my
plan 's the only one possible.'

'Oh, for Heaven's sake, cut all that!' groaned her brother. 'What do you want to do?'

'Start a school,' was the sufficiently startling reply.

'Start a school!' He stared at her. 'My good girl, that sort of thing requires capital—which we haven't got.'

'Yes, I know that as well as you do!' retorted his sister. 'At least, it does in England. But I wasn't thinking of England.'

'Then where were you thinking of?' he demanded, not unreasonably. 'Ireland? Shouldn't advise that! You might wake up one morning to find yourself burnt out!'

'Of course not! I've got *some* sense! And I do wish you'd try to be a little more sympathetic!' she returned rather heatedly.

'But, my dear girl, it's an awful undertaking to run a school. And you look such a kid! Who on earth would have you as Head? And anyway, you haven't told me yet where you want your blessed school!' he protested. 'You don't suggest coming out with me to India and starting there, do you?'

'No, of course not. Though, if there hadn't been Jo to consider, I might have done it. But we couldn't keep her there; and I won't leave her in England. So what I've thought of is this. D' you remember that little lake in the Austrian Tyrol where we spent the summer five years ago—Tiern See?'

'Rather! Topping little place, right up in the mountains, 'bout an hour's train run from Innsbrück, wasn't it? You went up in a mountain railway from some rummy little town or other—I forget its name!'

'Spärtz,' supplied his sister. 'Yes, that's the place. It was gorgeous air up there; and you could live for next to nothing.'

'Is that where you mean to have your school?'

She nodded. 'Yes. There was a big châlet there which would be topping. It was not too far from the lake; fairly near the steamer, and yet it was away from the paths. I shouldn't want a large number, not at first at any rate—about twelve at most, and counting Joey. I should want girls from twelve to fourteen or fifteen. I would teach English subjects; Mademoiselle La Pâttre would come with us, and she would take the French and German—and the sewing too. Music we could get in Innsbrück.'

She stopped and looked at Dick somewhat doubtfully at this juncture. A frown was robbing his face of half its boyishness. He knew very well that Madge had set her heart on this project, and that he had neither the strength of will nor the authority to turn her from her purpose. They were twins, and all their lives long she had been the one to plan for them both. If she had determined to start this school, nothing he could say or do could prevent her. Their only relatives

besides Great-Uncle William, before mentioned, were two aunts, both married, and
both with large families and small means.
Madge was not particularly likely to listen
to anything they might say. She read his
thoughts in his face.

'It's no use appealing to the aunts,' she
said. 'They'll have fits, of course; but it
can't be helped. Just consider how we are
situated. We are orphans, with a sister
twelve years younger than ourselves to be
responsible for. Our guardian got his affairs
into a frantic muddle, and then conveniently
—for him!—died, leaving us to face the
music. You're in the Forests, and your
furlough is up in three weeks' time; Joey is
delicate and shouldn't live in a wet climate;
and between us we seem to have some fairly
decent furniture, this house, and three thousand pounds in East India Stock at four per
cent.—or something over a hundred pounds a
year.'

'Twenty over,' interjected Dick.

'We can't live on that in England,' she
went on, unheeding the interruption. 'Even
if I did get a post in a school, it would mean
school-fees for Jo. But we could manage in
Austria. It's healthy—Tiern See, and it's
a new idea. I know of one child I could have
for the asking—Grizel Cochrane; and we'd
have to advertise for the others. I don't see
why we shouldn't make it pay in time.'

'What about apparatus?' suggested Dick.

'You'd want desks, and books, and so on, I suppose?'

'Get them in Innsbrück. My suggestion is that we sell most of the things here, keeping only what we absolutely need, and buy out there. I went over the châlet while we were there, Dick. A fortnight ago I wrote to Frau Pfeifen. Her answer came this morning. I wanted to know if the châlet was vacant, and, if it was not, if there was any other place she could recommend. It is vacant, and she thinks the owner-manager of the Kron Prinz Karl—that big hotel not far from the boat-landing—would let me have it all right.'

'If only I hadn't to go so soon,' muttered Dick, as he rapidly scanned the letter she had given him.

'I know! I wish you hadn't; but we shall have Mademoiselle.'

'I wouldn't have agreed to the idea if you had consulted me,' he replied. 'As it is, I suppose I must say " yes." You'll do as you like, whether I agree or not. I know that! But you've got to promise me one thing.'

'I'll see,' returned his sister cautiously. 'What is it?'

'That you'll cable me at once if anything goes wrong, and that you'll write at least once a week—oftener if you can.'

'All right. I agree to that. Now will you go and fetch Joey, and we'll tell her. I know she's a bit anxious about what's going to happen, but I couldn't say anything till I'd discussed it with you first of all. She's upstairs reading.'

'Jo reads entirely too much,' he grumbled as he went to the door. 'That's one thing I hope you'll alter a little.'

'She'll have plenty to take her out of doors,' replied his sister serenely. 'She really needs other companions. Call her, old thing.'

His yell of 'Joey!' resounded through the house a second later, and was answered by a shriek of 'Coming!' There was the sound of flying footsteps, a thud in the hall, and then Joey, or, to give her her proper name, Josephine, fell rather than ran into the room.

Anything less like Madge and Dick it would have been hard to imagine. Her cropped black hair was so straight as almost to be described as lank, her big black eyes made the intense whiteness of her face even more startling than it need have been, and her cheeks and temples were hollow with continual ill-health. Like her brother and sister, she had been born in India; but, unlike them, had come home at the early age of seven months. The frail baby who had never known her mother or father had thriven in the soft Cornish air of their home till she was four years old. Then a neglected cold had brought on an attack of pleuro-pneumonia, from which she had barely struggled back to life. Since then, her health had been a constant worry to those

who had charge of her. What made things
still more difficult was the fact that Miss
Joey possessed at least five times as much
spirit as strength, and fretted continually at
the restrictions they were obliged to enforce.
The exertion of her flight downstairs brought
on a bad fit of coughing, and until it was over,
and she was lying back on the Chesterfield,
whiter than ever with exhaustion, there was
no thought of telling her the news. Madge
flung an agonised look at Dick, even as she
gave the child a glass of water. He strolled
across the room to them, his hands in his
pockets.

' I say, old lady,' he began, ' you mustn't
sprint about like that ! '

Jo lifted her eyes to his. ' I 'm sick of
" don't ! " ' she remarked. ' Why did you
call me, Dick ? Anything settled about us
yet ? '

' I suppose so,' he growled. ' But just
listen to me for a minute. I 'm sorry you 're
sick of " don't," but I think you might have
a little more consideration for Madge. You
know how she worries when you cough.'

' Sorry, old thing ! ' Jo sent up a little
smile at her sister. ' I was so anxious to
hear, I forgot about not dashing round.
What are we going to do ? I can see it 's all
fixed.'

' Yes, it 's fixed,' replied Madge, as she
perched herself on one arm of the couch.
It 's my own idea, and I hope you 'll like it.'

' Well, what is it ? '

' Madge is going to run a school.'

' Madge run a school ! ' Jo sat bolt upright. ' *No !* She 's much too young ! Why, if her hair wasn't up she 'd look like a kid ! '

' I 'm twenty-four——' began Madge heatedly, when Dick interrupted her.

' You listen to me, my kid. Remember Tiern See ? '

' Rather ! '

' Well, you 're going there. Madge will open the school in that big châlet not far from the lake. Mademoiselle La Pâttre will come with you to look after you both, and help with the school.'

' What a simply ripping idea ! When are we going ? Before you do, Dick ? Who are the pupils ? '

' Don't be silly ! Of course you can't go yet ! There 's this house and furniture to see about, and Madge will have to buy her paraphernalia in Innsbrück——'

' *Dear* little Innsbrück ! ' Jo interrupted him. ' Shall we be there first, Madge ? How long ? Oh, it will be lovely to see Tiern See again ! When do we leave here ? '

' Don't quite know,' replied Madge. ' Dick, I don't think there 'll be much trouble about selling the house. You know, the Corah Mine people want a place for their managers to live in, and it 's within quite decent distance of the mine. Don't you think they might buy it ? '

'Good idea! Yes, I should think they might. It's the sort of place they want, of course. I'll take a stroll up to old Everson and get him to see it through. Since we're all going, the sooner we get the business over and quit the better.'

'I'll go and see the Cochranes,' decided Madge. 'I know they'll be thankful to get rid of poor little Grizel. What fees shall I ask, Dick? D' you think £120 a year would be too much?'

'Sounds rather a lot,' said Dick dubiously.

'It's only what most decent schools charge. I've got some prospectuses to see. Besides, the Cochranes can afford it; and I believe they'd pay even more to get rid of Grizel.'

'Mrs Cochrane would, anyhow!' chimed in Jo.

'What I can't understand,' said Dick thoughtfully, 'is why she ever married him if she didn't want a stepdaughter.'

'She knew nothing about it till she got here,' explained Madge. 'She nearly expired when she saw the poor kiddy! Oh, they'll let me have her all right. And it'll be the making of Grizel. You'll have to recommend me to your Anglo-Indian friends, Dick!'

'Aren't any where I am—not with kids of school-age, anyhow! Well, I'll get along and see old Everson while you interview the Cochranes. What are you going to do, Joey? It's too wet for you to go out.'

'I'm going back to finish *Quentin Durward,*'

returned Jo firmly. ' You 'll take all our books, won't you, Madge ? '

' Most of them, anyway. But you needn't start to pack them yet. This is only March, and we sha'n't be going till next month at earliest.'

Jo took little notice of this, but got off the Chesterfield, and returned to her little bedroom, where a blazing fire relieved the gloom of the rainy day, and her well-beloved books awaited her.

' Best thing in the world for her,' observed Dick when she had gone. ' Well, I 'm off to settle old Everson. He 'll fuss, I suppose; but, after all, there 's no one who can really interfere now our poor old Guardian 's gone, and as long as we agree, it 'll be all right.'

' Oh, rather ! ' Madge was struggling with her stout, laced-up boots. ' Insist on his doing things at once, Dick. I want to get off and be settled before the summer visitors arrive at Tiern See. He 'll want us to play round till September if I know anything about lawyers, and it makes no difference really, because I 've made up my mind to go. Mademoiselle will be thankful to get away from England too.'

' You 're sure it 's all right about her coming ? '

' Yes. I spoke to her a week ago, and she said if you consented, she would come. She 's not too happy at the Withers', and she 's not really tied to them at all. She loves us—

has done ever since I sat on Jean Withers for
being rude to her !—and she adores Jo.   I 'm
not mad keen on making a fortune.   So long
as we can keep ourselves, and save a little for
the chicken in case of accidents, I shall be
quite happy.'

'Righto !   Well, so-long !   Hope you get
the Grizel kid ! '   And with this, Dick turned
and left the room, while Madge ran upstairs
to get her raincoat and cap, before she, too,
ventured out into the hurricane of wind and
rain with which March had arrived that year,
to seek her first pupil for the Châlet School.

CHAPTER II.

GRIZEL.

SEATED at the old schoolroom piano, Grizel Cochrane was diligently practising scales and exercises. She had no real love of music, but her father insisted that she must learn; and since she must learn, then, also, she must practise. Her stepmother, whom Grizel hated with all the intensity of her childish soul, had decreed that, although this was her last day at home, the dreary hour of scales and exercises must be done as usual. Her music all lay at the bottom of her trunk, so anything else was impossible, for which she was devoutly grateful.

'Thank goodness, I shall be away from all this after to-morrow,' she thought as she pounded fiercely away at C sharp major. 'I love Miss Bettany, and Jo is a dear. I'm sure they won't make me practise three hours a day there. C sharp major, relative minor A sharp.' Automatically her fingers changed on to the relative harmonic minor as she went on with her thoughts. 'I'm glad I'm going away from England—glad I'm leaving them! They don't want me, and I can't endure them!' Tears pricked at the back of her eyes at this thought,

but she resolutely drove them back, and
attacked the melodic minor. At fourteen
and a half Grizel Cochrane had realised that
she was decidedly an unwanted member of
the Cochrane family. Her mother had died
when she was five. Grizel could just remember her as a fragile, complaining being,
who lay on a couch all day, and said ' Hush ! '
in fretful tones whenever her little daughter
ventured to raise her voice. After her death,
Mr Cochrane had sent the child to his
mother's, and led a bachelor life for the next
five years. On Grizel's tenth birthday he had
married again, most unaccountably, without
informing his second wife of the fact that he
had a daughter. That she discovered when
they reached home after the honeymoon, to
find Grizel awaiting them on the steps. To
say that the second Mrs Cochrane was indignant is to describe the state of affairs
much too mildly. At first, she insisted that
the child must go to boarding-school. Her
husband calmly replied that one reason for
his second marriage was that he wanted
Grizel under his own roof. He also pointed
out that if she were sent away at once people
would talk. Mrs Cochrane desired that less
than anything, so she gave way. Grizel went
daily to a big high school in the neighbour-
hood, and, nominally at any rate, received
the same care and attention as any of her
friends. But life at her grandmother's had
spoilt her in many ways, and before long she

and her stepmother were at daggers drawn
with each other. Mr Cochrane, never a
particularly loving parent, refused to interfere. Mrs Cochrane was never actively unkind, but she possessed a sharp tongue, and
she had never forgiven her husband for not
telling her of Grizel's existence. By slow
degrees the wilful, high-spirited child gradually became a frightened, nervous creature,
who did as she was bidden with a painful
readiness.

Later, she became the excuse for many
' scenes,' and on the day when Madge Bettany
set off in the wind and rain to secure her for
the Châlet School, Mr Cochrane had at last
given way, and agreed to send her away.
Then the great question had been ' where ? '
To them, considering the point, had come
Madge, and with her a complete solution of
the problem. It was satisfactory from all
points of view. Grizel's father realised that if
she were sent away with such an old friend
as Madge Bettany, it would give rise to no
gossip in the little town, which was beginning
to conjecture at the causes for her loss of
spirit. Mrs Cochrane rejoiced in the fact
that it would be sheer absurdity for her to
make the long journey from Innsbrück to
Cornwall for any holidays but the summer
holidays. Grizel herself only wanted to get
right away from her present surroundings,
and Madge went home thrilling to the fact
that she had gained her first pupil.

For the next fortnight or so everyone had been kept busy. Grizel found herself condemned to sitting and sewing name-tapes on to new stockings and gloves and handkerchiefs, as well as having to endure various 'tryings-on.' At any other time she would have resented all this intensely. Now it was, for her, just part of the joy of going away. Madge had been unable to say, at first, when they would go ; but Dick, having applied for and received a month's longer furlough, bustled their old solicitor to such an extent, that the middle of April found them with house and furniture sold, boxes packed, and everything ready. What was more, the Châlet School had two other pupils in prospect. Mademoiselle was bringing a little cousin, Simone Lecoutier, from Paris, and a business friend of Mr Cochrane's, an American, had been fired with enthusiasm over the school, and had written asking Miss Bettany if she could find room for his twelve-year-old Evadne next term.

Grizel was musing over all this as her fingers moved up and down the keys with accuracy and precision. It seemed almost impossible that it could be she who, on the morrow, would be taken up to London by her father, unusually indulgent, and there given over to Miss Bettany's charge. Madge and Jo had left their old home early in the previous week, in order to pay farewell visits to such relatives as remained to them.

'It's too good to be true!' thought Grizel ecstatically; 'and that's ten o'clock, thank goodness!'

She finished off the scale of A flat melodic minor in grand style, and then shut down the lid of the piano with a bang. She had heard her stepmother go out a few minutes previously, so she ran down to the kitchen, where the cook, who adored her, and spoilt her when it was possible, welcomed her with a wide smile, and made haste to proffer a rock bun.

'Just hot out of the oven, Miss Grizel, love,' she said.

Grizel accepted it, and, sitting on the table, munched it with good appetite.

'This time to-morrow I sha'n't be here,' she said, when it was disposed of.

'No, lovey. It'll be the train this time to-morrow,' replied the good woman in her soft, sing-song voice.

'And then Paris next day—and then Innsbrück next week!' Grizel spoke exultingly. 'Oh, Cookie! I'm so thrilled, I'm so thrilled, I can't keep still!'

'Eh, it's a lot you'll be seeing, Miss Grizel. And you'll write to Cookie and tell her all about the grand sights in them furrin cities, won't you?'

'Of course I will, Cookie dear! I'll write to you as often as I can.' And Grizel jumped down from her perch and, flinging her arms round Cook's neck, gave her a hearty hug. 'I'll write to you every week if I can.'

'There's a love! And—Miss Grizel, dearie, I was over to Bodmin last night, and I got this for you to remember your Cookie by.'

'Oh, Cookie! How dear and kind of you! Whatever can it be?'

Grizel took the narrow parcel, feeling its shape with childish curiosity before she opened it. A little scream of ecstasy broke from her as she realised what it was—a beautiful Waterman fountain pen.

'Oh, Cook! And I've always wanted one ever so!'

The tears stood in her grey eyes as she carefully examined it. Cook, looking down at the small flushed face, felt well rewarded for her long tramp of the night before, and for the sacrifice of a new spring hat, which had been necessary to buy the pen.

'I've nothing to give you,' said Grizel, sudden sadness in her tones.

'You'll be giving me your news, lovey—maybe a picture-postcard or two! That's all I'll be wanting from you. Now you'd better go, Miss Grizel. The mistress only went down to the butcher's, and she won't like it if she finds you here.'

Grizel nodded. Too well she knew the scolding that would be the portion of both of them if her stepmother caught her in the kitchen. With a final hug and a kiss, she turned and ran upstairs to her own little room, cuddling her new possession. Some paper lay on the little dressing-table, and she 'tried' the pen on it. Cook had had it filled ready, and it was a beauty—neither too fine nor too broad. She wrote her name with a flourish several times, and then, hearing Mrs Cochrane's step on the stairs, tucked it away into her attaché case, and screwed up the bits of paper, thrusting them into her pocket just in time. When her stepmother entered the room she was standing gazing out of the window, and whistling softly. Mrs Cochrane frowned at her.

'Grizel! I have told you before that I will not allow whistling! Kindly obey me! As long as you are under this roof you will do as I tell you!'

Grizel obeyed. The disciplining of the past three years had taught her the value of unquestioning obedience, if it had taught her nothing else.

'You had better put on your outdoor things and come with me,' went on her stepmother. 'You ought to say good-bye to the Rector and Miss Fareham; and I have to go to the Rectory. Hurry up now, and brush your hair, and be downstairs in ten minutes' time.'

She left the room, and Grizel did as she was bidden; but all the time that she was putting on the new blue travelling coat, and changing into her outdoor shoes, and wriggling her brown head into her scarlet tammy, she was murmuring softly to herself, 'Only to-day left! Only just to-day! To-morrow will soon be here now.'

She went on repeating it as she walked slowly downstairs. Mrs Cochrane caught the low murmur, and looked sharply at her.

'Why are you talking to yourself, Grizel? Please don't be so absurd.'

Grizel coloured up furiously, but she said nothing. Walking demurely at her step-mother's side, she went down the garden-path, which was already bordered with wall-flowers and tulips, gaily a-nod in the spring breeze, and out into the street, where they met two of the girls from her old school.

'You will want to say " good-bye " to your friends,' said Mrs Cochrane graciously—she was always gracious in public. 'I will wait for you at the Rectory; but don't be long, as there are still one or two things I want to do.'

She passed on, and Grizel was left with them.

'It's to-morrow you go, Grizel, isn't it?' said the elder of the two, a pretty fair child of fourteen, Rosalie Dene by name. 'Aren't you sorry to leave home?'

Hitherto Grizel's pride had kept her from making any revelations about home matters. Now, somehow, it didn't seem to matter. She would not come home for more than a year, for she was to stay with the Bettanys all the summer.

'Sorry?' she said fervently. 'I'm not sorry; I'm glad—glad, I tell you!'

'Grizel!' gasped Rosalie. 'Glad to leave home and go right away!'

''Tisn't like your home,' replied Grizel sombrely. 'You've a mother!'

'Well, but you have Mrs Cochrane, and I'm sure she's awfully sweet to you.'

'Yes, when there's anyone there to see it,' replied Grizel recklessly.

The two schoolgirls stood in horrified silence. They did not know what to say.

Grizel broke the spell. She held out her hand.

'I must be going,' she said briefly. 'Good-bye. Write to me sometimes.'

'Good-bye,' said Rosalie flatly. 'Of course I'll write if you will.'

'I'll send you some postcards,' responded Grizel. 'Good-bye, Mary!'

Mary, the other child, mumbled something in farewell, and then Grizel ran off, leaving them still staring after her.

'Well!' ejaculated Rosalie at last. 'Did you ever?'

'Never!' replied Mary with finality. 'I didn't think Grizel Cochrane was like that!'

'I wonder what mother will say,' said Rosalie thoughtfully.

What Mrs Dene actually said when she heard her daughter's story was, 'Poor little dear! I hope she will be happy in Austria, then.'

Meanwhile, Grizel hurried to the Rectory, where her stepmother was waiting for her,

and took leave of the Rector and his sister,
both of whom were fond of her. They had
farewell gifts for her too, in the shape of a
new Kipling and a big box of chocolates, and
she said ' good-bye' to them with real regret.
They had always been kind to her.

After the Rectory visit, Mrs Cochrane took
her into the town to do some shopping, and
it seemed to the little girl that never before
had they met so many acquaintances in one
morning. Everyone was very kind, and
wished her good luck and a pleasant journey.
One or two told her that they envied her her
visit to foreign countries, and most people
begged for postcards. Grizel promised them
to all and sundry, and all the time her heart
was beating madly with delight to think that
this was the last time for many a long month
that she would be here. Then they went
home to lunch, and after it was over, her
stepmother dismissed her to the moors, where
she ran about like a wild thing till the little
silver watch on her wrist warned her that it
was nearly tea-time, and she had better be
turning homewards. Her father came in for
tea, and brought with him a folding Brownie
kodak in a neat leather case with a strap
to sling across her shoulders. The general
atmosphere of kindness seemed to have infected even Mrs Cochrane, and so that last
evening passed off well. The next day Mr
Cochrane took her up to town, and gave her
into Madge Bettany's charge at Victoria.

CHAPTER III.

THE JOYS OF PARIS.

'RIEN à declarer ? '

'Rien à declarer ! ' replied Madge firmly, with one eye on her two charges. For all her self-confidence, she suddenly felt very young to be sole guardian of two girls of twelve and fourteen. The custom-house official grunted as he chalked the mark on the three suit-cases, which was all the luggage they had with them, Mademoiselle La Pâttre and Dick having gone out to Tiern See early in the previous week with the trunks and cases of books, ornaments and pictures, which were all they were taking with them from England. Experienced Joey promptly helped to fasten the cases again, while Grizel, flushed and excited, gazed round her, wonder in her big grey eyes. She had never been out of England in her life before, so even the draughty, prosaic *douane* of Boulogne, where everyone had to go in queue with their cases, was invested with a certain pleasure glamour for her. The hoarse voices of the *douaniers*, the clamour of their fellow-passengers, the unusual trains with their funny, high engines, and little steps up into the carriages, were all fresh and new to her. Madge cast an amused

glance at her absorbed face as they settled
down in their second-class carriage. The
only other occupant was a little fat man
in a loud check suit. He was mopping his
face with a white handkerchief adorned with
scarlet spots.

' Eh, it 's 'ot,' he said, his accent at once
betraying him for a Yorkshire man. ' 'Ot
for this time o' t' year it is.'

Years ago, Miss Madge's nurse had accused
her of being ' as friendly as a mongrel puppy.'
She had kept this quality throughout her life.
She was always interested in people, and,
having met nothing but friendliness in all her
twenty-four years, she had the same fearless,
somewhat confiding manner with strangers
as the pup to which nurse had likened her.
So, instead of snubbing the good-hearted little
man's advances with frosty good breeding,
she answered him pleasantly. He had had
little education, as was evident, but he felt a
kindly, if curious, interest in the trio in his
carriage, and when, a little later, they produced sandwiches and milk, he vanished, to
return with some magnificent gooseberries,
which he begged them to share with him
Again, Grizel looked for the icily polite snub
her stepmother would have given him.
Madge only thanked him for his kindness
with the direct simplicity which was so much
a part of her charm, and offered him sandwiches in return.

Over their meal they became quite friendly,

and, before they reached Paris, he had found
out that she proposed running a school in
the Tyrol. He commended the scheme, and
offered to try to find her pupils among his
customers—he was a wool manufacturer from
Bradford, as it turned out. They were quite
sorry to say 'good-bye' to him when they
reached Paris ; but he was going on to Lyons
that night, and they were to spend the next
two or three days in the gayest city in the
world. It was five o'clock—or seventeen, if
you cared to take French time—by the time
they had arrived, and both Jo and Grizel
were tired, so Madge made no attempt to do
anything that night. They went to their
hotel, a quiet one, not far from the Madeleine,
and after having arranged for the remainder
of the week, they were shown to their rooms,
where *thé à l'Anglais* was sent up. Then
they all three bathed and changed, and Jo
was packed off to bed, whither Grizel speedily
followed her. By nine o'clock they were
both fast asleep, and Madge, since there was
nothing else to do, followed their example.
They all woke early, and after *petit déjeuner*
of coffee and rolls, prepared to go out.
Naturally, since they were so near, the
Madeleine was their first objective. Jo had
seen it before, but she was perfectly willing
to visit the great church which Napoleon had
begun as a ' Temple of Glory,' and which he
was destined never to finish. Grizel looked
at it with wonder in her face.

' Somehow, I didn't think Napoleon was a religious man,' she observed thoughtfully. ' Whatever made him want to build a church ? '

' He wasn't ; and he didn't,' explained Madge. ' I forget what his idea was, but it certainly wasn't the idea of the average man. But then he wasn't an average man, of course ! Anyway, it's rather a wonderful thing, isn't it ? Not to be compared with Notre Dame, of course ! '

' Is he buried here ? ' asked Grizel.

' No, in the Invalides,' replied Jo, who was an enthusiastic admirer of the great Emperor. ' We'll go and see his tomb. But I must get some flowers. I always put them there to show that someone remembers him.'

' A good many people remember him besides you,' said her sister drily. ' He's not exactly in danger of being forgotten. And for goodness' sake, Jo, don't make the scene you made last time ! '

' I only threw the flowers over the railings,' protested Jo.

' I know what you did all right ! If only you hadn't been standing at the corner, and if only you could throw straight, it wouldn't have mattered ! As it was, you nearly let us in for imprisonment under the impression that you were flinging bombs about ! '

' If the idiot guide had ducked it would have been all right ! ' retorted Joey.

' How was he to know you were going to

throw flowers about in that way? Of course, if he 'd realised, I dare say he would have ducked, and then Guardian would have been saved an expensive *pour-boire*! If you want to put flowers on Napoleon's tomb to-day, you must be content with pushing them through the railings as far as you can. Well, I think we 've seen everything here, so we may as well go to the Champs-Elysées. We 'll take a bus there. Then we 'll go up it a little way, and get another bus to the Pont Alexandre. From there, it 's easy to get to the Invalides. When you 've done worship at the shrine, you two, we 'll have *déjeuner*, and after that, we go to the Louvre by the Métro.'

'And the opera to-night,' supplemented Joey. 'Oh, topping!'

Madge nodded. Mr Cochrane had given her an additional cheque, with the request that she would take Grizel about as much as possible. He was not a devoted father, but some strange feeling of regret that he meant so little to his only child had prompted him to do this. The money was ample, and he had bidden her take her younger sister as well.

'Children always enjoy that sort of thing better when someone of their own age is with them,' he had said. 'Please include Miss Joey in the party.'

'Are we really going to the opera?' asked Grizel incredulously.

'Yes. It 's *La Bohême* to-night. I don't know how much of it you 'll understand, but

the music is lovely,' replied Madge, as they
boarded a bus. 'Look out of the window,
Grizel. We're coming to the Place de la
Concorde, where the guillotine stood during
the Reign of Terror.'

Joey, the insatiable reader, murmured
softly, 'Sydney Carton!' But Grizel's knowledge of the French Revolution was confined
to that gained from the *Scarlet Pimpernel*
stories, and when, as they reached the famous
space, the younger girl softly quoted the
closing sentences from *A Tale of Two Cities*,
she paid no heed. The Champs-Elysées
pleased her far more with their bustle and
life. Madge chuckled softly to herself as she
walked between them. The outlook of the
two children was so totally different. Joey
always saw Paris through a rose-mist of
history and legend; Grizel, now that her
first wonder was over, so obviously took all
that side of it for granted, and devoted herself to its life and people. At the church of
the Invalides she did rouse to enthusiasm
over Napoleon; but it was only temporary,
and she stared at Joey when that faithful
devotee pushed a few sprays of lilies of the
valley between the railings that surround the
famous Emperor's tomb.

After Les Invalides, they had *déjeuner* at
one of the many restaurants, and then took
the Métro to the Louvre, which bored that
little Philistine, Grizel, almost to tears. The
opera, however, was an entire success. True,

neither of the children understood much of the story, but the exquisite music appealed to both, and even matter-of-fact Grizel felt a lump come into her throat when Mimi died. The next day was devoted to a trip up the river to St Cloud and Sèvres, which pleased Miss Cochrane far more than the Louvre.

' I like to see things done,' she explained to Joey. ' Of course, pictures and statues are all right, but they 're not half so interesting as seeing people do things now. And I think St Cloud is awfully jolly ! I wish we 'd been able to go up the Eiffel Tower, though.'

' You 've done quite enough for to-day,' declared Madge, with an anxious eye on Joey's white face. ' To-morrow we 'll go out to Versailles, and then on Monday we must be getting on. I'm going to send you to bed when we get back, Joey. You look done ! '

' I 'm all right,' replied Jo. Nothing would have induced her to own that her back and head were aching, and that bed was the one thing for which she was longing. However, her sister had not known her for twelve years without learning something about her, and to bed she went as soon as they reached their hotel.

On the next day they went to Versailles, and spent long, happy hours wandering about that magnificent extravagance of Louis XIV. The gardens filled them with admiration, and

Grizel thrilled at seeing the Hall of Mirrors, where the Peace Treaty had ended the Great War. From there, they went on to the Trianons, with their dainty artificiality, where poor Marie Antoinette and her court ladies had played at being milkmaids and shepherdesses clad in flowered silks, while, less than twenty miles away, the Paris mob was beginning to cry aloud for bread. The whole place was peopled with gay, exquisite ghosts for both Madge and Jo, and even Grizel became infected by them, and half expected to see some hooped and powdered lady, with raised fan and brilliant eyes, beckon to her from behind one of the statues. Madge was wise enough to take them back early, after they had seen the famous fountains playing, and the next day was spent in visiting Notre Dame and looking at the shops.

Grizel was anxious to buy nearly everything she saw, but Madge kept a tight rein on her. She would only allow her to change a little of her money into francs, and then she insisted that choice must be carefully made. Finally, at the Louvre a lace collar was chosen for Cook; several postcards were bought and sent off; then, at Jo's suggestion, they went to the Luxembourg Gardens, which lay bathed in April sunshine. Grizel was deeply interested in the French children who romped about there, carefully watched by mothers and nurses. The *carrousel*, with its lions and elephants, and gay little hurdy-gurdy, took her fancy completely, and she insisted on having several ' goes,' rather to the amusement of Jo, who strayed off to the fountain, where bare-legged and crop-haired small boys were sailing their boats to a general chorus of, ' Quel est beau ! ' ' Ah, mon Dieu ! ' ' C'est bien que possible ! ' ' Voleur ! C'est le mien ! ' And, more than once, ' Fermes le bec, toi ! '

Here Madge and Grizel found her when they came a little later, haranguing two small, bewildered-looking boys in a polyglot mixture of French and English.

' What on earth are you doing ? ' demanded her sister.

' Telling them to fight fair,' responded Jo calmly. ' Their boats got mixed up, and they went for each other. That one,' coolly pointing, ' tried to scratch the other, and *he* kicked *him*. I pulled them apart, and was just telling them not to scrap like girls, when you came ! '

The two little boys had been staring at her with horrid fascination. Now, as she reached the end of her explanation, they suddenly grabbed each other's hands and, taking to their heels, fled.

' You 've scared them ! ' laughed Grizel. ' Oh, Joey, I think it 's lovely ! I caught the ring five times, and the man said it was superb ! '

' Well, now let 's have *déjeuner*,' suggested Madge. ' I 'm hungry, if you aren't.'

Déjeuner over, they strolled along to the
Champs - Elysées, and joined in the merry
throng round 'Guignol,' which is a French
version of Punch and Judy.   After that, they
met the old woman who sells toy balloons and
zeppelins, and nothing would do but that they
must each have one.   Tea they had at a
pâtisserie, where Grizel rejoiced once more in
the delightful custom which ordains that each
customer shall take a plate and fork to the
counter and help himself to delicious sandwiches and cakes before settling down.

'So much more sensible than English
shops,' she said.   'They always bring the
things you don't want——'

'Like horrid spongy cakes with butter-
icing!' chimed in Jo.   'I loathe them!   Now
éclairs, I could go on eating for ever!'

'And beautifully sick you would be,' said
Madge firmly.   'No, you don't, Joey, my
child!   Remember, our train leaves at nine.
Finished?   Le comptoir, s'il vous plaît.'
This last to the pretty waitress who stood
near.   After that, they returned to their
hotel to pack up and have dinner, and half-
past eight saw them at the Gare de l'Est,
climbing into the Paris-Wien train express.

'Here start our Austrian adventures,' observed Jo, as she curled herself up comfortably in a corner.   'You can't count Paris!'

'Can't you?   I do!' replied Grizel.   'It's
all been absolutely thrilling, so far!'

'Go to sleep and don't talk,' ordered Miss

Bettany. 'We shall be in Switzerland, I hope, when you wake to-morrow.'

'Switzerland?' Grizel sat bolt upright in her excitement.

'Yes; we reach Basle about six in the morning. Now, be quiet!'

And she refused to say another word or to let them talk, so they subsided, and before long all three were fast asleep, while the great train hurled onwards through the darkness.

CHAPTER IV.

AUSTRIA AT LAST!

IT was half-past seven on the Wednesday evening when the Vienna express slackened speed before entering the Innsbrück Station. By this time Grizel was weary of the train, while Jo's tongue had long ceased wagging, and she lay in her corner of the carriage gazing dreamily out at the darkening landscape.

' We 're only an hour late,' observed Madge, as she collected their belongings together. ' We 've missed the last train of the mountain railway, so we 'll have to go to an hotel somewhere for the night.'

' I shan't be sorry,' replied Grizel decidedly. ' Will Mr Bettany meet us, or shall we have to fish for ourselves ? '

' Dick will meet us all right,' said Jo, rousing herself up to answer this question. ' Where shall we put up, Madge—at the Europe ? '

' I suppose so,' replied her sister. ' Or there 's the Kreide, only it 's farther away.'

' I hope it 's somewhere near,' returned Jo wearily. ' I should like to have a bath and go to bed ! Hello, we 're slackening ! '

' There 's Dick ! ' exclaimed Madge, as she

hung out of the window. But Dick had seen her, and was already running along by the side of the carriage, shouting a cheery greeting to them.

' Shove the cases through the window ! ' he called, as the train stopped. ' Bustle the kids out ! I 've got a porter here ! Rooms booked at the Europe ! '

Under the influence of his suggestions Madge bundled out their belongings, and five minutes later they were all on the platform making for the exit, while a short, good-natured-looking Tyrolean followed them with the suit-cases and rugs. Dick was an experienced traveller, and both he and Madge spoke German fluently, so they were soon past the barrier and out into the big square, where carriages intended for two horses, but drawn by one only, were waiting for hire, while the coachmen, picturesque enough figures in their short open jackets, full skirts, and little green Tyrolese hats with the inevitable feather at the back, leaned up against the wheels, shouting chaff to each other, or smoking their long china-bowled pipes. Beyond, they could see the great snow-capped mountains towering up on all sides, while round them thronged tow-headed, grey-eyed children, begging for *Krönen* with a persistence which suddenly died away as Dick addressed them with a ready flow of language.

' Awful little beggars ! ' he said as they

dispersed. 'They're nearly as bad as the natives at Port Said. Tired, Grizel? Here's our hotel; nice and handy for the station, you see! You kids had better have something to eat, and then hop it to bed. Plenty of time to see things in the morning.'

'Is everything all right at the Châlet?' asked Madge, as they entered the big hotel. 'Has Mademoiselle's cousin arrived? I've got another pupil—an American called Evadne Lannis. She's coming in September.'

'Good for you,' replied her brother. 'Yes, everything's all right, and the kid—Simone, her name is—arrived Friday of last week. Mademoiselle stayed down here till to-day, and sent up the things by rail. I got the place scrubbed out, and dear old Frau Pfeifen came along, and her eldest girl, and we've got it quite shipshape. There's a big room they had built on for a *Speisesaal*, and we've turned that into a classroom. I knocked up some shelves, and we've got the books up. Two little rooms we've given to you and Mademoiselle, and a huge loft affair we've put the kids' beds in. It holds eight easily, so you'd better buck up and get four more. There's a landing-stage just opposite, and the water's quite shallow. Old Braun at the Kron Prinz Karl says you can bathe from there in the summer. Now I'll get your keys, and then you can go and beautify yourselves while I order some food

for you.   Come down to the *Speisesaal* when
you are ready.'

'What's a *Speisesaal*?' asked Grizel, as
they went up in the lift.

'It's German for dining-room,' explained
Madge.   'Here we are!   Now buck up, you
two, and make yourselves tidy, and then come
and tap at my door.'

They hastened joyously, and in a marvel-
lously short time they were ready.

Then they went down to the *Speisesaal*,
where they found Dick and a delightful meal
awaiting them, together with a most obsequi-
ous waiter.

'Nothing really exciting,' said Dick.
'Only *Kalbsbraten*—all right, Grizel!   That's
German for roast veal!—and *Kartoffeln*,
otherwise spuds, and *Apfelntorte*, which isn't
apple-tart, although it sounds like it.'

'What is it, then?' Grizel wanted to know.

'Sort of cake with cooked apples on it,'
said Jo swiftly.   'Oh, it is nice to have the
funny things again!   I think foreign food is
much more interesting than English!   Must
we really go to bed after supper?   I don't
want to in the least.'

'It 'll be nine o'clock before you 're settled,'
retorted her brother.   'You can trot round
Innsbrück to-morrow if you 're so keen!   It
won't run away in the night, you know.'

'When do we go up to Tiern See?' asked
Grizel.

'Not till the half-past seven train to-morrow evening,' replied Madge. 'There are one or two things I want to get, and you really must see a little of Innsbrück while you are here. We will go to the Ferdinandeum Museum and the Hof Kirche, and you must see the old house with the golden roof.'

'Is it really gold ? ' asked Grizel in awe-struck tones.

'Oh dear no ! And it is really just the roof of the balcony to a window. But it's very famous, and you ought to see it.'

'Then there's the Mariatheresien Strasse with its swagger shops,' chimed in Dick, 'and the great Triumphal Arch. And you must go down and have a look at the Inn. You'll have plenty to do to-morrow, I can assure you. I'll go up during the morning, Madge, and take the cases, then you and the kids can come on later.'

Everyone agreed to this programme, and Jo and Grizel went off to bed quite happily, while their elders took a stroll up to the little station, where the electric railway, which is known as the Stubai Bahn, begins.

'You ought to take the kids up here some day,' observed Dick.

'Some day,' agreed Madge; 'but do remember that I'm here to start a school in the first place ! '

'Geography,' he said shortly, with a twinkle in his eye. 'You might make a week-end expedition of it in the summer and take them to the edges of the Stubai Glacier. You could get rooms in Fulpmes, and the Stubai valley is lovely.'

'I know,' said Madge, sighing. 'It all is! But oh, Dick! Supposing it isn't a success! Supposing I fail!'

'Tosh!' he said easily. 'You won't fail! You've too much grit for that. Other people might; but you'll go on! Buck up, old thing!'

'But I'm so young,' she said—'only twenty-four, Dick!'

He gave her arm a reassuring squeeze.

'You'll pull through all right! Keep your hair on, old girl! We'd better be getting back now. You're tired, and ought to be in bed.'

'Yes, I am,' acknowledged Madge. 'Oh, Dick, I shall be so thankful to get to our own house! I must say it sounds attractive. What is little Simone like?'

'Didn't see much of her,' he replied. 'She struck me as jolly quiet. Very dark, of course; not a bit pretty like that Grizel kid.'

'Yes, Grizel will be lovely when she's grown-up,' said his sister. 'I should think she's clever, too. Oh, Dick, she and Jo were too funny for anything in Paris! Joey was dreaming it all into history, and Grizel is so absolutely matter of fact. She simply couldn't understand Joey and her dream-pictures.'

'Jolly good job,' said Dick austerely. 'Jo dreams far too much.'

' Well, she hasn't had much chance to do anything else,' replied Madge. ' Perhaps Grizel and Simone, and Evadne when she comes, will make her different.'

' Oh, she 'll be better in the mountains,' was his answer. ' Half the trouble has been her health. She 's better already, I think, even though she 's tired.'

' It can rain at Tiern See,' Madge reminded him.

' I know that. But she 'll have companions of her own age. And don't you worry, my chicken ! Everything 's going grandly ! '

With this assurance the subject was dropped, and presently they reached the hotel, and Madge retired to bed.

The next day was spent in shopping and sight-seeing. Dick left them early in the day, and went up to Tiern See with the cases and the rugs, while the three girls explored the city to their hearts' content. Grizel, quick to learn, was already picking up phrases in German, and she took the greatest delight in practising them. Jo, whose German had been fluent in the past, found it coming back to her, even as her French had begun to do in Paris. She instructed her friend as they went about, and eventually poured so much information into her, that it was small wonder that Grizel became muddled. The result was a mistake that the Bettanys remembered against her for long enough.

Madge had decided to take both children

to have their hair shampooed before going up to the lake. She remembered, from their last sojourn in the Tyrol, a very good hairdresser's shop in the Museum Strasse, and thither she took them. The hairdresser had a little English, but not much. When the shampooing was over, he asked them whether the final rinsing should be of hot or cold water. The German for 'hot water' is '*heisses Wasser*.' Jo came through the ordeal all right, demanding a lukewarm rinsing for the last. Not so Grizel. She forgot what the German for ' cold ' was, but remembered, as she imagined, the word for ' hot.' The temptation to exhibit her knowledge of his language was too great to be resisted, and she reduced the man to horrified silence, and the Bettany girls to helpless laughter, by boldly demanding ' *heiliges Wasser*.'

It was the expression of outrage on Herr Alphen's face as much as anything that rendered it impossible for Madge to do anything but choke wildly ; while he himself, a most devout Catholic, decided that this was only one more example of the madness of the English. It struck him as profane in the extreme that anyone should demand to have her hair rinsed with holy water. Still, doubtless these poor creatures knew no better. With a resigned expression and outspread hands, he carefully explained that it was impossible to give her what she asked. He assured her, however, that he would put some

of his very best toilet preparations into what
was used if she would only say whether she
would have it hot or cold, or, like the other
Fräulein, lukewarm.

Of all this harangue, which was poured
forth at top speed, Grizel understood not one
word.   Finally Madge, choking back her
laughter with great difficulty, came to the
rescue, and the shampoo was finished.

'But I don't see what there was to giggle
at,' observed Grizel to Joey when they had
finally left the shop.   'And why did that
man get so fussy when I asked for hot rinsing water?   Did he think I should catch cold
after it?   I wanted a cold rinse, as a matter
of fact, but I couldn't remember the word for
it, so I asked for hot.'

'That's just what you didn't do,' Joey
informed her solemnly.   'You've shocked
poor Herr Alphen most horribly, and I'm not
surprised!   I only wonder he finished you at
all!'

'But why?   What did I do?' demanded
the bewildered Grizel.

'Oh, you only asked for a final rinsing of
holy water!   And he a Catholic—at least I
suppose so!'

'But I only said what you told me,'
protested Grizel.

'They're rather alike in sound,' admitted
Joey.   'The beginnings are the same anyhow.   I wonder if he's got over it yet?'

At first, Grizel was inclined to accuse her

friend of 'pulling her leg,' but when she finally realised that the mistake was her own, she cheerfully joined in the laugh against herself.

'Well, anyhow, that's one thing I sha'n't forget,' she said, as they made their way to the station. 'I couldn't if I tried after that!'

'I don't believe you could,' agreed Jo—Madge was buying their tickets to Spärtz. 'If you'd insisted, I wonder if he would have tried to get some for you! They're awfully obliging here, you know. Hullo, Madge! Got them all right? Doesn't it feel grand to count in hundreds and thousands?'

'No, rather a nuisance,' replied her sister. 'Now come along. Our train is over here. Have you got those books safe, Joey?'

The journey from Innsbrück to Spärtz is of no particular interest, with the one exception of the old-world town of Hall, famous for its salt mines now, though in olden days it had a great reputation as the centre of plots and wars. But the little mountain railway, which carries you up to a height of three thousand feet and more above the sea-level, is something to remember. Higher and higher they climbed, now and then stopping at a tiny wayside station, till at last they reached the great Alp, or rather Alm, as they are called in the Tyrol, and there before them, dark, beautiful, and clear as a mirror, spread the Tiern See, with its three tiny hamlets and two little villages round its shores, and

towering round on all sides the mighty
limestone crags and peaks of the mountains.

The railway terminus is known as Seespitz,
and here the steamer was waiting for the
passengers.   Dick was there too, ready to
help with the parcels.

'It's a jolly walk round the lake,' he said,
'but to-night I think we'll take the steamer.
It's about a quarter of a mile nearer from
the Briesau landing-stage than it is from here,
and I know you're all tired.'

The little steamer waited ten minutes,
then her whistle blew, and off she went—
first to Buchau at the opposite side of the
lake, and then to Briesau, where they were
welcomed by good Frau Pfeifen, who almost
wept for joy at beholding Madge and Joey
once more.   From the landing-stage to the
Châlet was a good ten minutes' walk, and then
they saw the welcoming lights, and heard
Mademoiselle's warm French greeting.   They
were at the Châlet School at last.

CHAPTER V.

THE CHÂLET SCHOOL OPENS.

BY degrees they settled down in the Châlet. The end of April found them ready to begin work. The huge room, which had been built to accommodate eighty people at meals, had been partitioned off into two good-sized classrooms. A third next to them had been made of a small room which had been used as a lounge—the former owner of the Châlet had tried to run it as a semi-restaurant. Another one, on the opposite side of the door, had been turned into a sitting-room, sacred to Madge and Mademoiselle. There were no carpets on the floors, but they were brought to a fine polish with beeswax and hard rubbing. The furniture, with the exception of the schoolroom appcintments, was all old. There was but little as yet; Miss Bettany intended buying here and there, and having it as good as might be. In the long kitchen at the back of the house Marie Pfeifen reigned, with a younger sister and a cousin to help her, while Brother Hans cleaned shoes and knives, and attended to the huge porcelain stoves which warmed the place throughout.

Dick Bettany's furlough was up on

29th April, and he had to say ' good-bye ' to
them, before getting the Paris express, since
he intended joining the boat at Marseilles.
Actual schoolwork would start on the following Monday, and Madge was very thrilled
over that, for, in addition to Joey, Grizel, and
Simone, she had four day-pupils whose
parents lived round about, because living was
cheaper in the mountains than in the town.
Hitherto the girls had gone into Innsbrück;
but now that the Châlet School was starting
at Briesau, it was both easier and less expensive to send them there. So they would
begin with a very fair number.

' And of course there are heaps of summer
visitors,' said Miss Bettany when she was
discussing it with Mademoiselle. ' When
they see how well our school is run, I 'm in
hopes that they will send their girls to us.'

Joey and Grizel were just as thrilled as she
was. Simone, though quite nice, was very
shy and quiet, and, since she had been
brought up very properly, was apt to be
shocked at the tomboyishness of her companions.

' Besides,' as Joey put it, ' if there are more
of us, we shall be able to have more games.'

So, when Monday came, they were all agog
to meet the strangers.

School began at nine-thirty, when a little
body of schoolgirls were to be seen coming
along the lake road, carrying books and
chattering.

'There they are!' cried Joey from her vantage-point at the window. Then a minute later, in amazed tones, she added, 'I thought Madge—my sister, I mean—said there were only four!'

'So she did,' replied Grizel, joining her.

'Well, there's six there anyhow, and one's quite a tiny one!'

'Let's go down and meet them,' suggested Grizel.

'Good scheme! Come along, Simone!'

Simone followed them slowly as they clattered gaily down the wooden stairs and out on to the path. Joey, who did not know what shyness meant, danced gaily along in front. Already the pure mountain air was having its effect on her, and a faint colour tinged her white cheeks. She ran up to the newcomers, holding out her hand in eager welcome.

'Hello!' she said. 'I'm Jo Bettany, and I know you are coming to the Châlet School. Do tell me your names, won't you? And why, there's six of you, when we only expected four.'

The girls thus addressed paused and looked at each other. Then one, who was obviously the eldest, came forward and took Jo's hand.

'How do you do?' she said in careful English. 'You are Fräulein Bettany's sister, are you not? I am Gisela Marani, and these are Gertrud Steinbrücke, Bernhilda and

Frieda Mensch, Bette Rincini, and my younger sister Maria.'

'These are Grizel Cochrane and Simone Lecoutier,' said Joey, waving her hand in their direction, while she looked eagerly at them.

The two Maranis and Bette Rincini were slight, graceful girls; Gisela and Maria very dark; Bette, brown, with wavy brown hair, brown eyes, and a warm brown skin. Gertrud was brown-haired, grey-eyed, and very pretty, and the two Mensches were of the fair German type. They were all between the ages of twelve and sixteen, with the exception of Maria, who was obviously not more than nine. Seeing Jo's eyes fasten on her small sister, Gisela apologetically explained her presence amongst them, and also Gertrud's.

'Mamma thought that perhaps Fräulein—ah, but you say "Mees," do you not?—Bettany would be so kind as to permit Maria to come also. She is younger than we are, but it would be dull for her at home, and she is clever. And Frau Steinbrücke has long wanted to send Gertrud to an English school, so she is with us, and her mother will come herself to explain.'

'Well, come in and take your things off,' said Joey, wondering to herself how Madge would take it. 'This way in. This is our cloakroom. Have you brought slippers to change? Righto! We sha'n't do much in the way of lessons to-day, you know! Just get to know what we know, and about books, and so on. You're the oldest, aren't you, Gisela?'

'Yes, I have sixteen years,' replied Gisela, 'and Bernhilda is next.'

Bernhilda smiled at Joey, but she was obviously too shy to say anything just at present. She and Frieda rather reminded Joey of two dolls with their fair hair, blue eyes, and rosy faces. She knew, because Madge had told her, that Bernhilda was fifteen and Frieda twelve. Bette looked about fourteen and a half, and Gertrud was evidently much the same age. When they had all changed, she led them into the first of the big schoolrooms, whither Grizel and Simone had already gone.

'Now we're all here,' she said. 'Shall we sit down? I expect my sister and Mademoiselle will be here presently.'

They sorted themselves out, Gisela, Gertrud, and Bernhilda taking three desks at the back, while Bette, Grizel, and herself sat in the next row, and Frieda, Simone, and little Maria occupied the front row. There was a minute's silence. Then came the sound of light, swift footsteps, and a moment later Madge entered the room, head well up, although her heart was beating rather quickly. She welcomed them all with a pretty, shy dignity, listened to Gisela's explanation of Gertrud and Maria, and assured her she was very pleased to have them, and

then turned her attention to the business of
the day. Prayers were something of a difficulty, since all the Tyrolese girls, and also
Simone, were Roman Catholics, while she and
Joey and Grizel were Church of England.
For the present, she solved it by a short
reading from Thomas à Kempis, and the
Lord's Prayer said in Latin. 'But I must
hurry up and decide what we are going to do
about it,' she thought. 'I must discuss it
with Mademoiselle.'

Prayers were followed by the working of
some exam. questions by all the girls, so that
she might have some idea as to how to
arrange them. As all lessons, save French and
German, were to be taken in English, she
found the foreign girls work rather more
slowly than would otherwise have been the
case, and little Maria did nothing at all. The
arithmetic was not done in the ways to
which she was accustomed, and there were
many quaint turns of speech in the short
English compositions; but, on the other
hand, both Joey and Grizel rather came to
grief over the French, while Simone's German
was dreadful, and Grizel's worse. Finally,
after much consideration, she decided to work
all of them, save Simone, Maria, and Frieda,
together in English subjects. Maria, Joey,
Grizel, and Bette would form one French
class, while the others would make another;
and for German, Grizel and Simone would
have to be specially coached. It was also

obvious that she must get another assistant as soon as possible. ' We are growing quickly,' she mused. ' I only hope it continues.'

At twelve o'clock she finished work for the morning, and bidding the Tyroleans to bring some sewing for the afternoon, dismissed them for two hours, during which she saw that the children had their dinner, insisted on Jo's practising for an hour, and, finally, entertained Frau Steinbrücke, a stout, cheery lady, who informed her that all Tiern See was talking about her, and who prophesied that, in the summer at least, she would have quite a large number of pupils.

At half-past two punctually all the girls were settled in their places again, each with some sewing, and Mademoiselle took charge. Here, both Jo and Grizel came off badly, since both hated their needles, and even little Maria was more expert than they were, while Gisela was doing some wonderful embroidery destined for her own underclothes. She sat with Grizel, and after watching that young lady's antics for a few minutes, put down her own work, and took the much-abused pocket-handkerchief the English girl was supposed to be hemming.

' But you should hold it so,' she said in her careful English. ' And your needle—it sticks. Here is another ; now we will try once more, please ! '

Thus encouraged, Grizel began again, with slightly better results.

'I hate sewing,' she said confidentially to her guide, who had taken up her own work again. 'I don't see why we should have to fag like this when there are sewing-machines that do the work twice as quickly!'

'But you would wish to know how to make the stitches?' replied Gisela.

Grizel tossed her hair with an impish grin. 'No fear,' she said. Then, with a sudden change of subject, she went on: 'I wonder who will be appointed Head Girl?—the first Head Girl of the Châlet School!'

'Ah, yes; I have read of the Head Girl in your English school-stories,' replied Gisela pleasantly. 'And also Prefects.'

'Yes. I know Miss Bettany means to have this exactly like an English school, so I expect we shall have them too.' Then she began to giggle. 'Rather weird to have Prefects when there are only nine of us!'

'But soon there will be more,' observed Bette Rincini, who up till then had worked in silence on Gisela's other side. 'Mamma said at *Mittagessen*——'

'"Dinner,"' corrected Gisela.

'Ah, yes, dinner—that already many of our friends are talking about us, and she makes no doubt that many more girls will come.'

'How jolly!' commented Grizel. 'I like a big school. Do you have big schools in Innsbrück?'

'But yes. The public schools are very

large. I did not go to them; Gisela and
Maria and I had a *Mamsell*. But our *Mamsell*
has gone away to be married, so Mamma is
very pleased for me to come here.'

'Bernhilda and Frieda went to the public
school,' observed Gisela, 'but they, too, are
pleased to leave it. My father says that
the English schools are deficient in education,
but they give girls a more healthy life, and
Herr Mensch agrees with him. There are
others, too, who think the same, so, as Bette
has said, we shall, without doubt, soon become a large school.'

'But our schools aren't deficient in education!' said Grizel, firing up. 'You get a
jolly good education at the High Schools!'

'But you have such a short period in
school,' returned Bette. 'You work for no
more than five or six hours. Now we begin
at eight o'clock in the morning and work till
twelve. Then we begin again at thirteen and
go on for another four hours.'

'How ghastly!' said Grizel sincerely.
'Almost as bad as Germany!'

'But in Germany, so my cousin Amalie has
told me, they work even harder than that.
And they have no games as you have.'

'Well, we certainly sha'n't work like that,'
replied Grizel decidedly. 'I'm sure Miss
Bettany would never hear of it!'

'No; she is English,' agreed Gisela.

At four o'clock the command came to fold
up the work, and then the six day-girls got

ready for their walk home.   The Maranis and
Gertrud lived at Torteswald, a small village
about twenty minutes' walk from Seespitz,
and the Mensches were at Seespitz Gasthaus
for the summer, while Bette had to go all the
way to Buchau. As it was a fine day, she
meant to walk instead of taking the steamer,
and Grizel and Jo volunteered to accompany
them to the Seespitz landing—Simone had
disappeared as soon as they were dismissed,
and they could not find her, though Joey ran,
calling, through the house.

It was a delightful walk, and they found
each other very friendly, although shy Frieda
only smiled and scarcely spoke at all.   Gisela,
Bette, and Gertrud were anxious to find out
all they could about English schools, and they
asked many questions. The two English
girls found that they had read quite a number
of school-stories, and were very ready to take
in all they could on the subject of Prefects, and
Head Girls, and games.

' Then I understand that though most of
you are very honourable, it is not always so,'
said Gertrud finally.

' What do you mean ? English girls
always play the game ! ' cried Jo sharply.

' But some cheat, and look at examination
papers beforehand, and take what is not
their own,' returned Gertrud.

' Tosh ! I 've never met any ! ' declared Jo.

' But it says so in the books I have read,'
persisted the elder girl.

'But that's only to make the story,' explained Jo. 'We don't really do such things —honest Injun, Gertrud!'

'I should hope not!' came from Grizel, who was walking a little in front with Gisela and Bernhilda.

Gertrud's face cleared. 'Ah, I see. I am glad, for I should like to think that all English girls are honourable. We are grateful to you, you know, for my father says that it is the great loans England has made to Austria that are making it possible for us to become a nation once more.'

Jo and Grizel neither knew nor cared about the loans to Austria, but they realised that the others wanted to be friendly, and they were ready to meet them half-way. They chattered on about school topics till they reached the Seespitz Gasthaus, where Bernhilda and Frieda said ' good-bye ' to them.

'Will you, perhaps, come and eat an English tea with us on Saturday?' asked Bernhilda, just before they parted. 'Mamma would be so pleased if you would come; and Simone also.'

'Thank you, we'd love it,' replied Joey.

'Our first invite,' she said gleefully to Grizel as they trotted back to the Châlet. 'Well, what do you think of them all?'

'I like them,' returned Grizel with fervour. 'Gisela's a dear, isn't she? Do you think Miss Bettany will make her Head Girl?'

'Oh, I expect so; she's the eldest. I say,

if we 're going to go on growing like they
say, Madge 'll have to take another place,
won't she ? ' said Joey with considerable lack
of good grammar. 'And get some more
mistresses too ! There 's Simone ! Hullo,
Simone ! Why didn't you come with us ? '

'I went for a little promenade,' replied
Simone.

'Well, why didn't you promenade with
us ? ' demanded Grizel. 'There 's no need
for you to go off by yourself like that ! '

'You had enough,' returned Simone.

'Oh, tosh ! ' declared Joey in friendly
fashion. 'You mustn't go raking off by yourself. There 's only us three boarders at
present, and we must stick together ! '

Simone looked wistfully at them, but made
no remark, and as they had reached the
Châlet, the conversation dropped.

CHAPTER VI.

JOEY GIVES A PROMISE.

BY Saturday it was quite obvious that the Châlet School would have to enlarge both its premises and its staff. It had started actual work with nine pupils. In five days' time these had swelled to seventeen, two of them being English girls whose parents wanted to go to Norway, and were not anxious to take their children on such a tiresome journey. So, as Joey said, there were two more boarders straight off.

Amy and Margia Stevens were nice little people of eight and eleven, who had spent most of their short lives in travelling, since their father was Foreign Correspondent to one of the great London dailies. Margia, the elder child, was a motherly person, who adored her small sister; Amy was a dainty, fairylike little creature, who thought Margia was all that was wonderful.

'It really is time they mixed with other children,' said Mrs Stevens, as she sat talking to Madge and Mademoiselle; 'but until this year, Amy has been so delicate, I did not like to leave her anywhere, and it was out of the question for Margia to go alone. We must go to Bergen, but I did not want to send them to a convent school.   When we heard of you, it seemed quite providential.'

Bette Rincini's cousins came from Innsbrück to live at Buchau with their uncle and aunt for the summer months, and it was taken quite as a matter of course that they should come with her.   Then two sisters came from Scholastika at the other end of the lake, and two small children came from the Kron Prinz Karl, where they were staying with their parents.

'It is awfully thrilling!' said Joey to Madge on the Saturday morning as she sat curled up on her sister's bed.   'I didn't think schools grew as quickly!'

'They don't generally,' replied Madge, who was brushing out her curly locks.   'It just happens that we've made a lucky pitch.'

She laid her brush down, and began to twist up her hair.   Suddenly she turned from the mirror and faced her sister.

'Joey, is Simone Lecoutier happy?   She's such a quiet little thing, and those eyes of hers look naturally tragic.   Are you and Grizel kind to her?   I hope you don't go off together and leave her alone?'

'Do you really think we'd be so mean?' demanded Joey, righteously indignant. 'Why, we haul her along wherever we go when we can find her!   But she's so weird!   Soon as ever lessons are over, she slides off by herself, and where she gets to is more than I can say.'

It was on the tip of Madge's tongue to

inquire, 'Are the others decent to her?' but she remembered in time that no headmistress can expect to be respected if she starts questioning her pupils about each other; so she let the subject drop, and suggested instead that Joey had better go to her own quarters.

'I see so little of you now,' grumbled the younger girl as she wriggled off the bed. 'Early morning is the only chance I get nowadays.'

Madge laughed. 'Sorry, Joey, but I'm afraid you'll have to put up with that during term-time. I'll make it up to you in the holidays. Run along now. The breakfast-bell will be going in a minute.'

Joey left the room and went downstairs to the big dining-room, where Marie was just putting a big dish of honey on the table. Simone was there already, looking, as she usually did, almost painfully tidy in her blue and white checked frock and long black pigtails. The Châlet School uniform was to be a short brown tunic with tussore top, but so far, Joey and Grizel were its only members to have them, although the others were getting them made, and Simone's, at any rate, would be ready by Monday.

Her sister's question had aroused fresh interest in the little French girl in Joey, and she regarded the younger child gravely as she saluted her with the pretty Tyrolean greeting, 'Grüss Gott!'

'Bon jour,' said Simone soberly. She was rather white, and her eyes looked as though she had been crying.

'Why don't you give me "God's greeting"?' asked Joey laughingly. 'I think it's such a nice thing to say to anyone.' She came closer. 'Simone, why have you been howling? Aren't you happy?'

'I am ver' 'appee, zank you,' replied Simone with dignity.

'Then you don't look it,' retorted Jo, in her most downright manner. 'If you're happy, why don't you chirk up a bit?'

Simone lifted tragic dark eyes to her face, but anything she might have said was lost, for Grizel came running in at that moment, followed in more stately fashion by Mademoiselle, and Simone promptly became muter than any oyster.

As a matter of fact, all that was wrong with her was that she was dreadfully homesick. She had never been away from her mother before in her life, and wanted her badly. She said nothing, because her people were poor, and had jumped at this chance of getting her educated so cheaply; for Mademoiselle insisted that the only return that she desired for her services was her small cousin's education. To little Simone, it would have been terrible ingratitude for all Cousine Elise's kindness if she had let her see that she was not quite happy. Then again, neither Grizel nor Jo wanted to leave her out of things, but they had a trick of referring to their past good times together which had the effect of making the little French girl feel that she was not wanted. Perhaps Grizel was the worst offender in this way. It was the natural reaction from the effects of her home-life. The pity was that Simone should be the sufferer. On this morning she slipped off again as soon as breakfast was over, while the other two were concluding an amicable wrangle as to which of them should practise on the sitting-room piano. Jo missed her presently as she went off, quite cheerfully, to what was, for the moment, known as the Junior form-room.

'Slipped off again!' she thought. 'Well, my practice must just wait—though it's a shame to be indoors on such a gorgeous day! But I must find her first. Simone! Si—mo—one!' She raised her voice in a long melodious call, but no Simone answered it. 'Si—i—i—mo—one! Where are you? Simone!'

No response came, so she dropped her music on to the nearest chair, and dashed upstairs—in complete defiance to rules—to see if the small girl had taken refuge in the dormitory. But when she pulled aside the pale yellow cubicle curtains, she found the cubicle quite empty. A scamper downstairs, and a hasty rush through all the living-rooms, helped her no further, for Simone was not there. Marie, when questioned, declared she

had not seen the young lady since breakfast,
and she was sure she was with neither
Mademoiselle nor Fräulein Bettany, for they
had gone off to Spärtz half an hour before.
So that accounted for the fact that no one
had wished to know why she was running
about the house instead of practising, thought
Jo, as she wandered out into the warm sunshine, and turned to gaze at the Bärenkopf,
a mountain which greatly took her fancy,
although they had not climbed it yet, since
it was considered dangerous, at any rate for
amateurs.

'I'll have a shot at that some day,' she
thought, as she looked at the bold, rugged
outlines. Then she gave an exclamation,
for among the trees which clustered at the
foot of the slope of the Bärenbad, another
mountain, she had caught a flash of the blue
and white frock which Simone wore.

'So that's where she goes!' she thought,
as, practice now completely forgotten, she
raced across the flower-besprinkled grass
which lay between her and the woods. She
soon reached them, but by that time Simone
had disappeared, and although Joey shouted
again and again, there was no answer.
Finally, just as she had decided to give up
the hunt and return home, she stumbled
over the root of a large tree, and went headlong on to a nest of old leaves, and there was
Simone, sobbing as if her heart would break.
Joey had a horror of tears, and never quite

knew what to do with people who cried.
Still, it was obvious that she could not leave
the little French girl like that, so she wriggled
over to her and began to pat her shoulder.

'Simone! What's up? Don't cry like
that, old thing! Aren't you well?'

At the first sound of her voice Simone had
half sprung up, then she collapsed again into
the little huddle she had been when Jo
found her.

'Is anything up?' asked the latter again,
as she made a valiant effort to pull the other
child into her arms. 'Tell me, Simone, old
thing!'

'I want my mother!' sobbed Simone in
French, so that it was all Joey could do to
make it out. 'I want my mother and my
home!'

'You poor kid!' Simone was exactly ten
weeks younger than Joey, but for the present
the English girl felt very maternal towards
her. 'You poor kid! There, don't cry, old
dear! You'll be all right soon!'

Simone stretched out a hot, sticky hand
and grabbed Joey's.

'I am so lonelee!' she sobbed. 'You and
Grizel are such friends!'

'I say, we didn't mean to make you feel
out of it,' replied Joey, whose conscience was
very busily at work. 'Honour bright, we
didn't!'

'You are of the same nationality,' went on
Simone, who, once she had started to make

confidences, evidently meant to go on. 'You
live in the same town, and know each other
well, and me, I am only one. And now
there will be two more, and I shall still be
only one.'

Here her sobs choked her, and she was
unable to go on for a few minutes. Joey sat
stroking her head in silence, the while she
was rapidly turning things over in her mind.
Finally she decided.

'Simone,' she said aloud, 'I'm awfully
sorry Grizel and I have been such beasts. I
quite see we have been beasts, even though
we didn't mean it! Now I want you to mop
up—here's a hankie!—and come back with
me, and we'll start again. I'm sure Grizel
will see it, and we'll all be pally together.'

But this was not what Simone wanted.
Truth to tell, she had conceived a violent
affection for Jo, and Grizel, with her vivid
prettiness and more obvious qualities, repelled
her. So she sobbed on, while Joey sat,
nearly distracted, and not knowing what to
do.

'Simone, I do wish you'd stop!' she said
finally. 'Do stop crying, old thing! I'll do
anything I can for you; honest, I will!'

Simone made a big effort. 'Will you be—
my friend?' she choked out.

'Of course I will! I am! We both are!'

'No; I mean—my *amie intime*! Oh, Jo,
if you only would, I think I should be happier!
Grizel makes friends with everyone. Gisela

Marani loves her, and so does Bette Rincini!
I don't want her; I want only you! I love
you so!'

Anyone less sentimental than Joey Bettany
it would have been hard to find; and now
she sat rigid with horror while Simone made
this little speech. Her first impulse was to
say, 'Don't be so idiotic!' But you can't
do that when a person has lifted a pathetically
tear-stained face to you, and is looking at
you with eyes full of a doglike affection.
At least you can't if you are like soft-hearted
Jo, who promptly hugged the younger girl,
saying, 'Righto! we'll be pals. And now,
do mop up, there's a gem!'

'You will be my *amie intime*?' persisted
Simone, even as she scrubbed her eyes hard
with Joey's handkerchief. 'You will relate
to me all your secrets, and walk with me, and
love me?'

'Yes, as long as it doesn't interfere with
other people,' responded Joey. 'I can't tell
you other people's affairs, Simone! And
look here, you mustn't come rushing off by
yourself. It might come on a thunderstorm
or anything, and we shouldn't know where
you were. At least, I should now, but the
others wouldn't, and it might worry them.'

'I will p—romise to do it no more,' replied
Simone soberly. 'And now, Joey, please kiss
me. You have never kissed me yet.'

Joey hastily brushed Simone's cheek with
her lips, then she said, 'I don't kiss anyone

very much. You mustn't go feeling hurt
'cos I don't kiss you every day. We don't
in England.'

'I think England must be very cold and
hard,' sighed Simone, as she accepted the
hand Joey stretched out to her, and got on
to her feet. 'But I will remember, Joey, that
it is not because you do not love me that you
do not kiss me, but that it is your custom.'

'You're all leaves; you'd better let me
brush you down!' said Jo, changing the
subject hurriedly. She had had quite enough
of it. 'You'll have to change before we go
over to the Mensches this afternoon; you
can't go in that frock now! It looks as
though you'd slept in it!'

They went slowly down the slope, and
crossed the grass to the Châlet, where they
were met at the door by Grizel, who had just
finished her practice.

'Hello!' she said. 'I've just finished.
What shall we do?'

'I'm going to practise,' replied Jo. 'I
haven't touched the keys yet!'

'Not practised? But you went when I
did!'

'Well, I changed my mind. I've been out
with Simone, so I've got to do it now instead;
and she's got to change her frock. Come on,
Simone!' And Joey vanished into the
house, leaving Grizel looking after her in
startled fashion.

Simone followed her, and Grizel was left

alone to wonder, first, what on earth the
French child had been crying about ; second,
why Joey had left her practice till this hour.
She could come to no satisfactory conclusion,
so she gave it up, and wandered off to the
landing-stage to see if any visitors were
coming, as the steamer was just crossing
from Buchau. She was rewarded for her
interest by seeing a party, unmistakably
English, leave the boat, and, giving their
luggage in charge of the porter, make for the
Tyroler Hof, one of the largest hotels in
Briesau. What interested her most was the
fact that, besides a lady and gentleman who
looked very bored, there was also a girl of
about her own age.

' I wonder if they are staying long ? ' she
thought to herself, as she turned and went
back to the Châlet to see if the other two
were ready to come out. ' P'r'aps it 'll be
another pupil for the Châlet School. Oh, I
do hope so ! '

CHAPTER VII.

THE TIERNJOCH.

'SOME new people came this morning,' said Grizel.

They were all five—Joey, Simone, Bernhilda, Frieda, and herself—gathering flowers in the stretch of meadow that lies between Seespitz and Torteswald. The flowers in the Tyrol are wonderful, and now, in mid-May, the place was a veritable fairyland. Even Grizel and Joey, fresh from Cornwall, where the wealth of bloom is almost as rich as it is in Devon, were thrilled with the riches at their feet, and gathered armfuls of gentian, anemone, hepaticæ, heartsease, narcissi, and daisies, which they would later arrange in the bowls and jars at the Châlet.

There had been a good deal of chatter about school affairs—or rather, Joey and Grizel had done the chattering, and the others had put in an occasional word. Now Grizel changed the conversation.

'Some new people came this morning.'

'How interesting!' said Bernhilda politely. 'Were they English?'

'They looked like it,' replied Grizel. 'There were three of them—father, mother, and a girl about fourteen, I should think.'

'Perhaps another pupil for the Châlet School,' suggested the elder girl, glancing at her watch as she spoke. 'I think, if you do not mind, that we had better return now, as we shall have tea at——'

'Four o'clock!' put in Joey. 'You told us the time before, Bernhilda, and it is so muddling when you talk of sixteen o'clock.'

Bernhilda laughed. She was a rather sedate, well-mannered girl, and Miss Bettany had already decided to appoint her as Second Prefect. Gisela was to be Head Girl, and Bette and Gertrud would be subs. Madge would have preferred an English girl as head, but Grizel was too irresponsible, and Joey too childish for her to dream of it.

Bernhilda now led the way to the *Gasthaus*, her arm slipped through Grizel's, while the other three followed, Joey keeping up a lively flow of conversation, to which shy Frieda only responded by smiles. Simone had remained glued to her side the whole afternoon, and it was beginning to dawn on Joey that she might have undertaken a friendship which was to prove rather tiresome on occasion.

In this order they reached the hotel, where kindly Frau Mensch was awaiting them with tea, accompanied by great platefuls of delicious-looking little cakes which, Joey knew, must have come from Innsbrück, since such things were unprocurable in the lake villages. She welcomed them cheerily, and soon they were all sitting round the table, while their hostess inquired, 'Thee mit Citron oder mit Rhum ?'

With a sudden shock Joey realised that she was being asked whether she would have tea with lemon in it or rum. She hated the one, and had no idea of taking the other, so she was not very sure what to do. Luckily, Bernhilda came to the rescue.

'Oh, Mamma,' she said, 'I think Joey and Grizel prefer *Thee mit Milch*—do you not ?' turning to them.

'Yes, if you please,' replied Joey promptly.

Frau Mensch smiled kindly. 'Of course, if that is what you desire, my children. Kellnerin,' she called to the waitress, 'bitte, Milch !'

The milk was brought and the tea was made, the Mensches taking it in the same way, though Frieda evidently disliked it. Towards the end of the meal Herr Mensch appeared. He was a big, jolly man, with fair hair and grey eyes, and, since he was in one of the big banks in Innsbrück, his English was much more fluent than his wife's. His children obviously adored him, and he sat down, pulling Frieda on to his knee with a loud and hearty kiss.

'What hast thou done to-day, Mädchen ?'

'I have studied my lessons for Monday,' replied Frieda seriously, 'and I have helped our guests to gather flowers.'

'Such glorious flowers !' put in Joey eagerly. 'I do think Tiern See is lovely !'

' Thou lovest it already, Fräulein ? ' He looked pleased. ' It is my home—where I was born. I fished yonder '—he pointed at the blue lake waters—' many a day ere I was thine age. I climbed the Tiernjoch when I was but eleven, and brought my mother home some edelweiss. *Ei!* But my father was angry ! I had gone in disobedience, you understand, and his stick was ready for me ; but my mother begged me off, and there was no punishment that time.' He broke into a great roar of laughter, and the girls joined with him.

' Why should you be punished for climbing the Tiernjoch ? ' asked Grizel curiously. ' Which is it, Herr Mensch ? '

' The Tiernjoch is dangerous for all but the most experienced climbers,' he replied, ' and the edelweiss grows only in one part, which is the most dangerous of all. Thou dost not know it, *mein Kind* ? Come then, and I will show it to thee. We will walk to Buchau— canst thou walk so far ? And Fräulein Joey, and the little one ?—then we will go to Buchau, and from there I will name you the mountains, and all three shall see them. Mamma '—he turned to his wife—' you will come too ? '

Frau Mensch declined, however, saying laughingly that she was too old and fat for the walk there and back, and there would be no steamer for some time. So the others set off through the thick grass, listening eagerly while Herr Mensch told them about the time when he was a boy here, more than thirty years before, and the little lake had had no big hotels, but one simple *Gasthaus* to each little village, where the inhabitants of the Tyrolese towns used to put up for a night or two in the summer when they took their annual holiday, spent, for the most part, in climbing.

'We did not then think of the hundreds of tourists from all countries who would come and visit our little lake,' he said. 'And now we have even a school!'

'Papa, Grizel saw some English people come to-day,' said Bernhilda. 'They are at the Tyroler Hof, and there is a girl of our age. Perhaps she may come to the Châlet School.'

'That would be very pleasant—another compatriot,' he replied seriously. 'But it is early yet for English visitors. They do not generally come till June is here. Now see, my children, there is the Tiernjoch, that large one who lifts his head into the clouds. In front of him stands the Bernjoch, and that one, to the side, is the Mittelberge—all very difficult to climb. That one that seems to watch over Briesau—see how he bends protectingly!—is the Mondscheinspitze, quite easy to climb, and there is a hut on the Alm where one can obtain milk and butter and cheese. We will climb there some day if Fräulein Bettany will permit it. It is a walk up the valley, and then it is very pleasant on the mountain, with flowers growing, and butterflies so tame, they will not flutter when one approaches.'

'How topping!' said Joey. 'I should love that!'

'I want to climb the Tiernjoch,' said Grizel suddenly. 'I like difficult things!'

The kindly giant—he really was almost a giant!—looked down at her with a smile. 'Na-na, mein Kind! A good Mädchen will wait till there is time for a whole day and a guide. That cannot be until the summer. Then, perhaps, it may be possible. But the little expedition up the Mondscheinspitze can be made on a Saturday, and we will take the herdsmen some tobacco, and drink of their milk, which is very rich with cream, and so come back. To climb the Tiernjoch one must start very early in the morning before the sun has risen, and climb for six—eight hours before one reaches the summit. But the Mondscheinspitze, that is a nice little climb.'

Grizel said nothing further, but her lips set in obstinate lines, and Joey, looking at her, felt assured that it would take more than Herr Mensch's speech to make her change her mind.

'I wish we hadn't said anything about it,' she thought to herself. 'I know Grizel will think of nothing else now, and I shall have to spend half my time trying to persuade her not to!'

How heartily she was to wish this thing

before the summer was over Joey did not
then know—which was, perhaps, just as well.
Now she turned her attention to Herr
Mensch, who was pointing out the mountains
behind them, and naming them : 'Sonnenscheinspitze, Alpenglückjoch, Maria—The-
resienspitze, Wolfkopf, Schneekoppen. But
these are not such mountains,' he went on, ' as
the Dolomites. Some day you will doubtless see those too.'

' Papa took us there two years ago,' observed Bernhilda. ' We stayed in the *Gasthaus* at Primiero, and our cousins came too.
It was very pleasant there, and they have
many lovely flowers. You would like those,
Grizel.'

' Did you climb any of them ? ' asked
Joey.

' Oh, no ! The Dolomites are very difficult
to climb,' explained her young hostess. ' But
Papa and Onkel Paul used to go for days.
Once or twice they took my brother with
them——'

' Brother ! I didn't know you had
a brother ! ' interrupted Grizel, somewhat
rudely, it must be admitted.

' Oh, yes ; my brother is eighteen, nearly
nineteen. He is at the University of Bonn,'
replied Bernhilda. ' He will be a doctor some
day, and perhaps I shall be his *Hausfrau* till
he marries.'

' Perhaps he won't,' suggested Joey. ' I
know Dick, my brother, says he won't. He

says the Deccan is no place for women, and he loves his work too well to give it up.'

'Oh, I hope Gottfried will marry some day!' said his sister earnestly.

'We all hope that,' said her father. 'And now we must be returning, for there is quite a long walk, and the little one looks weary.'

He reached out a big hand and pinched Simone's cheek as he spoke.

She blushed, and edged nearer to Joey, who felt suddenly cross with her. If Simone was going to be so idiotically shy, and stick to her like glue all day, Joey felt things were going to be tiresome. And why, oh, why didn't she talk instead of standing there deathly silent?

'It's been awfully jolly of you to show us all these things, Herr Mensch,' she said, with a surreptitious poke at Simone. 'It makes it seem twice as nice to know the names of all the places; doesn't it, Simone?'

'Yes,' replied Simone faintly.

'We are going to go up the Bärenbad Alpe some Saturday soon and have cream,' went on Joey. 'Marie—Marie Pfeifen, who does the work for us, says that it is awfully nice cream; and it's an easy climb, so we shall all be able to go, even the new little boarders. Did you know we were to have two new boarders on Monday, Bernhilda?'

'No, I had not heard of it,' responded Bernhilda.

'Well, we are—Margia and Amy Stevens. Margia is eleven, and Amy is about the same

age as Maria Marani. That makes five of us
boarders, and p'r'aps we shall get some
more.'

Suddenly Grizel caught her arm. 'Look!'
she cried. 'There are those people I told you
about this morning that I saw going to the
Tyroler Hof! See—coming this way!'

They all looked with interest at the trio
who were walking in their direction—a tall,
bronzed man, with erect, soldierly bearing;
a small, slight woman, sallow of skin and
fashionable of dress; and a schoolgirl of
fifteen or thereabouts, whose most noticeable
features were a pair of enormous dark eyes,
and a long, fair pigtail swinging to her waist.
She was walking slightly behind the others,
and there was a sullen, unhappy look in her
face. Just as the two parties met, the woman
turned to her, saying sharply, 'Juliet! Hold
yourself up! Good gracious me, child, you
look positively deformed! Put your
shoulders back at once!'

The sharp, scolding tones brought back
her stepmother to Grizel, and involuntarily
she shivered. Joey, noticing, slipped an arm
through hers with a little squeeze. The girl
Juliet looked at them curiously as she passed
them. She had made no effort to straighten
herself, and Bernhilda commented on this
when they were out of hearing.

'But how disobedient!' she remarked.

'I can tell you their name,' said her father.
'He is a Herr Captain of the Indian army—

Captain Carrick. He came into the bank this morning to change some money.'

'I don't think he looks kind,' said Joey. 'What a pretty name the girl has—Juliet! Don't you think so, Grizel?'

'I thought she looked dreadfully unhappy,' replied Grizel. 'And how funny to have fair hair with those dark eyes!'

'Do you think so?' asked Bernhilda. 'There are a great number of people living in Wien who are like that. But as for unhappy, she did not do as she was told.'

Herr Mensch approved of this. 'The young should always obey,' he said. 'Is it not so, my little Frieda?'

Frieda, who would as soon have thought of flying as of disobeying her parents, said in her shy, soft voice, 'Yes, Papa!'

Grizel made a little impatient movement, but Joey's hand on her arm checked any remarks she might have made, and they went on to the *Gasthaus*, talking about the mountains. The girls went in, and the three boarders got their flowers and said 'good-bye' to Frau Mensch, who was sitting placidly knitting some stockings for Frieda. She kissed them all, and told them to come back whenever they liked. Then, accompanied by Bernhilda and Frieda, they went out, to find Herr Mensch waiting for them at the boathouse.

'Come!' he said. 'It is a long walk, and *die Kleine* looks tired! I will row you

across to your own landing-stage. Bernhilda
and Frieda, you may come too. Run, Frieda,
and tell Mamma ! '

Frieda ran quickly back, and presently
returned, and they pushed off.

It was glorious on the lake. The day had
been very warm for mid-May, but now, with
the evening, had come a little cool breeze
that ruffled the surface of the water into tiny
ripples, and set the curly ends round Grizel's
face dancing gaily.

They rowed out into the centre, and then
Herr Mensch rested on his oars, and nodded
towards the mountain he had named for them
—Alpenglückjoch.

' Look ! ' he said. ' Alpenglück to-night ! '

They turned and looked. As they did so,
they saw the grey limestone crags flush into
rosy life with the reflected light from the setting sun. All along the westward side of the
Tiern See the peaks caught the glory. It reflected on the silver thread of a mountain
cataract high up in the Sonnenscheinspitze,
and even cast a faint glow over the lake. For
five minutes the wonder lasted, then it began
to fade, and Herr Mensch took up his oars
again and rowed them in leisurely fashion to
the Châlet landing-stage.

' It is beautiful ! ' said Joey in low tones.
Her imaginative temperament had been fired
by the loveliness of what she had just seen.
' I have seen it once or twice from the
windows, but never from the water before.'

'Yes, it is a glory,' replied Herr Mensch; 'but it always brings bad weather with it. We shall have rain to-morrow.'

He brought the boat up to the landing-stage as he spoke, and helped them out. Madge had seen them coming, and came running down the path to meet them. When the Mensches had gone and were beyond calling range, she turned to the three.

'Girls,' she said, 'I have news for you! We have another day-girl. She is an English girl, whose people are Anglo-Indians. They have just come to Tiern See. When they heard of us, they came at once, and she starts on Monday. She is fifteen and a half, and has only been to school in the Hills. Her people are army people, and her name is——'

'Juliet Carrick!' burst out Grizel impatiently. 'Oh, Miss Bettany, is it—is it? Do say it is!'

Madge looked at her in amazement. 'Yes, it is,' she answered; 'but how do you know?'

They explained to her about the meeting near Buchau, and Grizel enlarged on the way Mrs Carrick had spoken to the girl.

'I believe she's her stepmother!' she concluded.

'No,' said Madge, 'she isn't. Don't get wild ideas into your head, Grizel. If they only came to Tiern See to-day, I expect they are tired, and that is why Mrs Carrick scolded.'

Grizel said nothing further, and Madge

thought no more of it. But when Herr Mensch heard, he looked thoughtful.

' I hope things will go well with Fräulein Bettany,' he said to his wife. ' I did not like that man—I do not trust him.'

And he resolved to advise Madge to write to her brother at the earliest opportunity, and see if any information could be gathered about these people who had come so suddenly.

However, when he spoke about it some days later, he found that she had done that very thing already.

' I know it seems mad to take anyone so abruptly,' she said, ' but they were so anxious, and—well—somehow he persuaded me. And they have paid a term's fees, of course, and if I find from my brother that she is not a desirable pupil, I can get rid of her quite easily by saying that we are full up. Anyhow, it is probably for this term only, as they expect to go to England in September ; but they had heard of Tiern See, and thought they would like to see it, so they broke their journey home.'

And after that the good-natured Austrian felt he had nothing left to say for the present.

CHAPTER VIII.

A FIRST PREFECTS' MEETING.

'GISELA!'

    'Yes? Do you want me, Gertrud?'

'I should be glad if you would summon a Prefects' meeting.'

Gisela put down her pen, which all this time she had been holding, and lifted a surprised and inquiring face to her friend.

'A meeting, Gertrud? Oh, but why? Nothing has gone wrong?'

'No,' agreed Gertrud, 'but I am afraid something will go wrong very soon.'

In her earnestness, she forgot the school rule which said that, during school-hours, and save in French and German lessons, nothing but English was to be used, and dropped into her native tongue.

'Oh, Gertrud! You have forgotten,' said Gisela reproachfully.

'I am sorry, Gisela! I was thinking about the meeting,' apologised Gertrud. 'Shall I enter my name in the Order Book?'

'No,' said the Head Girl firmly. 'It is not good for the Juniors that they see a Prefect's name there. You had better report yourself to Miss Maynard. And now, tell me, why do you wish this meeting?'

'There is mischief going on in the school,' returned Gertrud, perching herself on her friend's desk. 'It is partly that new girl, Juliet Carrick, but I think Grizel Cochrane is making it also.'

'How tiresome!' Gisela knitted her black brows at this information.

During the seven weeks that she had been Head Girl, there had been no real difficulty to meet. This was partly because of the novelty of things to all the girls; but also her own personal character had a great deal to do with it. Miss Bettany had chosen wisely in choosing her as Head of the girls. Bernhilda made a very good second, and Bette and Gertrud were rapidly learning their duties as Subs, but the most reliable person was Gisela. She now collected her papers together, and hastily stuffed them into her locker, while Gertrud stood, looking out of the window at the meadow-land, where half a dozen of the Juniors were playing cross-tag, with Joey Bettany as instructress.

'Ready?' she said presently, turning her head. 'Then shall we call the others? They are by the landing-stage.'

'Yes. Would you ask them to come to our room, Gertrud?' said Gisela. 'I will await you there.'

Three weeks previously, Madge Bettany, after a long discussion with Mademoiselle and Miss Maynard, who had been added to the staff as mathematics mistress, had given over

to the Prefects a small room on the first floor
for their own.

'Even if they have just four chairs in it, it
will give them a feeling of being a little different from the rest of the school,' she said.

Miss Maynard, herself a High School girl,
had agreed, and the four delighted girls had,
accordingly, that possession of which they
had read so much in their English school-
stories—a Prefects' room.

Miss Bettany had explained to them that,
beyond chairs and a small table, she could
give them no furniture yet; but they had
promptly joined forces. While Gisela
brought some pictures and a couple of bowls
for flowers, Gertrud produced a set of bookshelves which she had induced her brother to
make; Bernhilda contributed a pretty blue
and white tablecloth and a fancy inkstand,
and Bette presented a little clock and a
bracket on which to place it. Among them,
they had made a dainty little sanctum, and
Gisela always felt a thrill of pleasure when she
was in it. They were very anxious to have
things as like an English school as possible,
and many had been the consultations over the
question. In one book Gertrud had read of
the 'Prefects'' notice board. Careful questioning had soon drawn from Joey all
there was to know about this, and now a
similar board hung over the bookshelves,
with notices of various kinds on it, all written
in Gisela's pointed Italian handwriting, which,

by the way, was much less clear than it had
been when she first came, the reason being
that she was trying to copy her headmistress's
pretty High School script. The two big
bowls were full of Alpen roses, and on this
sunny afternoon it was as charming a girls'
room as could be wished. The Head Girl
pulled up the four chairs round the table, and
seated herself at the head, paper and pencil
before her. Presently there came the sound
of footsteps on the stairs, and then the other
three entered. Very smart and business-
like they looked in their school uniform,
which every girl now wore as a matter of
course. Gisela looked at them with approval.
The most English of English Prefects could
not have looked more orthodox, she thought.

'Gertrud tells me you wish a Prefects'
meeting,' began Bernhilda, as she took her
seat on Gisela's right hand. 'What is it that
you wish to discuss with us?'

'It is Gertrud's idea,' replied the Head
Girl. 'She thinks that things are going
rather——'

'Wonky,' supplemented Bette, as Gisela
paused to search for the right word. It was
a mystery to them all how Bette contrived to
pick up so much slang and to use it so cor-
rectly. All the foreign girls were far quicker
at English than either Grizel, Juliet, or the
two little Stevens had shown themselves at
French and German. Joey having merely to
renew her acquaintance with these two

languages, already spoke fluently and even colloquially! Bette's accent, too, was, save for a slight trill to her 'r's' and a trick of giving each word its full value, almost perfect. The other girls spoke with a fair fluency, but even Gisela was sometimes at a loss for a word; Bette, never.

The Head Girl now made a little bow to her Sub, and continued:

'Apparently Gertrud fears that Grizel Cochrane and Juliet Carrick are about to cause trouble. Myself, I have noticed nothing.'

'But I have,' said Bette composedly. 'I quite agree with Gertrud, and I think Juliet Carrick is at the bottom of it.'

'Why should you think that?' demanded Gisela.

'Because, until she came, Grizel Cochrane never rebelled against our authority. But now she is tiresome,' replied Bette. 'She is even rude.'

'How so? She has not been rude to me as yet. How has she been rude to you?'

'I told her to go and put her shoes away,' said Bette, 'and she said it was sickening having fussy foreigners always at you.'

'That was very rude,' said Gisela slowly. 'What did you do?'

'I said I was sorry she looked at it in that way,' returned Bette, 'but as I was a Sub-Prefect, and one of my duties was to see that the cloakroom was kept tidy, I was going to see that it was kept tidy.'

'What did she say then?' queried Bernhilda with interest.

'Said I thought myself everybody,' replied
Bette. 'I told her not to be impertinent, and
saw that she put the shoes away, and that was
all.'

'I think it was sufficient,' said Gisela
quietly. 'And you, Gertrud?'

'Talking after the silence-bell had been
rung,' said Gertrud. 'I told her to be quiet,
and she looked at Juliet and laughed.'

'What did Juliet do? Laugh too?'

'Yes, and shrugged her shoulders. It is
not good for the Juniors to see that in a girl
as old as Grizel or Juliet.'

'I don't think you need worry about the
Juniors,' said Bette. 'Amy and Margia
would never behave like that, and Maria is
too fond of you, Gisela, to worry you that
way. Nor would Suzanne and Yvette.
Giovanna will be good, because she doesn't
want a fuss with me, and I couldn't imagine
either Frieda or Simone doing anything but
keeping the rules. Joey, of course, will do as
she's told too. It really is only Grizel, and
she wouldn't if Juliet didn't encourage
her!'

'Well, I must make a punishment,' said
Gisela. 'I am sorry, but Grizel must not be
rude to the Prefects.' She thought deeply
for a minute. 'I shall send for her and make
her apologise to you, Bette, and you, Gertrud.
Then I shall say she is to learn some German

poetry in her play-hours. Yes, that is what
I shall do! Will you fetch her, Bette?'

Bette got up and left the room, to return
ten minutes later by herself.

'She refuses to come,' she said briefly.

'Refuses to come?' There was conster-
nation in Gisela's voice. 'But did you tell
her that the Prefects wanted her?'

'Yes,' said Bette. 'She just laughed, and
said if we wanted her we could go to her;
she wasn't coming to us!'

There was a silence. No one had foreseen
that Grizel would go to quite such lengths
as this, and they were uncertain how to deal
with it. It was, had they but known it, the
testing-point of the Prefect system in the
Châlet School. Had they given way, or taken
no notice of the English girl's defiance, it would
have been 'good-bye' to all hope of self-
government. Luckily for the school, Gisela
Marani was made of too fine stuff to throw
up the game weakly. To her mind there was
only one course to follow, and she followed it.

'I must report the matter to Miss Bettany,'
she said quietly. 'Bette, will you come with
me? She will want to hear what you have to
say.'

'Shall we wait till you come back?' asked
Gertrud.

'Yes, I think it would be better, if you do
not mind. We will make haste.'

The two girls left the room, and went downstairs to the sitting-room.

Madge Bettany, enjoying a much-deserved rest, looked up with surprise when, in answer to her ' Come in ! ' they entered, closing the door.

' Well,' she said with a smile, ' what is it that you want ? Anything wrong, Gisela ? '

' I have come to make a report to you,' replied Gisela steadily.

Madge's face sobered. ' To report a breach of rules ? Must you, Gisela ? '

All indecision had vanished from Gisela's mind now.

' Yes, I must,' she answered firmly.

' Well, what is it then, dear ? Sit down, both of you, and tell me.'

They sat down, and then Gisela unfolded her story, looking every now and then to Bette for corroboration. Miss Bettany grew more and more serious as they progressed, and when, finally, they had finished, she sat for a minute or two without speaking. As a matter of fact, she had herself noticed a change in Grizel's manner of late. She realised, of course, that after four years of such rigorous training as the child had had, reaction must follow with the greater freedom ; but she had not expected anything quite so bad as this. She had no desire to punish Grizel, but this sort of thing could not be allowed. As for Juliet, she sincerely hoped that September would see her far enough away from the Tiern See.

' I will send for her,' she said at length.

'Where are you? In the Prefects' room? Very well, then! I will come back with you, and she shall come and apologise for her rudeness to you. I am sorry this has occurred, Gisela.'

'I, too, am sorry,' replied Gisela. 'I wish it had not been necessary to trouble you with it, Madame.'

'You were quite right to report it,' returned her headmistress. 'We cannot have this sort of thing occurring. Will you find a Junior, Bette, and send her for Grizel? Then I will follow you upstairs.'

Thus dismissed, they left the room. In the passage they met Amy Stevens.

'Please tell Grizel Cochrane that Miss Bettany wants her in the Prefects' room at once,' said Bette, while Gisela passed on in silence.

'Yes, Bette,' said little Amy. 'In the Prefects' room? All right.'

She ran off, and Bette followed Gisela upstairs. They were greeted by a duel of 'Well?' as they entered the room.

'Miss Bettany has sent for Grizel, and she is coming here herself,' replied Gisela.

A minute later the headmistress appeared, looking sterner than they had ever seen her before. She had just taken her seat, when there was a tap at the door, and Grizel entered with an air of somewhat forced defiance.

Left to herself, she would never have behaved as she had done. But there was a

certain weakness in Grizel's character, and she
was easily led. Juliet Carrick was just the type
of girl to exercise a good deal of influence over
Grizel.   In the first place, the child's generous
pity had been aroused by what she had seen
and heard of Juliet's family life.   There was
no doubt that Captain and Mrs Carrick found
their daughter a good deal of a nuisance, and
the girl had a most unhappy time.   Then
again, Juliet had grown up in the class
of Anglo-Indian society that considers the
English the only nation worth mentioning,
and her training in a Hill school, where nine-
tenths of the girls were Eurasians who looked
down on their native cousins with a bitter
contempt, had helped to foster this feeling.
She had sneered at 'foreigner Prefects,'
asserting that they could not possibly act
adequately.   Grizel was feeling sore at what
she considered Joey's extraordinary fancy
for Simone Lecoutier—and all the time poor
Joey would have given much to be rid of
this friendship !—and she therefore followed
Juliet's lead, with disastrous results to herself, and to others later on.

Madge wasted few words on her when she
appeared.

'You have been rude to the Prefects,
Grizel ? ' she asked.

A mumble was the only reply. Madge took
it as meaning ' yes.'

'You will apologise at once,' she said
coldly. 'I will allow no rudeness from you

younger children to my Prefects. You had better understand that at once. Ask their pardon, and then do whatever they give you for punishment.' There was a silence. ' Come, Grizel ! '

There was that in the headmistress's voice which compelled Grizel to obedience.

Without raising her eyes, she muttered, ' I 'm sorry ! '

Miss Bettany was wise enough to realise that it would be well to accept this. She waited till Gisela had accepted the apology, and had set the culprit a short German poem to learn. Then she said, ' You may go, Grizel ! ' And when the child had dashed away, she left the room.

As for Grizel, she had rushed off to the pine-woods, where she vowed, amidst her tears of shame and anger, that she would pay them all out for treating her in this way.

CHAPTER IX.

SIMONE'S EXPLOIT.

IF any of the girls had been inclined to
defy the Prefects, Miss Bettany's prompt
action over Grizel Cochrane's behaviour had
put an end to any such ideas. The school
was rapidly settling down, and the twenty
girls who made it up already felt a great pride
in it. All the day-girls stayed for dinner now,
arriving at the Châlet by half-past eight in
the morning and staying till six o'clock in the
evening. Lessons began at nine and went on
till twelve, when there was a break for the
midday meal. At two o'clock they started
work again, and went on till four. Tea was
at ten past four, and then, from five to six,
the Seniors did preparation and the Juniors
practised. Twice a week Herr Anserl came
up from Spärtz and gave music lessons to the
more advanced pupils, while the others
learned with Mademoiselle. Miss Maynard
taught mathematics and geography through
the school, and Miss Bettany herself under-
took the English subjects. French, German,
and sewing were Mademoiselle's department,
and she was form mistress of the Junior form.
At present they had only the three forms—
Senior, Middle, and Junior; but already

Madge was looking joyfully forward to the time when she would be able to have at least five forms.

Two days after the Prefects' meeting, a long letter came from England from Mrs Dene. Mr Dene had been the senior curate of the Parish Church at home, but he had accepted a chaplaincy in the West Indies, and they were not anxious to take Rosalie there. Then Mrs Dene had thought of the Châlet School at Tiern See, and she wrote to ask if Rosalie might join them in September. If so, would Miss Bettany also have room for Rosalie's cousin, Mary Burnett?

Miss Bettany wrote back saying that she would be pleased to have them both.

The same day, an Italian lady whose acquaintance she had made came to make inquiries with regard to her little daughter. Signora di Ricci was a charming person, and she was obviously very anxious that Vanna should come. Madge knew Vanna, and liked her; so, with Evadne Lannis, there were four more pupils for the Châlet School.

Sitting on her desk in the Middle school-room, Joey Bettany proclaimed the news of the coming of two more English girls in the autumn.

'It's topping to think Rosalie and Mary are coming!' she said enthusiastically.

'How old are they?' asked Margia Stevens.

'Rosalie's about fourteen and Mary's twelve,' replied Joey.

' Oh ! One for the Seniors and one for us,'
observed Frieda Mensch, who was beginning
to get over her shyness. ' That will be jolly ! '

' Tophole ! ' agreed Joey. ' We are spread-
ing, aren't we ? You 'll love Mary, Frieda.
She 's such a dear, steady old thing ! I 'm
glad she 's coming ! '

Simone, who was, as usual, glued to her
side, changed colour at this, but for once
Joey took no notice. Truth to tell, she was
getting thoroughly tired of Simone's jealousy
and all-in-all friendship, and there had already been more than one scene, when Simone
had accused Jo of hurting her on purpose,
and not liking her any more. The last time,
unsentimental Jo had very nearly declared
that she didn't ; that she was fed-up with all
these fusses ! But Simone had melted into
tears at the least harshness, and cried so
piteously, that Joey hadn't the heart to do it.
Now, unheeding of the little French girl at
her side, she went on enthusiastically : ' Mary
was a form below me at the High School, but
they lived near us, and we used to play
together. We were in the same net-ball
team too.'

' And the other girl—Rosalie ; is she, too,
pleasant ? ' asked Frieda.

' Oh, yes, quite jolly ! ' replied Joey.
' She 's awfully pretty too, and jolly clever
as well ! Oh, bother ! There 's the five-to-
nine bell, and I haven't got my books out !
Mind, Simone ! '

She brushed past Simone as she jumped down, and dashed to her locker to collect her possessions. The French child looked at her with big, mournful eyes, but Joey took no notice. She was intent on finding her history, which seemed to have vanished. Just in time it turned up, and then they all had to go in to prayers and call-over.

At lessons that morning Simone seemed unusually stupid. All her arithmetic was wrongly worked; her dictation was full of mistakes; and she knew no one word about history, although, as Joey well knew, she had thoroughly prepared it on the previous evening. The lesson was an easy one too—the story of the Bartholomew Massacre. As question after question passed the little girl, and she either did not answer at all, or else talked utter rubbish, Miss Bettany's brow grew blacker and blacker. She had just left the Seniors after a tussle with Grizel, who seemed to have taken leave of her senses lately, and she wondered whether that young lady's spirit of lawlessness were infecting Simone. Finally, she closed her book with an angry snap.

'Simone! Why have you not prepared your work? It is simply disgraceful that you should know so little of your own country's history! I am surprised at you! You must do this lesson over again at half-past four, and please never give me such disgraceful work again!'

Simone said nothing. She felt utterly miserable and unhappy, and only longed to fly away somewhere where she could cry her heart out. The others were looking at her with startled faces. It was so unlike Simone to have to be spoken to like this. Meanwhile the bell rang, and, under their Head's watchful eyes, they were forced to file out of the room in proper order. Nor were they able to speak until they had escaped with their glasses of lemonade into the open air.

Then Simone was discovered to have disappeared.

'What on earth can be the matter with her?' demanded Joey of a select group, composed of herself, Margia Stevens, Frieda Mensch, and Suzanne Mercier. 'D' you think she's ill or anything?'

'She was all right at first,' replied Margia. 'She was talking like anything at breakfast, and she ate heaps!'

'But look here! She knew that history last night—I know she did! And she never gets returned work! Why, she's top of the form every time!' protested Joey, whose own work had, at any rate, the merit of not being monotonous, since it was either very good, or else so bad as to be beneath contempt.

'She may have a headache,' suggested Suzanne, as she nibbled daintily at her biscuit. 'Sometimes they begin suddenly.'

'I 've never heard of Simone having headaches,' said Joey doubtfully.

'Let's try and find her,' proposed Margia. 'If she isn't well, Miss Bettany ought to know. She might be going to have measles or anything'

At that moment the bell for the end of break went, so they had to return to their form-room and French composition. Simone did not put in an appearance; but then, as Joey said afterwards, they all thought that she must be poorly and have gone to tell the Head, who had sent her to bed. Mademoiselle herself did not miss the child. Simone was always so very quiet and inconspicuous, and naturally, she did not require nearly as much attention as the others. The last lesson was geometry with Miss Maynard, and as the little French girl's arithmetic was appallingly backward, it had been decided that, for the present, she should concentrate on that. When, however, she did not put in an appearance at *Mittagessen*, Miss Bettany promptly inquired where she was.

'In bed, I think,' replied Joey with equal promptness.

The Head's black brows were drawn together in a frown of perplexity.

'Bed? But why? Who sent her? Isn't she well? Mademoiselle——'

'I know nothing,' replied Mademoiselle. 'I have not seen her since this morning.'

'Nor I,' replied Miss Maynard. 'She came to my arithmetic lesson, of course, but she doesn't take geometry, and I haven't seen her since before recreation.'

Miss Bettany got up, looking disturbed. ' Joey, why do you think she has gone to bed ? Did she tell you she felt poorly ? '

' Oh, no,' replied Joey. ' Only, she got all her work wrong, and it isn't like her, so we thought she must be ill.'

' Run upstairs and see if she is there.'

Joey vanished, to come back a few minutes later looking flushed and startled.

' She isn't there, Madge,' she said, using the forbidden Christian name in her earnestness. ' There's no one there. But in her cubicle I found—this ! ' And she held up a long, thick plait of black hair.

A gasp sounded through the room. Madge, Mademoiselle, and Miss Maynard stood as if they were transfixed to the spot, while Joey Bettany stood holding that awful relic of Simone before their eyes.

Amy Stevens broke the silence by a whimper. ' Oh, is Simone killed dead ? Has someone chopped off her head ? ' she wailed.

As if someone had released a spring which was holding her, Mademoiselle leaped forward and snatched the plait from the trembling Joey.

' And where, then, is Simone ? ' she shrieked in her native tongue. ' What has become of her ? '

' Nothing very terrible can have happened, Mademoiselle,' said Madge, coming forward hastily. 'She must have done it for a joke or for mischief, and now is probably ashamed to show herself!' She turned to the girls with anger in her face. 'Girls, do any of you know anything about this?' She was looking hard at Grizel and Juliet as she spoke, but it was quite obvious that they knew no more about it than anyone else. They all looked dumbfounded.

Mademoiselle turned on Joey. 'Josephine, you are the friend of Simone! Why has she done this thing?'

Joey shook her head helplessly. 'I don't know, Mademoiselle—honest Injun, I don't! I'd have stopped her if I'd known.'

Things certainly seemed at a deadlock. Amy had stopped crying, mainly because no one was taking any notice of her, and the rest just sat in stricken silence.

'Well,' said Miss Bettany at length, 'we had better try to find her. Miss Maynard, will you take the table while Mademoiselle and I go to search? Yes, Joey, what is it?'

'Oh, please, may I come too?' asked Joey breathlessly. 'I've just remembered where she might be—in the pines. I can find it in a second.'

'Very well,' said her sister. 'Mademoiselle and I will go through the house, and you can try this hidey-hole you say she has in the pine-woods. Put your hat on, though—the sun is very hot to-day.'

Joey only waited long enough to snatch her

hat from its peg in the cloakroom before
dashing off to the pine-covered slopes at full
speed. As she ran, her brain busied itself
with the question of why Simone should have
cut her hair, of which, as a matter of plain
fact, she had been rather vain. No good
reason came to her as she clambered over the
roots of the pine trees, occasionally sliding a
little on the slippery earth. It was very still
in the woods, for there was no breeze to stir
through the pine-needles, and the very birds
seemed to have hushed their hymns of praise.
Overhead, through the dark branches, she got
glimpses of a sky, blue as lapis lazuli, un-
flecked by a single cloud. But although she
worshipped beauty, Joey had no time to
spare for the wonderful tranquillity of this
summer noon. She was intent on finding her
friend. She reached the hollow between the
big roots, where she had found Simone before,
but it was empty. There was no sign at all
of the little French girl, and Joey's heart
stood still for a moment. She had been so
sure she would find Simone there. As she
stood, wondering whatever she should do now,
a little sob caught her ear. At once she swung
round, and scrambled over the sticks and dead
pine-needles in its direction. There, in a little
heap, lay Simone, crying as even Joey had
never seen her cry before. The ends of her
hair where she had sawn off her plait stood
up like little drakes' tails, an effect which
would have made her friend giggle helplessly

at any other time. Now, however, she only
tumbled down beside her, flinging an arm
round her, and hauling her up on to her knee.

'Simone! Oh, Simone! What is the
matter with you?'

'Go away!' sobbed Simone, in her own
language. 'Go away, Joey!'

'No fear!' replied Joey. 'I'm not going
till you're ready to come with me. And
anyhow, I want to know why you've chopped
your wig like that. You once told me you
wouldn't have your hair bobbed for anything.
Why on earth did you do it?'

'I—I thought you would like it!' Simone
choked out. 'You have often laughed at me
because my hair was long, and I thought if I
cut it short you would love me, and not leave
me when those new English girls come next
term!'

'Well!' Joey sat back and gasped. 'Of
all the mad ideas!' she said, when she had got
her breath back. 'I don't care whether you
wear your hair cropped like a convict or
trailing round your feet like Lady Godiva!
Really, Simone, you are a perfect idiot! And
why did you rush off here like that? I
nearly had a fit when I went to find you in
your cubicle and found only your pigtail!'

'I look so terrible!' sobbed Simone. 'And
then I thought of what Cousine Elise would
say, and how Miss Bettany would be angry,
and you and all the other girls would laugh,
and so I ran away.'

' Well, now you 're coming back,' said Joey
firmly. ' I don't know what Madge will say
to you, or Mademoiselle ! But you can't
stay here for ever, and I want my dinner—I
came out in the middle of it ! As for laughing
at you, I sha'n't ; and I don't much suppose
the others will either. Now do stop howling
and come on ! '

At first Simone refused to budge, but finally
Joey succeeded in getting her to come back
with her, and they reached the Châlet, both
of them feeling hot and tired. After one
glance at the French child's face, Miss Bettany
packed her off to bed without one word of
scolding ; and when she had finally dragged
the whole ridiculous story out of her sister,
she sent that young lady up to her cubicle
with strict injunctions to go to sleep. Then
she betook herself to Mademoiselle and unfolded the tale to her.

' In a way, it 's just as well,' she said, ' for
all that mass of hair was far too much for
her in hot weather ; but of course she had no
business to cut it herself like that. You had
better take her over to the Kron Prinz
to-morrow and let the hairdresser there trim
it. Now I must go to my class.'

The next day Simone was taken to have
her hair properly cut, and, much to her relief,
the other girls said very little about the whole
affair, although her cousin scolded her roundly.
Besides that, she had to write a letter home to
tell them what she had done, and *Maman's*

grieved reply was very hard to bear. Altogether, Simone deeply regretted the fact that she had ever touched her hair—the more so, since Joey Bettany, instead of being impressed by what she had done, characterised the whole thing as ' idiotic nonsense ! '

CHAPTER X.

THE CINEMA ACTRESSES.

IT was a mercy, as Madge Bettany said, that for the next week or two everything went quite ordinarily. Grizel and Juliet gave the Prefects no further trouble; Simone ceased, for the moment, to behave in a sentimental way; Amy Stevens gave up crying on the smallest provocation; and there was peace in the Châlet School. The only event of any note was an accident Bernhilda had with the red ink.

All the stationery was in one cupboard, the key of which Miss Maynard kept. Bernhilda had been appointed Stationery Prefect, and she went every Friday and gave out the new stationery as it was required. It was not a very heavy task as yet, since everyone had started with new books at the beginning of the term. Scribblers and little notebooks and pen-nibs were what were mainly required, with a very occasional exercise-book, and Grizel Cochrane, in her capacity as ink monitress, came on Mondays for the week's supply.

On the Monday following Simone's exploit, Grizel came as usual with her ink-can. She found Bernhilda, who took her duties very seriously, engaged in tidying the top shelf of the cupboard. The Prefect, sitting on the top of the step-ladder, looked down at her Junior.

'Oh, Grizel, will you please take the ink?' she said. 'I want to finish this before the bell rings! It is in the big jar at the bottom.'

'All right, Bernhilda! Don't you worry; I'll get it all right,' replied Grizel cheerfully. Juliet had been absent on the Thursday and Friday of the previous week, and had not yet turned up, so Grizel was a much nicer child in consequence.

Having directed the Junior's attention to the big ink-jar, Bernhilda returned to her task, while Grizel, pushing back the long, thick curls which, despite the ribbon that tied them back, would get in her way, uncorked the jar, and, carefully tilting it on one side, began to fill her can. Both were absorbed in their work. Grizel had very nearly finished, when Bernhilda gave a sudden shriek, and dived forward, nearly collapsing on to Grizel, who echoed her shriek. At the same time there was a crash as the large pint bottle of red ink fell heavily against the step-ladder, and smashed, sending a fountain of red ink in every direction. Bernhilda's tunic suffered, but the one who came off worst was Grizel, who was almost directly underneath. In her dive forward, the Prefect managed to catch the bottom portion of the bottle, and the rest fell clear of the Junior; but the ink deluged her—hair, frock, hands, even her legs

were dripping with it. As Madge said afterwards, a more gory-looking spectacle it would
have been hard to find anywhere.

The combined shrieks of the two drew
the staff hastily to the spot. Mademoiselle,
under the impression that there had been a
fearful accident, rushed forward with a cry
of ' Where, then, is the injury ? '

Miss Maynard and the headmistress, who
had both realised almost at once what had
occurred, were hard put to it to keep from
laughing, although the latter promptly produced a handkerchief, and set to work to try
to wipe off some of the ink. By this time
Bernhilda had reached the ground, and was
giving a somewhat incoherent account of what
had occurred.

According to her story, she had turned
some books round sharply, and had caught
the ink-bottle with a corner. She had tried
to catch it, but had not been in time to prevent its breaking. The rest they could see
for themselves. Grizel, who had not been
actually hurt, was furious.

' I 'm all ink, and my gymmer is ruined ! '
she said in choked accents.

' No, I don't think so,' replied Miss
Bettany gravely. ' You must get out of it
at once, of course, and Marie must wash it
immediately. Then I think it will be all
right. Luckily it 's your cotton tunic. And
you must go and get a bath. I 'll come and
wash your hair, and then you 'll be all right

by recreation. Don't look so distressed, Bernhilda. It was an accident, and you couldn't help it. But I advise you, for the future, to put all liquids on the floor of the cupboard.'

Accordingly, Grizel was marched off to sundry ablutions, and Bernhilda was requested to give up her tunic so that it, too, could be washed. While it was drying, she put on a skirt of Miss Maynard's.

When recreation came, a very clean and exceedingly indignant Grizel joined the others, secretly expecting to be well teased about her unexpected bath. Luckily for her, however, she found everyone buzzing with excitement over some news Juliet Carrick had brought that morning.

It appeared that a certain well-known firm of film producers had decided to use the Tiern See as part of the setting for a film which should give *Life in the Austrian Tyrol*. It was one of a series of educational films that they were doing; and since it was not, of course, always possible to get the natives of the country to pose for them, they had sent the ' principals ' over from America. These six important people, together with the director, the camera man, and a business manager, were making the Tyroler Hof their headquarters for the time being. They were going to use all the villages and hamlets round the lake as settings, and also some of the Alms, where the cowherds lived during the

summer in wooden huts, while the cows
browsed contentedly on the sweet, short
grass of the upland pastures. They intended
to go beyond the lake and, following the
course of the little Tiern, take some of the
hamlets and villages on its banks. Just why
they should have hit on the Tiern See was
hard to say. Juliet was not occupied with
that question. It was the whole idea which
appealed to her, and she was full of it.

' They are going to the Ziller Thal after
this,' she chattered eagerly, ' and Kufstein as
well, before they go south to the Dolomites.
They 've done Innsbrück and the Stubai Thal
and round about there, and Mr Eades—that 's
the camera man—said they had some glorious
close-ups of Hall and Spärtz. He was awfully
interested in us, and I think they mean to ask
Miss Bettany to let them take us. Isn't it
thrilling ? '

Miss Bettany, however, when approached
on the subject by the said Mr Eades and a Mr
Sindon, the business manager, refused to hear
of it. She was icily courteous and absolutely
decided. Nothing would induce her to re-
consider the matter, and the two gentlemen
left the Châlet, realising that, as one of them
later expressed it to Juliet, ' It was abso. N.G.
Nix on the "movies" stunt ! '

Most of the girls cared very little either
one way or the other, but Juliet herself,
Grizel, and one or two of the more thoughtless
ones were bitterly disappointed. They had

already, in imagination, seen themselves on the screen. People all over Europe and the British Isles, at any rate, would know them, and now it was all spoilt by Miss Bettany's refusal.

' It 's a shame ! ' cried Juliet, to a select gathering on the afternoon of the day on which she learned of her headmistress's decision. ' Why couldn't we be filmed ? Big schools like Eton and Winchester are ! But Miss Bettany always does that sort of thing ! She 's thoroughly narrow-minded ! '

' No, she isn't ! ' returned Grizel, who had moments when she realised that her present behaviour was anything but what Madge had the right to expect of her. ' It 's different photographing boys at sports, and doing us here by the lake. Oh, I can't tell you how, but it is ! ' And from this position she refused to budge.

Juliet gave it up, for she was clever enough to realise that once Grizel had made up her mind to a thing, wild horses wouldn't move her. However, Anita Rincini, Sophie Hamel, and Suzanne Mercier were more easily swayed, and were soon persuaded into thinking that they had a grievance against Miss Bettany. The manager of the ' movies ' also felt he had a grievance. He had foreseen a glorious advertisement in the school. It was, so far as he knew, an entirely fresh idea, and the girls looked so fresh and dainty in their uniform, and the whole thing would have made an excellent foil to his continental scenes.

'If only I could get just one or two of your kids!' he said to Juliet. 'It would be an easy matter to rig up a schoolroom scenario. And we could take you sculling, and swimming, and so on.'

These words gave Juliet an idea. 'Could you really do it?' she asked. 'If I got some of the girls together in our uniform, could you really manage?'

'Of course I could!' he said impatiently. 'Come to that, I suppose I could rig up something in the States when we get back.'

'But it wouldn't be the same scenery,' said Juliet earnestly.

'We could fake it near enough for the public,' he replied.

'But it would be better with the same backgrounds, wouldn't it?' she asked.

'Of course it would! But that school-ma'am of yours won't even listen to the idea, so where's the good of talking about it?' he returned irritably.

'Supposing I were to get two or three of the others to come, couldn't you take us?' queried Juliet.

Mr Sindon's face lit up at the idea. He was not so thick-skinned that he could not feel the disdain in Miss Bettany's icy voice when she had refused his suggestion, and it seemed to him that here was a chance to get even with her.

'I could manage it, of course,' he said slowly. 'When could you arrange for it? Because we are off next Friday, so it would have to be before then.'

'Would Saturday do?'

'Yes, that would do very well. Saturday, then, at ten o'clock in the morning. Bring your swimming suits, and we'll get you in the water.'

Juliet tackled her four satellites, and by dint of flattery, coaxing, and, in the case of Sophie Hamel, frank bullying, got them to agree to join her. As she had expected, Grizel was the hardest of them to capture. If it had not been for the fact that she had been caught talking in the dormitory the previous night after 'lights out,' and had been roundly scolded by the Head that morning, she would probably never have done it. As it was, she gave in when Juliet had alternately scolded and pleaded with her for nearly half an hour, and agreed to be at Geisalm, a little hamlet a mile and a half up the lake shore, on Saturday morning. It would be an easy matter for her to be there; for, on Saturdays, they were left very much to themselves, Madge Bettany having a theory that it was better to trust girls than to watch them continually. They were not allowed to bathe or go boating unless a mistress was there; but otherwise no one interfered with them, and so far there had been no necessity for interference. Therefore, ten o'clock on

Saturday morning found Grizel, in company
with Juliet, scrambling along the narrow
rocky path that leads from Briesau to
Geisalm.

' Aren't you thrilled ? ' demanded Juliet, as
they stopped to rest on the great ' fan ' of
alluvial rock which marks the half-way between
the two places. ' I am ! I 've never acted
for " movies " before.'

Grizel did not suppose Juliet had, and her
conscience was beginning to wake up very
thoroughly, which may have accounted for
the vehemence with which she said, ' Oh,
rather ! Awfully ! '

Juliet shot a quick glance at her from her
queer, dark eyes, but she said nothing beyond,
' Well, we 'd better be getting on ! '

They went on their way—slowly and carefully, for at this part the path was not very
wide, and went almost sheer down to the
water, whose vivid blueness told how deep it
was. At any other time Grizel would have
enjoyed that scramble over the rocks, and the
rapid run past the place where the mountain
water dripped from a crag that overhung the
path. She had enjoyed this very walk a score
of times. But now she felt half angry and
wholly unhappy, and I think that if it had not
been for her fear of Juliet's mocking tongue,
she would have turned back even then. So
absorbed was she in her uneasiness, that she
never noticed a broad-bottomed rowing-boat
with four people in it heading for Scholastika.

Juliet, who, at the moment it passed, was gathering a bunch of purple scabious and white moon-daisies, did not notice it either.

The occupants of the boat glanced up, attracted by the splash of brown against the green of the Alm which they had reached. Juliet they passed over, but as Joey Bettany's eyes lingered on the other gym-frocked figure, she gave a gasp.

' Herr Mensch ! ' she cried. ' That's Grizel ! Whatever is she doing here ? '

Herr Mensch turned a placid face towards the place, but the two girls had vanished behind the clump of trees which protects the footpath from the lake at this point.

' So ? ' he said politely. ' Then that is why we could not find her when we came to fetch you ? But is it wrong for her to be here ? '

' I 'm sure my sister doesn't know about it,' declared Joey. ' She thought Grizel must have gone to buy apples from the old woman at Seespitz, 'cos she said so ! '

Herr Mensch's fair, German-looking face became troubled.

' That is very wrong of das Mädchen,' he said gravely. ' Would you like us to land at Geisalm and take her into the boat ? '

Joey thought rapidly for a moment. They had never been told that they were not to go to Geisalm by themselves, but she knew that Madge was always a little nervous about that path, especially the narrow bit of it. She also knew that Grizel would be furious at being interfered with—and she had been furious so often lately! But Joey Bettany was not the kind to shirk doing what she ought to do just because other people would be furious with her, so she nodded her head.

'Yes, please! I think it would be better, if you don't mind!'

Without a word, the good-natured Austrian turned the boat towards the little green triangle with its big white *Gasthaus*, which forms Geisalm. A group of people were standing there talking together. Joey recognised the cinema folk, but still she didn't guess what was up until Bernhilda cried, 'Why, there are Sophie and Anita. How strange for so many of the Châlet girls to meet here to-day!'

Then Joey understood.

'Oh!' she said, and her face, pale no longer, but tanned by the hot sunshine, flamed with sudden anger. 'Oh! How can she, when Madge said not!'

'How can she do what?' asked Bernhilda, who was slow at grasping things. 'And of whom are you speaking, Joey?'

'It's Grizel! Juliet's done it, of course! She's mad on them!' replied Joey incoherently. 'Oh, Herr Mensch! Please stop them! Madge will be so angry, and it isn't fair when she said she wouldn't!'

Herr Mensch was quicker than his daughter. With a final pull he brought the boat neatly to the landing-stage and sprang out.

'Stay here!' he said curtly to the three girls with him, and then he strode off to the group by the *Gasthaus*.

Mr Sindon was considerably surprised when he found himself confronted by an angry giant of a man, who requested to know, in very good English, if he intended taking photos that day. Something in the angry giant's voice warned him that he had better give an answer at once, and to the point, so he replied that he was. It was at this moment that Grizel and Juliet came upon them. Herr Mensch took not the slightest notice of the elder girl, but he turned to Grizel and, in tones which literally scared her, told her to go to the boat at once. With her he sent Anita and Sophie. Then he spoke to the paralysed Mr Sindon.

'I am sorry, mein Herr, if in taking these young ladies away I am causing you any inconvenience, but they are here without the knowledge or permission of their parents and guardians. I wish you good-day!' And with this he turned and strode back to the boat, where Anita Rincini, who happened to be the daughter of his own great friend, had dissolved into tears. Sophie looked scared, and Grizel was beginning to recover sufficiently to feel furiously angry at having been treated in this summary fashion. But Herr Mensch took no notice of her at all.

'How did you get here?' he asked the other two in their own language.

Sophie pointed to the light rowing-boat moored to the landing-stage. 'We rowed across from Scholastika,' she explained.

'I see,' he said. 'Well now, you will row back with me.' Then he turned his attention to the English girl. 'You will come with us,' he said. 'Get into the boat.'

Grizel gave him one look—and obeyed. Sophie and Anita had already started. In a grim silence they pulled up the lake to Scholastika. Bernhilda and Frieda were too much afraid of their father's anger to speak, and Joey was busily engaged in trying not to say what she thought—yet.

At Scholastika, Herr Mensch grimly marched them before him, first to the Rincinis' villa, and then to the hotel where the Hamels were staying. While there, he rang up the Châlet, and told Madge that, as they had met Grizel, he was taking her with the others to Maria Kirche to see the famous church there, and they would all return in the afternoon. Then he went back to the girls, and sending Bernhilda and Joey on in front, took each a hand of Frieda and Grizel.

It was not a pleasant expedition. And when they returned in the afternoon, Herr Mensch had a long conversation with Miss Bettany, which ended in a more serious scolding for Grizel than she had ever known since she had left England. What hurt her more than anything was the knowledge that she was not to be trusted by herself—at any rate for the present. As for Juliet, Captain Carrick had made arrangements only that morning for her to be a boarder for the remainder of the term, as he and his wife were going to Munich to visit some friends, and did not want to take her with them. Miss Bettany resolved to keep a watchful eye on the new boarder.

CHAPTER XI.

'JOEY! Are you busy, or may I come and talk to you?'

Joey Bettany raised her head with a start at the sound of the voice. Looking down from her perch on the fence which shut off the Alm of Briesau from the Geisalm path, she saw Gisela Marani standing beside her, book in hand, a very serious expression on her charming face.

'Hullo, Gisela! What's the trouble?' she said cheerfully, as she closed *John Halifax, Gentleman*, which she was reading for the third time in succession.

'It is this book,' explained Gisela, tapping it. 'Will you come with me to the seat by the boat-landing? I wish to discuss it with you.'

'Rather!' Joey slid down from her seat with great goodwill, and, slipping her arm through Gisela's, strolled along by her side.

'Look!' she said suddenly. 'There's some new people from the Kron Prinz Karl. They came last night. Father and mother, and two girls and two boys, and a grown-up girl. Don't they look jolly?'

Gisela glanced idly in the direction in which

Joey, in complete defiance to good manners, was pointing. Then her face suddenly changed, and her lips curved up in a smile of surprise and pleasure.

'Wanda!' she cried.

The elder girl, a slim, fair person of about fifteen, turned round at the sound of her voice. Then she uttered a little cry and ran towards them.

'Gisela!' she exclaimed.

The younger girl and a small boy of about seven looked up too, and in a minute they also were racing up to the little group.

Gisela embraced them all, while Joey stood on one side, feeling rather in the way. But the Austrian had no idea of leaving her out.

'Wanda — Marie — Wolfram — this is my English friend, Joey Bettany. I am now at her sister's school in the large châlet over there. Joey, these are Wanda and Marie von Eschenau, and their brother Wolfram. I was at school in Vienna with Wanda and Marie when we lived there.'

Joey had never been a shy person; she had travelled about too much for that. So now she came forward and shook hands easily.

'Hullo!' she said. 'Are these your holidays?'

The elder girl, whom Gisela had saluted as Wanda, smiled.

'But no; not holidays,' she said, and her careful speech reminded Joey of the first few weeks of the Châlet School. 'We have

left our *lycée* in Wien '—which is what the
Austrians call Vienna—' and we are resting
here until Mamma finds us one where we can
be always—ah! you call it " boarding-
school," I remember.'

' Oh, Wanda ! ' cried Gisela. ' You must
come to the Châlet School ! '

' That would be very pleasant,' said Wanda
politely. ' Listen ! I hear Mamma calling.
Come, Marie ! Wolfram ! We shall hope to
see you again, Gisela ; I must tell Mamma you
are here. *Auf wiedersehen !* Good-bye, Fräulein Joey.'

And she hurried off, followed by the other
two, who had looked at the two Châlet girls
in deathly silence all the time.

' What *pretties*, Gisela ! ' said Joey enthusiastically, as she and Gisela made their way
to the little white-painted stand near the
landing-stage, where people liked to sit and
watch the passengers getting on and off the
boats. ' What did you say their name was ? '

' Von Eschenau,' replied Gisela. ' Their
papa is Herr Rittmeister von Eschenau of the
Imperial Guards. It would be very jolly if
Wanda and Marie came to the Châlet School,
for they are nice girls ; and if Miss Bettany
could say she had the daughters of a Herr
Rittmeister at her school, then she would get
many more pupils.'

' Would she ? ' Joey had the vaguest ideas
about the Austrian class-feelings. Also, she
was not sure just what a Herr Rittmeister

might be. Gisela did not enlighten her, either. She was, at the moment, much more engrossed in the book which she had been reading than in the arrival of her old friends, and as soon as they were comfortably established on one of the white seats, she began her discussion at once.

'Papa brought me this book two days ago,' she said, exhibiting to Joey's interested eyes a girl's school-story with a gay paper jacket.

'*Denise of the Fourth*,' read the English girl. 'Who's it by? Muriel Bernardine Browne? Never heard of her! What's it like?'

'I find it interesting—in parts,' replied Gisela, 'though some of it seems to me impossible. But there are descriptions of two things which interest me very much, and I was wondering if we also could not have them.'

'Don't say " we also " like that!' corrected Joey, who occasionally found the English of her continental friends rather boring. 'It isn't a bit English! And what are the two things?'

'Thank you, Joey, I will try to remember,' said Gisela, referring to Joey's correction of her English. 'And the two things are a magazine, first. In the school of this story, the girls had a most interesting magazine. It gives examples from it. See!' And she rapidly found the place, and gave it to Joey, who skimmed through the chapter with a widening grin on her face.

' It is amusing ? ' queried the Head Girl.
' You find it funny ? '

' It 's a shriek,' pronounced the critic.
' Fancy anyone writing sentimental tosh like
that sunset !   How old is Denise, anyhow ? '

' She is fourteen,' replied Gisela.   ' You call
it sentimental ? '

' And tosh !   Why, just listen to this ! '
And Joey read aloud : ' " The glory of the sun
lingered long o'er tree and flower ; his molten
rays kissed the silvery river as it slid silently
past, crooning a tender lullaby to the fragile
flowers which bent to kiss their reflections on
its surface.   In the pale lilac skies, one silvery
star—the perfect star of eve—shimmered
and glowed——"   Is there a lot of kissing in
the book ? '

' They do kiss each other very often,'
returned Gisela.

' I thought so !   And that isn't even good
English !   She 's used " silvery " and " kiss "
twice in about five lines !   But it 's rather an
idea.   We ought to have a magazine.   The
only trial is, it will be so frightfully difficult to
decide what language it will be in.'

' But of course it will be in English,' said
Gisela.   ' We are an English school.'

' It would be rather fun,' mused Joey.
' Who 'd be editor ?   You, I suppose ? '

Gisela shook her head.   ' Oh, no,' she said
earnestly.   ' I do not know enough about it.
Perhaps Miss Maynard would do it.'

' She might ; but it ought really to be a

girl. Well, go on ! What 's the other scheme you liked so awfully ? '

' The Head's birthday,' replied Gisela, turning over more pages. ' See, Joey ! In this they had a dance, and they gave the Head beautiful presents, and had a splendid time ! Here is the picture.'

Joey looked thoughtfully at the coloured illustration which depicted a white-haired headmistress receiving a magnificent chain and pendant from a Head Girl of fabulous beauty ; while a small child nearby looked almost swamped by a huge bouquet of lilies and roses.

' We haven't anyone as gorgeous as that,' observed the English girl thoughtfully. ' Even that friend of yours, Wanda What 's-her-name, isn't as lovely as that, and she 's the very prettiest girl I 've ever seen ! Besides, it 's idiotic, of course ! Head Girls don't go round with their hair all over the place like that ; they wouldn't be allowed to—not in a decent school anyway ! And I 've never heard of a school where the girls gave the Head a slender gold chain on which was swung an exquisite pendant studded with diamonds ! The most we ever rose to at the High was a really decent reading-lamp. But the holiday stunt is all right, and so is the dance. Madge's birthday does come this term, as it happens. I vote we ask her for the holiday, anyhow.'

' But she must also have a gift,' protested

Gisela. 'And flowers as well. What day is it, Joey? Soon?'

'It's July the fourth,' replied Joey—'next Thursday. It would be a ripping scheme to go for an expedition somewhere, wouldn't it? Tell you what! We might go up the Mondscheinspitze and have a picnic there, and then come down and have the dance in the evening! Oh, gorgeous!'

'And the gift?' persisted the Head Girl. 'We all admire and love Miss Bettany so much, we would wish to give her something.'

'Oh, well, that's for you to decide!' returned Joey, wriggling uncomfortably.

'But of course we will! You will want to give your own souvenir; we won't ask you to join unless you wish it. But I know the others will. What would Miss Bettany like?'

'Oh, any old thing! She'd like whatever you give her!'

'The flowers will be easy,' pursued Gisela thoughtfully. 'We have a garden, Bette has a garden, Anita and Giovanna have a garden, and so has Gertrud. We shall have roses, lilies, and marguerites.'

'It's a tophole scheme. Let's go and ask the others,' proposed Joey. 'It's nearly time for prep. anyhow. You'll have to ask my sister for the holiday, you know, and you'll have to give whatever you do give her.'

Gisela coloured faintly. She was rather inclined to be shy.

'In *Denise of the Fourth*, Mervyn, that's

the Head Girl, asks them to cheer the head-mistress,' she said. ' I should have to do that too ? '

' Of course ! What do you think ? Here's Gertrud and Grizel coming. Let 's tell them now, shall we ? '

' Don't you think it would be better if we waited till everyone was together ? ' suggested Gisela diffidently. ' And should I not ask the Prefects first ? '

' Ye—yes, I suppose you should,' conceded Joey reluctantly. ' All right ! You go and call a Prefects' meeting, and I 'll go and see what Simone is up to. I haven't seen her since *Mittagessen*.'

Joey skipped off, leaving Gisela to follow at a more stately rate, as befitted a Head Girl who is weighed down with responsibilities.

Simone greeted her friend with mournful eyes.

' I looked for you everywhere, Joey,' she said reproachfully.

' Well, I was reading on the fence,' responded Joey briskly. ' Then Gisela came to talk to me about a new book she was reading. Oh, Simone, do you remember those people who came to the Kron Prinz Karl last night by the last boat ? We 've just met them ; they 're friends of Gisela's—come from Vienna, and they 're here for a while. You remember the two pretty girls like fairy princesses ? Their names are Wanda and Marie, and they went to a *lycée* in Wien !—It always seems a mad idea to me to chop the end of Vienna

and spell it with a " W "!—Gisela wants
them to come to the Châlet School. She says
it would be topping for my sister if they did,
because their father's a Herr Rittmeister,
and—— What's the matter?' staring in un-
disguised amazement at Simone, who looked
as if she were about to burst into tears.
'Aren't you well?'

'Oh, Joey,' said Simone pathetically, dropping into her own language in her agitation
—'oh, Joey, don't have any more friends!
Please, Joey, don't! You've got Grizel, and
Gisela and Bette love you, and I've only got
you! And now you want those two new
girls that you don't know at all! Oh, Joey,
don't be so selfish!'

Joey stood stockstill in her amazement.

'Selfish!' she repeated. 'Selfish! It's
you who are selfish! I've told you over and
over again that I'm going to have all the
friends I want, and it doesn't make one scrap
of difference to my being pally with you! I
don't mind *your* having other friends—I don't
see why you don't! Margia would chum
with you if you gave her half a chance, and
she's a jolly nice kid! It's no use looking
like that, Simone! It doesn't make one
scrap of difference! If I like Wanda and
Marie, I'm going to like them. If they do
come to the Châlet and we want to be pally,
I shall be!' Then she relented somewhat
at the look of misery in Simone's great dark
eyes, and slipped an arm round her shoulders,

giving her a gentle little shake. 'Do buck up, Simone, and be—be a man! You'd be twice as jolly if you only would! Look here! There's five minutes before the bell goes—I forgot my watch is fast—and there's just time to tell you what Gisela was talking to me about. Come along and let's go and sit by the boat-slip and I'll tell you about it. It's awfully thrilling!'

But although Simone allowed herself to be drawn towards the little wooden landing-stage beside the Châlet, the dumb wretchedness of her expression did not relax, and all the time that Joey was enlarging on Gisela's 'topping' idea, she sat without making the slightest effort at cheering up. Finally, even happy-go-lucky Jo Bettany gave it up in despair. What could you do with a girl who refused to be interested in birthday-parties and sat looking like a chunk of solid misery?

Joey was thankful when the bell went, and she was able to go off to her own form-room, where there were plenty of people interested in all she had to say about the newcomers at the Kron Prinz Karl.

'It would be splendid for the school if they did come,' said Anita Rincini. 'I have heard Papa talk of Herr von Eschenau. They are very well born.'

'What a silly reason!' said Grizel crushingly. 'The real question is, Will they be all right in school? Are they good at games, for instance?'

'They will not know cricket,' laughed Sophie Hamel, coming to the rescue, for Anita was too much squashed by Grizel's remark to say anything. 'You will have to teach them that, Grizel. Two more, perhaps, for your team.' For Grizel, who was keen on cricket, and had been a shining light of the Junior Eleven at her last school, had been appointed cricket captain, and was proving a very capable coach. Perhaps one reason for her success was that the other girls were all so keen on being an 'English' school, that they took her criticisms and sarcasms in good part, and really tried to learn the game. As for the Juniors, they spent most of their free time in fielding practice. The games mistress at the High had been very insistent on the necessity for smart fielding, and Grizel, quite a good, steady bat, had nevertheless excelled in bowling, which naturally made her more determined to have good fielding than if it had been the other way round.

They had tennis, too, for most of the girls played it quite well, and Gisela Marani and Gertrud Steinbrücke were exceptionally good. The courts were not all that could be desired, since they had, until two months ago, been ordinary meadow-land. But Herr Braun of the Kron Prinz Karl had lent them his roller, and even sent one of his men over at odd times, first to cut the grass, and then to roll it, and, as Miss Bettany had remarked a day or so previously, it really would be quite good in another year's time. However, there could be no doubt about it, cricket was the more popular game.

Now, in answer to Sophie's remark, Grizel spoke quite graciously.

'We sha'n't be playing cricket next term. I don't quite know what we shall play; do you, Joey?'

'Not an earthly!' returned Joey promptly. 'I should think it'll be hockey, though. My sister was awfully good at it when she was at school. But isn't there heaps of snow here in the winter?'

'Oh, yes,' said Anita readily. 'The lake is frozen, too, and there is much skating.'

'Girls! Why are you talking?' said Gertrud's voice at that moment. 'You ought to be working! Sit down, please!'

They went to their seats, while Gertrud, who had come to take preparation, arranged her books to her liking on the mistress's table. Then there was silence while they got on with their preparation in the cool, quiet room.

As soon as the bell for tea went, Joey literally pitched her books into her locker, and fled along the passage to find Gisela. She wanted to know what Madge had said about the birthday-party. However, she had to possess her soul in patience, for the Head Girl was in the Prefects' room.

Luckily, those great people had decided to make all arrangements as soon as possible, and when their own tea, which they were allowed to have by themselves, was over, they came down to the *Speisesaal*, where the others were, and Gisela, blushing furiously, murmured a request to Miss Maynard, who was taking tea. Miss Maynard nodded, and got up at once.

'Yes, certainly, Gisela! We have just finished, so I will say "Grace" and then leave them to you.'

She said 'Grace,' and then went out of the room.

'Will you all please to sit down,' said Gisela, when the door was shut.

They all sat down, Joey squeezing her hands together in her excitement; for, of course, this must mean that Madge had agreed, and they would be able to go up the Mondscheinspitze, which she had been longing to do ever since Herr Mensch had told them about it.

Gisela was quite brief. She explained to them about the English custom of celebrating the Head's birthday, and told them that she and the Prefects had thought it would be a good plan to celebrate Miss Bettany's. Miss Bettany had no objection to their having the holiday, and, subject to the weather being fine, had agreed to their making an expedition up the Mondscheinspitze. If it was wet, they were to have a party in the Châlet.

'Miss Bettany has been very good to us,' went on Gisela, 'and I think you would all

like to join to give her some souvenir of the
first term of the Châlet School; would you
not? So any who wish it may bring contri-
butions to Bette Rincini or myself to-morrow,
and on the Saturday we will go into Innsbrück and purchase something. And on
Thursday, will those of you who can, please
bring flowers, and come early, so that we may
also give her a bouquet.'

Then she ceased speaking, and waited.
But the burst of enthusiasm which answered
her told her that the idea was most popular,
and, as Joey said later on, 'That was that!'

CHAPTER XII.

SHOPPING—AND A MEETING.

SATURDAY proved to be a gloriously fine day. The sun shone brilliantly from a blue, cloudless sky, and everything glowed in the mellow warmth. A fresh little breeze rippled the surface of the lake, lying like a piece of lapis-lazuli in the heart of the great limestone mountains that have kept watch over it for centuries. Joey and Grizel in their short white tennis frocks, with bare brown legs, looked delightfully cool, and the others in their brown gym tunics regarded them enviously.

'You look so nice and fresh!' said Margia Stevens. 'I wish I was going into Innsbrück to-day!'

'You needn't,' laughed Madge from the foot of the table, where she was buttering Amy's roll for her. 'It will be stewing hot in Innsbrück to-day. Remember we're three thousand feet above sea-level as it is, and there's a delightful breeze from the lake; but there won't be a breath of air down in the valley. What it will be like by noon I can't think. Luckily, Gisela and Bette have enough common sense to make you keep quiet then, or I wouldn't let you go. Finished? Very

well. You 'd better run along or you 'll miss
the train, and make the others miss it too.
Your biggest hats, girls; and have you got
plenty of money ? '

'Heaps !' declared Joey. 'Come on, Grizel,
buck up ! Good-bye, everybody. Expect us
when you see us ! '

With this she danced out of the room,
followed more slowly by Grizel, and soon they
were hurrying along by the lake-path towards
Seespitz and the mountain railway, where
Gisela and Bette awaited them impatiently,
while Fräulein Helfer, the Rincinis' *Mamsell*
—or mother's help, as we should call her in
England—was already sitting in the train.

'Come ! You are very late !' cried the
Head Girl. 'I had fear that we must await
the next train, and Papa says that it will be
so hot in Innsbrück later on.'

'Awfully sorry,' returned Joey in unruffled
tones. 'I think our clocks must be wrong,
because we thought we had oceans of time.
Good-morning, Fräulein Helfer. Hope we
haven't given you spasms ! Isn't it a glorious
day ? '

Fräulein Helfer, who understood about half
of this speech, bowed and smiled nervously,
as Joey, still chattering, clambered up beside
her, followed by the others.

'Joey, have you yet learned what it is
Madame desires ? ' inquired Gisela presently,
as the train puffed its way importantly down
the mountain-side.

Joey shook her black head vigorously. 'Not an idea. I think it 'll be best if you just get what you think. Whatever it is, she 'll be sure to like it, because you 've given it. Hullo! Some people at Wachen! I say, what a crowd!'

'Summer visitors,' said Bette. 'Germans, most of them. That woman in the tartan dress comes from Berlin—I heard her say.'

'What a size she is!' commented Grizel, as the lady in question lumbered into the car. 'I shouldn't think one seat would do her! Are there many Germans here in the summer, Gisela?'

'A great number generally,' replied Gisela. 'We like the Bavarians—they are polite, and like ourselves in many ways; but the North German people, and especially the Berliners, are not.'

'Papa says that it was they who caused the war,' Bette chimed in.

'Oh, well, everybody knows that!' said Joey easily. 'What a tremendous way up we are! What would happen if anything broke, Gisela?'

'I do not think it could happen,' replied Gisela seriously. 'I have never heard of it. But if it did, we should plunge over the side and on to the path to Spärtz, which lies down there.'

'Wouldn't it be awful if the lake were suddenly to overflow? It would come down here like a mill-race, wouldn't it?'

'Joey! What horrid things you imagine!' protested Grizel.

Joey laughed, and stopped her imagining to gaze at the lady from Berlin. She certainly was enormous—far fatter than Frau Mensch. She looked uncomfortably hot, too, in a dress of scarlet, green, and yellow tartan, with a little straw hat adorned with scarlet and green bows perched on the top of her head. Her yellow hair was scraped back off her wide face, making it seem larger than ever, and she stared in front of her with eyes like grey glass. Suddenly, as if attracted by Joey's interested regard, she glared at the small girl.

'Engländerin!' she snorted in guttural tones.

'Rather!' responded the irrepressible one. 'And proud of it too!'

'Joey! Be quiet!' said Gisela firmly.

'Why should I? She spoke first!'

'It makes no matter. She is much, much older than you!'

Gisela had not intended her remarks to be overheard, but her voice was of the clear, carrying order, and the lady from Berlin not only heard, but understood.

'Schweine!' she said, and then heaved her bulk round, nearly upsetting her opposite neighbour, an inoffensive little Tyrolean who was going to market in Spärtz.

'Isn't she rude?' observed Joey. 'All right, Gisela! I'm not going to say anything

more. Did you say your father was going to
meet us at Innsbrück?'

'Yes. Fräulein Helfer wishes to visit her
parents, and Papa is going to be our escort.
He will see us at the station, and will take
us to the shops. Then we are going to have
lunch at the Mariatheresien Restaurant, and
afterwards we shall go for a drive along the
Brenner Road, and go back by the last train.
There is a *Gasthaus* up the Brenner where
we can have coffee, and we will take cakes
with us. Do you like it?'

'Topping! Isn't it, Grizel?'

'Rather!' said Grizel. 'It's tophole of
Herr Marani to do it!'

'I am so glad you are pleased!' said Gisela
courteously. 'Ah, we have arrived at Spärtz,
and there is our train to Innsbrück on the
other side of the platform! Come! We
must hurry!'

But it was easier to say that than to do it.
Frau Berlin, as Grizel had christened her, took
her own time about getting out, and as she
blocked the doorway, the girls had, perforce,
to wait until she was well on to the platform.

'I've a good mind to climb out of the
window!' said Grizel as they watched her.
'Would there be a fuss?'

'Of course there would!' returned Bette
promptly. 'We should probably all be
detained at the police court.'

'A case of "more haste, less speed," in
fact,' grinned Joey. 'Thank goodness, the

old freak's out at last! Come on! We
shall miss the train if we don't buck up!'

They nearly did miss it, for *Mamsell* was
not accustomed to dashing from one train to
another, and had it not been for Grizel and
Gisela, who hauled her up the steps and into
the carriage with little ceremony, she would
have been left on the platform. As it was,
she was gasping and scared.

'But never mind that; we've caught the
train!' said Jo practically.

It was full, as it was the Wien-Paris train,
so they had to content themselves in the
corridor; however, it was only for a short
time, and then they reached the outskirts
of the capital of the Tyrol, where tall, flat
houses faced them, with *plumeaux* hanging out
to air from the open windows, while the hot
valley air rushed to meet them as they
whirled past.

'Here we are!' exclaimed Grizel, as the
train drew up beside the busy platform.
'And there's your father, Gisela. Let's get
out! There's no horrid fat Frau Berlin to
stop us this time!' As she spoke, she swung
herself down on the platform, bumping into
someone who was going heavily past. The
someone turned and glared at her. Horrors!
It was Frau Berlin herself! What would
have happened it is hard to tell, for she
had obviously heard and understood Grizel's
indiscreet remarks. Luckily, at that moment
Herr Marani came up, and quickly grasping

what had occurred, he raised his hat, apologising courteously to the furious lady for the English child's clumsiness. Frau Berlin was not to be placated, but she rolled onwards, after directing a venomous glare at the impenitent Grizel.

'You must be more careful, my child,' said Herr Marani, after he had assisted the others out of the carriage and through the barrier. 'You might have hurt that lady very much indeed.'

'I'm sorry,' murmured Grizel untruthfully; while Gisela added, 'Indeed, Papa, she was very rude as we came down, and called us *Schweine.*'

'Hush, *mein Liebling*! I do not like to hear such words from thy lips,' said her father, as they crossed the station square, which lay white and hot in the brilliant sunshine. 'Let us talk of our errands instead. We need not think of an ill-bred Berliner, but only of what is pleasant to us all.'

'There is a shop in the Museum Strasse where one can buy beautiful china,' said Bette, as Gisela seemed to be reduced to silence by her father's gentle rebuke. 'We had thought if we gave Madame a little coffee-service. We have collected enough money for a small one. Would she like it, Joey? Or we can get her a necklace of carved ivory beads.'

'It's topping of you!' said Joey cordially. 'She'd rather have the china, I believe. She doesn't care a great deal for jewellery.'

'The coffee-service then, by all means,' agreed Herr Marani. 'I must go in here for two little moments to buy some cigars. Then we will go to the china shop and purchase the coffee-service.'

'How shall we carry it home?' asked Grizel practically, as they waited for Herr Marani outside the shop. 'Oh, look at those plums! Only six hundred *Krönen* the kilo! I must buy some!'

'But there is no need,' objected Bette. 'We are going to have *Mittagessen* when we have bought the present. If you eat plums now you won't be hungry for it.'

'But we might take some home,' suggested Joey. 'We can get them when we come back. Don't buy any now, Grizel. They'd only be an awful nuisance to cart about. Gisela, is there anywhere where I can buy a picture of the Tiern See? I think M—my sister would like that best.'

'Yes, of course! There is a very good shop in the Mariatheresien Strasse where they have pictures and photographs too. We can go there as we go to the restaurant.'

'Here is Onkel Florian,' observed Bette at this juncture.

Herr Marani came out of the shop at that moment, and taking Joey's hand, and with Bette on his other arm, said, 'And now we are all ready for the important part of our holiday. Let us go to the shop.' He turned off as he spoke down one of the side-streets

that lead from the Landhaus Strasse to the
Museum Strasse.

There is much more camaraderie between
Austrians and their children than between
Germans and theirs, and the Tyrolese middle
class and upper middle class treat their boys
and girls with a freedom nearly conforming
to English ideas.   Herr Marani, a tall, Italian-
looking man, was devoted to his two daughters
and his pretty niece, and Joey and Grizel felt
no shyness with him, so that all their tongues
were soon going at full speed.   He good-
naturedly paused to let them look at the
shops, and answered their questions as well
as he was able, promising them a visit to the
Ferdinandeum Museum in the autumn, and
also one to the theatre when there should be a
good play.

'But not now,' he said.   'Now the sun
shines, and it is well to be out in the fresh
air.   When the winter cold comes we will
have our inside amusements.   Now this is the
shop where the china is sold.   Let us go in and
choose.'

It was all very well to say it, but it was
dreadfully difficult to decide among so much.
There was one coffee-service bespattered with
pink roses on a black ground, and another
with a purple clematis pattern all over it,
and they paused a long time before one in
gold and black.   However, they finally agreed
on one with a blue and yellow design on a
white ground, which had a quaintly foreign

air to both Joey and Grizel, and Herr Marani
told the woman in charge to pack it up and
have it ready for them to take to the station
when they should return from the Brenner
drive. Then they left the shop, and turned
out of the Museum Strasse into the Mariatheresien Strasse, which is a fine, wide
street with very good modern shops. Whether
you look down or up it, you see the mountains
with which Innsbrück is ringed round. At
the south end stands the triumphal arch
and gate, and. beyond them, the Herzog
Friedrich Strasse, with its crowning glory of
the *Goldenes Dachl* or ' Golden Roof.'

Grizel loved the great wide sweep of the
more modern street ; Joey preferred the
history-steeped narrowness of the Emperor
Frederick's day—and there you have the
difference between the two girls. Herr Marani
had discovered it long since, but it amused
him to see it once again in their arguments
about the two most famous thoroughfares of
his beloved native city. However, time was
getting on, so he hushed their arguments, and
led them across the road to the shop on the
opposite side of the street, where Joey soon
succeeded in choosing a charming picture of
the Tiern See for her sister. Then they
crossed once more, and entered the Mariatheresien Restaurant.

They did not pause in the crowded room
which faces on to the street, but went right
through to the Garden Room, where palms, a

fountain, and creeper-hung trellises gave an open-air atmosphere which was very delightful. Electric fans whirling round kept the air fresh and cool, and they all sat down with sighs of relief. It really was boiling in the streets !

When she was comfortably settled, Joey looked round, and gave a little squeal.

' Gisela ! Look ! There 's that horrid fat woman ! '

Gisela, who was opposite her, promptly turned round, nearly overturning her chair as she did so, and saw, sitting a few yards away, their late enemy of the train. She had not seen them, for she was buried in a current number of the *Fliegende Blätter*, which is the German *Punch*, and she looked hotter than ever.

' Horrid old freak ! ' murmured Grizel. ' Doesn't she look awful ? '

' Like a scarlet hippopotamus ! ' suggested Joey. ' If I were as fat as that I should go and drown myself.'

Herr Marani, who had been discussing the menu with the waiter, turned at this moment, and caught the last speech of his youngest guest.

' Josephine ! ' he exclaimed in horror.

Joey had the grace to blush. ' I know it 's rude of me,' she mumbled, ' but—she is fat, isn't she, Herr Marani ? '

' Hush, my child,' he replied. ' It is wrong to say such things of one so much older. She is not, perhaps, so charming as one would wish, but we must forget that. Now let us discuss our drive up the Brenner Road. I propose that we go to the Alte Post, where we can get coffee and rolls and butter. Perhaps we may be able to find a zither-player, and then you shall hear some of our mountain songs amidst the grandest scenery on earth. Then, when we have had coffee, and you have gathered your flowers, we will come down, and stop at the shops for our parcels, and then we must catch the train. You like that? Yes?'

'Oh, rather!' said Joey enthusiastically. 'It's jolly good of you to give us such a ripping treat, Herr Marani.'

He laughed. 'I, too, like a little holiday. Here comes the soup.'

Joey's eyes widened at the thought of soup on so hot a day, but when it came, she discovered that it was iced, and very delicious. From her seat she could see Frau Berlin gobbling up soup also, with small regard for good manners. However, Herr Marani kept her attention occupied, and she soon forgot the fat lady. Frau Berlin, on the other hand, had just seen them, and she looked furious. In her indignation she allowed her temper to overcome her discretion, and she spat vehemently in their direction, just as the head waiter passed between them.

There was an instant uproar; for he, in the shock of the moment, stepped heavily backwards, almost upsetting Gisela, whose

plate of soup went flying. Herr Marani
sprang to his feet, and a couple of Italians
who were lunching near joined in at once,
pouring forth a flood of questions and exclamations, and, when the angry manager
appeared on the scene, explanations of the
whole affair. Several people who were sitting
near stood up to see better what was happening. The author of all the disturbance snorted
out something about *Verdammte Engländ-
erinen*, and demanded her bill. Ten minutes
later she had gone, everyone had sat down,
the head waiter's feelings had been soothed by
a gift of *Trinkgeld* from Herr Marani, and the
manager had vanished, with only a very hazy
idea of what had occurred, but convinced by
everyone that the fault lay with Frau Berlin.

'I hope that is the last time we shall see
her,' said Gisela.

'She has been horrid all round!' declared
Grizel with conviction. 'But it was rather
fun, wasn't it?'

'Yes, it was,' agreed Bette; 'but, like
Gisela, I hope we shall see her no more.'

However, they were destined to meet her
again, though this they could not possibly
know just then.

They finished their meal without further
disturbance, and then Herr Marani took them
back to the Station Square, where they got
into one of the quaint open carriages which
always amused the English girls so, and set
off for their drive into the mountains.

CHAPTER XIII.

AT THE ALTE POST.

'OOOH! Isn't this gorgeous?' Joey Bettany drew a long breath as she gazed round her at the mountains which rose on every side in majestic splendour, while below, the pine forests swept down to the valley, where the Inn went brawling past, hurrying down to join Father Danube. At first they had passed houses and châlets, and people leading heavily-laden mules had stopped to look after them; but for the last half-hour they had met no one. Herr Marani smiled kindly down at the little girl. Her enthusiasm pleased him, for, like all Tyroleans, he loved his country devotedly.

'It is finer farther up,' he said. 'As we get higher and higher, we see the peaks at the other side; and if we go high enough, we can see the Stubai Glacier. We must take you there some day.'

'If it's fine, we're going up the Mondschein-spitze on Madge's birthday, you know,' said Joey eagerly.

'So? That is a pleasant little climb.'

'I want to climb the Tiernjoch,' put in Grizel. 'I mean to some day, too!'

Now Grizel had said nothing about climbing

153

the Tiernjoch lately, so Joey had imagined she had forgotten about her desire to make its ascent, and she was thoroughly dismayed at Grizel's remark.

'I wish Herr Mensch had never said anything about it!' she thought.

Herr Marani raised his eyebrows at Grizel's words. 'The Tiernjoch? It is not a girl's climb. Best leave it alone—for the present at any rate,' he said decisively.

'I mean to go,' said Grizel stubbornly. 'And I'm not a baby, Herr Marani.'

'But will Madame permit it?' put in Gisela somewhat tactlessly. 'It is, as Papa says, a very difficult climb—I have not done it yet! It would tire you, Grizel.'

Grizel made no answer, but her mouth took its old obstinate lines, and Joey made haste to change the conversation.

'Oh, Herr Marani! Look at that little boy crossing his fingers at us! Why ever does he do that?'

'He is making "the horns,"' laughed Herr Marani; 'just in case any of us have the evil eye. That will drive away the danger.'

'What cheek! As if we could! I never heard such nonsense!'

Gisela laughed at Joey's vehemence. 'We are strangers, and those living in the mountains are very superstitious, naturally. Some of the children see no one but their own relatives all the year round. But all the same, they must see people go past in automobiles,' she added, 'for this is the high road into Italy.'

'It's the road Napoleon came by, I know,' said Joey. 'I'm awfully glad to see it on that account.'

'You admire him? But he allowed his soldiers to be terribly cruel!' cried Bette. 'Think of what they did to Andreas Hofer when they took him prisoner!'

'Yes, we of the Tyrol find it hard to forgive the treatment meted out by the French to our great patriot,' said Herr Marani. 'We are proud of him, for he died for freedom.'

'But Napoleon couldn't know what a great man he was,' pleaded Joey. 'He didn't know how the soldiers were treating him till it was too late!'

'He need not have ordered his death,' replied Bette.

'But they were at war, and Andreas Hofer was the leader.'

'You must agree to differ,' said Herr Marani, seeing that the two were becoming very heated.

'And anyway, they've both been dead ages,' Grizel chimed in. 'I never can see why you make such a fuss about people who are past and done with, Joey. They can't possibly make any difference to you one way or the other now.'

Their kindly host burst out laughing at this

extremely matter-of-fact view of things, and then pointed out to them a huge, white, barn-like building up the mountain-side.

'That is the Alte Post,' he said. 'We shall be there in half an hour now, and then we will have our coffee——'

'Papa!' Gisela interrupted him with a cry of dismay. 'The cakes! We have forgotten the cakes! Now we shall only have rolls and butter.'

'Gott in Himmel! But how thoughtless!' Herr Marani looked as perturbed as his daughter.

'Perhaps they will have *Kuchen* at the inn,' suggested Bette, not very hopefully.

'And anyway, it doesn't matter,' added Joey. 'We can get cakes any day when we're in the town.'

The big Austrian's face cleared at that. 'That is true, *Bübchen*. You shall have cakes for Fräulein Bettany's birthday to make up for your disappointment to-day. My mother makes delicious honey and nut cakes, and I will ask her to make some for you.'

'Oh, that would be ripping of you if you will,' said Joey fervently.

'Topping!' agreed Grizel.

'Grandmamma makes wonderful cakes,' said Gisela. 'We all love them.'

'Madge will be bucked!' murmured Madge's small sister. 'She is going to have a jolly birthday!'

'It won't be a bit like English birthdays,'

observed Grizel. 'Except the presents, of course, and the flowers!'

'And the birthday cake,' added Joey. 'She and Mademoiselle have made a huge one, all rich and plummy, with a threepenny and a button and a ring in.'

'But why?' demanded Gisela. 'I do not understand.'

'Don't you? Why, whoever gets the threepenny will be rich, and the ring means marriage, and the button an old maid,' explained Joey. 'We always did it at home; and candles round the cake too—as many candles as you are years old.'

'Is Miss Bettany going to have candles?' queried Grizel with interest.

'I don't know; she didn't say. I expect she will, though. Oh, Herr Marani! Just look at those flowers! Can't we get out and gather some?'

'Best to wait till we return,' he advised. 'Then your flowers will be fresh to take home. We are almost there now. Just one more turn and we reach it.'

'I say! Wouldn't it be awful if Frau Berlin were to be there?'

All the others turned to Grizel, who had made this charming suggestion.

'Goodness! I hope not!' This vigorously from Joey.

'What a dreadful idea, Grizel!' Thus Gisela.

While Herr Marani said decidedly, 'Oh, I should not expect it!'

'Still she might be,' persisted Grizel. 'We 've met her once already.'

'Then, if she should indeed be there, I shall trust you to say nothing, do nothing that may upset her,' said the Austrian gravely.

'Supposing she spits at us again?' suggested Joey. 'She might!'

'Then you will remember that you are English, and an Englishwoman is not revengeful. Gisela and Bette, you must be careful of what you say. I do not wish a disturbance which might mean that we could not have our coffee at the *Gasthaus*.'

'And here we are!' exclaimed Bette. 'We will remember, Onkel.'

They jumped down as the carriage drew up before the inn, and Joey at once gave eager attention to the scrolls which were painted above the doorway in green and gold; while Herr Marani gave orders about the coffee to a pretty dark-eyed girl who had come out on hearing the noise of the wheels.

'Coffee?' she said, in the low-German patois of the country. 'Yes, I can give you coffee, very good, and bread-and-butter too.'

'Have you any cakes?' asked Herr Marani.

She shook her head. 'Na; Kuchen, nein! Aber Marmelade,' she added good-naturedly, seeing the disappointment on the four girlish faces. 'Marmelade ist sehr gut.'

'We will have that, then,' decided Herr Marani.

She nodded. 'Im Speisesaal—fünf minuten.'

She held up the five fingers of her left hand to emphasise her remark, and then ran off.

'I always think it's so funny to call jam "marmalade,"' observed Grizel idly. 'What a pretty girl, Herr Marani! But she looks quite Italian. Look! There are some more! What heaps of children!' as four or five tow-headed urchins came shyly round the corner of the house to stare wide-eyed at the visitors.

'All probably grandchildren of the inn-keeper,' said Gisela. 'Sometimes three or four families will live together in a place like this. Papa, see! How near the mountains seem!'

'It is only seeming,' said her father. 'Look, Josephine! That is the way you came to Innsbrück. There is the line, over there, across the river. And now, our five minutes are up. Let us go and see if our coffee is ready.'

Bette and Grizel ran on in front, bursting into the *Speisesaal*, only to draw up in amazed silence. There before them sat Frau Berlin, drinking coffee and eating bread at one of the tables!

She looked up as they entered, and her already purple face deepened in colour as she glared at them.

'My only aunt!' gasped Grizel, finding her voice at last.

Herr Marani was equally thunderstruck; but before anything else could be said, Frau Berlin heaved herself to her feet.

' I will *mit* English pig-dogs not eat ! ' she announced in thunderous tones.

' Well, we don't want to eat with you ! ' retorted Grizel before Gisela could stop her.

The woman glared at her in stupefied silence. Herr Marani put out a hand, and dragged the English child back with small ceremony.

' Be silent ! ' he said sternly. ' Go outside, all four of you ! '

However indulgent he might be in some ways, Gisela knew that her father insisted on obedience, so she hauled Grizel out into the open air, followed by Bette and Joey, who were half scared, half inclined to giggle.

' Grizel ! ' exclaimed the Head Girl when they were outside. ' How could you speak so rudely ! She has right to be annoyed now ! '

' I 'm not going to be called " pig-dog " by any measly old German ! ' retorted Grizel.

Gisela threw out her hands with a little gesture of helplessness.

' You are an idiot, Grizel ! ' remarked Joey casually. ' You 're spoiling our fun by being so stupid ! If you 'd left it alone, she 'd have been in the wrong ; now it 's us ! '

' Well, you can let that fat old pig call you names if you like,' flashed Grizel, ' but I won't ! You aren't a bit patriotic ! '

' How dare you say that ! ' Joey was becoming heated now. ' I 'm as patriotic as you, but I 've a little more common sense ! If you 'd held your tongue, she would have been in the wrong. But now you 've been

abominably rude and let us down! Patriotic!
Huh! If that's your patriotism, I'm glad I
don't possess any of it! A nice name she'll
give all English girls now, thanks to you being
" patriotic"!' She stopped for sheer lack of
breath, and Gisela promptly interfered.

' It is of no use to quarrel now. It is done,
and it is a great pity, but it cannot be helped.
Joey, will you come with me to gather some
of those flowers? And Bette, perhaps you
and Grizel will go the other way and see what
you can find.'

' Certainly,' said Bette promptly. ' Come
along, Grizel!'

Grizel's quick passion had died by this time,
and she was feeling rather ashamed of herself,
so she meekly followed Bette; while Gisela,
taking no notice of Joey's lowering expression,
walked up the road, chatting easily about the
flowers which grew in glorious splendour
everywhere. By the time they returned to
the *Gasthaus* in answer to Herr Marani's call,
the storm had blown over, and they were able
to enjoy the excellent coffee, *Butterbrod*,
and *Pflaume Marmelade*, which the pretty
girl of the inn laid before them on a table
outside. She also produced some apples, and
they made an excellent tea. Herr Marani was,
apparently, quite undisturbed by his encounter
with Frau Berlin, whom they could see in the
Speisesaal thunderously drinking her coffee,
with her enormous back ostentatiously turned
towards them. However, Grizel was not to

get off quite so lightly, for when the meal was over, and they were gathering flowers to take back to Tiern See, their host called her to him.

'Mein Kindchen,' he said gently, 'another time, please do not be so violent in your patriotism. There is no real harm done this time, but it has not made our little expedition the pleasanter, and I do not think Miss Bettany would like it.'

'No,' agreed Grizel meekly. 'I'm sorry I was so rude, Herr Marani.'

'Then we will forget,' he said cheerfully. 'Come, I will get you some of those ferns for your bouquet, and then we must return, or we shall be too late to catch our train, and I am sure you do not want to walk up the mountain-road from Spärtz.'

'Don't forget we must call for the picture and the china, Papa,' said Gisela, as they were once more seated in the carriage, rattling down the mountain-side. 'The others will wish to see what we have chosen.'

'Of course,' he said. 'I can understand that.'

'It's getting hotter, isn't it?' remarked Joey. 'There was a lovely fresh breeze up by the Alte Post, but down here it's quite hot.'

'That is because we are lower down,' laughed Bette. 'Onkel, did you see Herr Rittmeister von Eschenau yesterday? He had bought Wanda and Marie six books of English school-stories, all new. Wanda said she would lend them to us.'

'Ah, that reminds me,' said her uncle. 'Josephine, Frau von Eschenau has told me that she wishes to send Wanda and Marie to the Châlet School. Do you think your sister will be able to have them for boarders?'

Joey's face flushed as she said joyfully, 'Oh, how gorgeous! I like Wanda and Marie so much; don't you, Grizel? Yes, I'm sure she can have them. Oh, what splendacious news!'

'We are growing! We'll be a big school soon,' said Grizel. 'There are four more girls coming next term, and with Wanda and Marie, that will make us twenty-two, and there may be more yet!'

'Are we going to live at Tiern See all the winter, Papa?' asked Gisela.

'Yes, I think so,' he replied. 'I shall spend the week with *Grossmutter* in town, and come for the Sunday. Herr Mensch is going to do the same; and Bette, I think you are to live with us.'

Bette clapped her hands. 'How delightful! Oh, Onkel Florian, I am so glad! It would have been so lonely in Innsbrück without you all!'

'Hasn't this been a day of happenings?' said Joey presently as they reached the town. 'Where do we go? Down here? Oh, I do love Innsbrück! It is such a dear town!'

They retrieved their purchases and made for the station, where Herr Marani left them for a moment in order to buy a paper. As

they stood in a little group waiting for him,
Grizel suddenly uttered an exclamation. 'Oh,
see! Joey! Look! There is Captain
Carrick over there!'

Her clear accents carried high above the
other noises, and the man at whom she was
pointing, in defiance of good manners, heard
her, and turned. It was, indeed, Captain
Carrick. Raising his soft hat, he came over
to them.

'Well, girls! Fancy seeing you here! I
found I had to run into Innsbrück to go to the
bank. I have left Mrs Carrick waiting for me
in Munich. How is Juliet? She is not with
you, I see.'

'No; we came in to buy a birthday
present for Miss Bettany,' explained Grizel.
'We are going back now.'

'And so am I—going back to Munich.
But your mention of Miss Bettany reminds me
that I have a note for her from my wife—
something about her summer frocks, I think.
I wonder, Miss Joey, if you would mind taking
it for me. I forgot to post it, and she will get
it all the sooner.'

'Oh, rather!' Joey took the note, and
then the Captain bade them 'good-bye' and
strolled away.

'Joey, you look puzzled,' said Bette.
'What is it?'

'Nothing,' said Joey briefly. 'Here's Herr
Marani.'

They accomplished the rest of the journey

without any further happening, and were met at Seespitz by Madge, Miss Maynard, Simone, Juliet, and the Stevens.

'We thought we'd stroll round to meet you,' explained Madge. 'What lovely flowers! For me? Oh, thank you, girls!'

'Madge, this is for you!' said Joey, producing the note. 'It's from Captain Carrick. I saw him in Innsbrück, and he gave it to me to give to you, because he had forgotten to post it. He came in to go to the bank, and was going back to Munich to-night, he said.'

Madge's black brows had been drawn together in a quick frown at the sound of the forbidden Christian name, but something in Joey's tone checked her. She glanced irresolutely at the note.

'Read it!' urged Joey. 'Read it now, Madge!'

'Oh, yes, Miss Bettany, please read it!' echoed Juliet, who had gone suddenly white on hearing Joey's news. 'Yes, read it!'

With a murmured word of excuse, Madge opened the envelope, and began to read, a little puzzled frown on her face. Suddenly she gave vent to an exclamation.

'Oh, how dreadful! What am I to do?'

CHAPTER XIV.

JULIET, THE INCUBUS.

AT once they all closed round her—all, that is, save Juliet. She stood on the outside of the little circle, with white face and eyes full of dread. None of them noticed her; they were too much interested in Madge and the letter.

'What is it?' demanded Joey. 'What's the letter say?'

Madge, reading the closely written words on the sheet of thin, foreign paper, did not answer her, so Joey shook her arm slightly.

'Madge, what is it?'

With an effort the elder girl pulled herself together, and realised the startled little crowd of children round her.

'Never mind, Joey,' she said sharply. 'Miss Maynard, will you take the girls home, please? Tell Mademoiselle I shall be back presently. Herr Marani, I must have a man's advice.'

'Certainly, Fräulein. I shall be pleased to do anything for you that I can. Will you not come back with us? It is difficult to talk business here. Gisela, you may go to Buchau with Bette, but make haste to return.'

The various parties set off, Miss Maynard

taking the Châlet girls by the lake-road to Briesau, while Bette and Gisela struck off across the water-meadows in the direction of Buchau, on the opposite side of the lake, and Miss Bettany and Herr Marani turned towards Torteswald. No one even noticed that Juliet stayed where she had dropped in the long grass in a little heap, shaking with silent sobs.

Herr Marani left the subject of the letter severely alone until they reached the Villa Hubertus, a pretty wooden house just outside Torteswald. Arrived there, he put Madge in a chair on the verandah, and disappeared indoors, to return presently with a cup of coffee, which he insisted on her drinking before they discussed any business whatsoever.

'You have had a shock,' he said. 'Drink the coffee, Fräulein.'

Miss Bettany drank it, and felt better. He took the empty cup from her, placing it to one side, and then sat down beside her.

'And now, Fräulein, tell me what has troubled you in this letter.'

For answer, Madge held it out to him. 'Will you read it?' she said.

He took it from her, and read it slowly through.

'DEAR MISS BETTANY,' Captain Carrick had written,—'Perhaps you will be surprised at what I am going to say. Possibly you will think and say very hard things about me.

That is my misfortune. However, let me
break to you at once the news that I am
presenting you with my daughter Juliet.
Circumstances over which I have no control
force me to leave Europe at once with my
wife. A sulky schoolgirl will only be an
encumbrance to us, added to which I have
very little money. At least you have been
paid a term's fees, and I dare say you can
make the girl useful to you, and repay yourself for her food and clothes in that way.

' If, in the future, I find myself able to
afford to keep her again, I will send for her.
Until you hear from me to this effect, she is
in your hands and at your mercy.

' I regret that I am forced to these measures,
but I see nothing else for it. Of course, if you
like, you can send her to the nearest orphan
asylum ; but I have more faith in your goodness of heart. For your own convenience, I
may as well tell you that neither my wife nor
I have any relatives, so search for them will
be as useless as search for us. Juliet can tell
you that much herself.—Au revoir !

' LINDLEY F. C. CARRICK.'

Herr Marani swore deeply in German when
he had finished reading this heartless letter.
Then, realising that Madge could understand
him, he apologised hastily.

' I crave your pardon, Fräulein. It is the
callous impudence of this man ! He is not
worthy of the name of either " man " or

"father!" That poor child, to be abandoned thus!'

At these words, a slight figure rose out of the bushes which came up to the edge of the verandah, and a sobbing voice said, 'Miss Bettany! Oh, have they left me again?'

'Juliet!' cried her headmistress. 'How did you come here?'

Herr Marani made three strides, and was off the verandah and beside the child in a moment. He gripped her by the arm and drew her in to Miss Bettany, who looked at the red-rimmed eyes in the white face with a softening glance.

'What did you mean by "again"?' demanded the Austrian.

Juliet flung herself down on her knees by Madge's side.

'Oh, I was so afraid when they made me a boarder!' she sobbed. 'They did it once before in the Hills; but that time the Head found them and made them take me back. Then we came here, and ever since he told me I was to be a boarder, I have been afraid they meant to leave me. In one way, I'd rather be with you, because you are kind to me. But oh, it is so dreadful to be thrown on people's charity!' she finished with a little dry sob.

Madge slipped an arm round her. 'You poor kid!'

It was such a pitiful existence the child had shown her in that little gasping, sobbed-out speech! She was furious at the letter, but she could not vent her anger on the girl kneeling beside her.

'Don't cry, Juliet. We'll fix things up somehow. It's very hard luck on you.'

With these few words she had won Juliet's passionate allegiance, though she was not to find that out till afterwards. Now she turned to her host.

'Herr Marani, I must think what to do. Perhaps you can help me. Meanwhile, Juliet ought to be at home—it's getting late. Here is Gisela coming. I just want to know if you can tell me whether it would be possible to get on to Captain Carrick's tracks. Could we wire them at Munich Station?'

Herr Marani shook his head. 'I do not think he will have gone back to Munich. He is much more likely to have gone east to Wien, or else straight through to Paris. We can try, but I do not think it would be worth it. Take Juliet home now, and I will think what is best to do. Yes, that is the best plan.'

Madge, seeing that it certainly was, got up, pulling Juliet on to her feet too.

'Thank you, Herr Marani. We will do as you say. Come, Juliet, it is supper-time now. Stop crying, child, and come along.'

'You will permit me to row you across the lake?' said their host. 'It is growing late, and the last steamer has gone.'

Madge thanked him with her prettiest smile. She was, as a matter of fact, thankful to have

him with them, for he was right in saying that
it was growing late. The walk along the lake-
side road would be dark by now, and though,
as a rule, the Tiernseer were a peaceable folk,
little given to late nights or disturbances,
still, there were many visitors now, and all of
them did not bear the quiet character of the
Tyroleans among whom she was living. The
journey across the quiet lake to their own
little landing-stage was distinctly preferable;
more so, since she had been out all day, and
was feeling tired out with exertion and the
shock Captain Carrick's letter had given her.
So she fell in readily with the kind Austrian's
suggestion, and even meekly accepted the loan
of a huge shawl belonging to his wife when he
brought it to her with the remark that her
gown was thin and that, on the lake at any
rate, it would be rather chilly now. Juliet
was muffled up in a similar wrap, and then
they set off down the quiet road over which
the occasional châlets cast dark, gloomy
shadows in the bright moonlight. Feeling
the child beside her still quivering with an
occasional sob, Madge slipped one hand from
under her shawl, and clasped the thin fingers
in a reassuring grip.

' It is very good of you, Herr Marani,' she
said, addressing her host. ' Indeed, I think
everyone is kind in Austria.'

' Oh, *bitte sehr*,' he said, glancing down at
her with a smile. ' We should be a rude
people indeed if we were not grateful to the

lady who is doing so much for our girls. And we are not Prussians, you know!'

'It's funny,' said Madge slowly, 'but the only discourtesies I have met with have been from Prussians. The Bavarians I know are all delightful, and as for the Tyrolese, I cannot say how much I like them. But the Prussians seem to be filled with a hatred as bitter and venomous as vitriol.'

Herr Marani laughed. 'We had a good example of that to-day. The little Grizel makes a worthy opponent.'

'An opponent? Why, what do you mean? What on earth has Grizel been doing?' demanded Madge with a feeling of dismay.

'Oh, she was not really to blame,' he replied. 'It was a Frau Berliner who created most of the disturbance, and das Mädchen is patriotic—and hot-headed. Here is the boat, mein Fräulein. Will you sit in the bows, please, and steer?'

He helped them in, and pushed off from the land. When they were well away, he told them of Grizel's encounter with the fat lady of Berlin, describing it with a good deal of humour, and glossing over Grizel's behaviour as much as might be.

'Oh, dear! I'm afraid Grizel has been dreadfully rude,' sighed the young headmistress. Then, with a sudden change, she began to laugh. 'I should like to have seen it, all the same! I can just imagine it! She is a thorough little John Bull—the result, I suppose, of never having left her own country before. Joey, my little sister, is much more of a cosmopolitan. But then, she has travelled fairly widely.'

'It was very funny,' agreed Herr Marani with a reminiscent chuckle, as he drew up by the Châlet boat-landing. 'No, thank you, Fräulein,' as Madge invited him to come in for coffee. 'I must return. My wife is away, and the children will be expecting me. Auf wiedersehen!'

'Auf wiedersehen,' called Madge softly, as the boat shot out into the moonlight once more. Then she turned to Juliet. 'Come, Juliet! It's appallingly late, and you ought to have been in bed an hour ago.'

Juliet clung to her arm a moment, her face gleaming white in the dusk.

'Miss Bettany, you've been awfully good to me! I'm so sorry I was ever horrid to you! If you'll keep me, I'll do my level best to help you and—and not be a nuisance! I promise you I will!'

Madge looked down at her with a little smile. 'I shouldn't turn you out even if we were in England, Juliet. Certainly not in a foreign land. Your father guessed rightly when he guessed that!'

Juliet looked at her with an expression in her eyes which made the elder girl exclaim sharply, 'Juliet! What are you thinking?'

'I was thinking—oh, Miss Bettany, do you think they are really my father and

mother? Do you think perhaps I am a
foundling, and that's why?'

'Nonsense,' replied her headmistress firmly.
'That's all rubbish, my dear child. Of
course they are your father and mother!
Now come along in, and then you must have
some hot milk and go to bed and to sleep.
Come!'

She turned towards the house as she spoke,
and Juliet, her mind set at rest on this point
which had troubled her for long, followed
obediently. At the door they were met by
Mademoiselle, who was looking anxious.

'I had begun to have fears for you, *ma
chérie*,' said the little Frenchwoman as they
entered. 'It is so late, and Juliet will be
so weary. Go straight upstairs to bed, *ma
petite*, and I will bring thee a cup of warm
milk. Go quietly, for all are now asleep.'

'Yes, Juliet, go,' said Madge. 'Good-
night, child! Sleep well, and don't worry!'

'Good-night, Miss Bettany,' replied Juliet.
'And—and thank you.' She turned and
vanished up the stairs, while Madge and
Mademoiselle went on to their sitting-room.

'There is a cablegram, Marguérite,' said
Mademoiselle, as the English girl dropped
limply into the nearest chair. 'Drink this
coffee, *ma mignonne*. Thou art weary.'

'I'm completely done,' replied Madge
candidly, as she opened the cablegram.

She read it aloud. '"Have nothing to do
with Carrick. Writing.—Dick." Oh, well,

it's done now! Read this, Elise, and see what you think of it.'

She tossed Captain Carrick's letter across to her friend, and then turned her attention to the coffee, eggs, and rolls Mademoiselle had provided for her.

Meanwhile, the Frenchwoman read the remarkable communication with many ejaculations, but of horror and surprise. When she had finished it, she turned back to the beginning and read it over again.

'But, *ma mie,*' she cried in her own language, 'it is villainy, this!'

'Villainy pure and simple,' agreed Madge. 'As for that poor child Juliet, what do you think she had got into her head? That she was a foundling, and that was why they had done it. Apparently it isn't the first time either. They did it once before in India, she says.' And she repeated Juliet's pitiful story, while Mademoiselle uttered little cries of sympathy.

'Of course he is quite right,' finished the girl soberly. 'I shall most certainly keep her! But imagine the poor child's feelings! Of course it's a silly, morbid idea, and there is no foundation for it except this abominably callous treatment of her; still, that's what she was thinking.'

'Oh, there can be no truth there,' agreed Mademoiselle. 'There is a most clear likeness to both parents. But, my Marguérite, have you thought that there will be now

another mouth to fill and another body to
clothe ? Soon it will be winter—already it
grows colder at nights—and she has no winter
garments at all.'

' Well, what do you propose I should do ? '
demanded Madge. ' Follow the delightful
suggestion he offers as an alternative to keeping her, and place her in an institution ?
You *know* you wouldn't hear of it ! No, I
shall keep her. Next term I shall let her
help with the little ones, so that she need not
feel under too great an obligation to us. She
can do quite a lot without interfering with
her own work, and as she will be the oldest
of our boarders, it need surprise nobody.
Now I vote that we go to bed. It 's eleven
o'clock, and I 'm dead tired. What a blessing
to-morrow is Sunday and we can take things
easily ! Light the candles and come along.
I 'll put out the lamp.'

At the head of the stairs she turned before
going to her own room.

' Don't let the others know about this,'
she said earnestly. ' It would make it so
dreadfully uncomfortable for Juliet. I will
go and see her to-morrow early, and warn her
to say nothing. *Bonne nuit*, Elise.'

' Bonne nuit, ma mie. Le bon Dieu te
garde,' responded Mademoiselle.

Then they went to their own rooms, and
presently darkness and silence reigned over
the Châlet.

CHAPTER XV.

SUNDAY.

THE boarders of the Châlet School always declared that Sunday was quite one of the best days of the week. To begin with, they could stay in bed until nine o'clock if they were so minded. Then, after their breakfast of coffee, rolls, and honey, they all assembled in the meadow which ran up from the lake edge to the pine wood, and Madge read aloud to them for an hour. The Catholics generally attended High Mass, when it was celebrated, in the little whitewashed chapel which stood near the Kron Prinz Karl; but as the priest had also to minister to Torteswald and Buchau, the service was held only once in three weeks. After the reading, they were allowed to wander about as they liked, so long as they kept within call, and they were summoned to dinner at twelve o'clock. In the afternoon, they generally took books and lay outside, reading, or talking quietly, or sleeping; and in the evening, Madge took the English Church girls, and Mademoiselle the Catholics, and they had quiet talks which never lasted more than an hour. Then they were once more free to do

as they pleased until Marie's bell called them
to supper and bed.

'We have such *gentle* Sundays,' Margia
Stevens had once written in a letter to her
mother, and the quaint epithet exactly expressed the feeling all the girls had for it.

On this particular Sunday, the first person
to awaken was Jo Bettany. She had a funny
trick of opening her eyes to their widest
extent and then sitting bolt upright, wide
awake in an instant. This morning, as she
sat up in her little wooden bed, gazing straight
out of the window, she suddenly remembered
Madge's expression as she had read Captain
Carrick's letter the night before, and her
hands clenched.

'If he's worried Madge, I—I'll take it out
on Juliet!' she thought. 'I hate him—
horrid man! Poor old Madge! I wonder if
I could wake her? What time is it?' She
burrowed under the pillow and found her
watch. Seven o'clock, and much too early
to disturb anyone on a Sunday! Joey tucked
it back and turned her attention to the book
at the bedside. It happened to be Lockhart's
Life of Napoleon, with which Dick had presented her just before he had departed for
India. The little girl was reading it slowly,
a chapter at a time in order to make it spin
out. Usually she became buried in it at once,
but this morning she could not fix her attention
on the woes of the great Emperor. The sight
of the green covers of the book recalled her

brother's cablegram to her memory, and she began to wonder what news it had contained. Obviously it had been nothing serious, or her sister would have let her know before this. Perhaps the English mails had been late, and Dick had begun to worry about them. That had happened once before, and he had cabled them to know if they were all right.

'I don't expect we can cable from here,' mused the little sister. 'Someone will have to go into Innsbrück, I should think. Herr Marani or Herr Mensch would perhaps take it for us on Monday, but that would make it a long time for Dick to wait.'

At this point the sound of a light footstep aroused her, and, turning her head, she saw Madge come in, moving cautiously as she skirted the other beds. Her face lighted up as she met Joey's gaze.

'So you are awake!' she said in low tones. 'I thought you might be. Fetch your things along to my room, and we'll dress and go out. I want to talk to you.'

Noiseless as any ghost, Joey slipped out of bed, clutched at her garments, and then tip-toed along to her sister's room. Miss Bettany was standing in front of the mirror brushing out her long curls. She turned round as her small sister entered, and smiled involuntarily at the funny little figure in the yellow dressing-gown. Joey's hair, rumpled with sleep, stood bolt upright, and her clothes were crumpled up anyhow in her arms. Her wide, dark eyes

intensified the startled air this gave her, and
so did her parted lips.

'You do look a fright, Jo!' she said in true
sisterly fashion. 'Now hurry up and get
dressed. I had my tub before I came to
fetch you, and I've filled it up again for you.
Hurry! It's all ready, and if you're quick,
we'll have a jolly time together.'

Joey deposited her clothes on the bed and
departed, to return in five minutes fresh and
glowing from the sting of the icy mountain
water. Madge was almost ready by that
time, fresh and dainty in her plain white
frock. She gave her little sister's wild locks
a thorough brushing, and then left her to make
a raid on the larder. When she came back,
bearing two large chunks of currant cake, Jo
was ready, and her bed had been stripped and
the *plumeaux* hung over the balcony. The
Bettanys were not demonstrative as a rule,
preferring to show their affection by deeds
rather than words, so Madge understood
what that act was intended to convey, though
all she said was, 'Here, catch! That's all I
could find. There isn't any milk either, so if
you're thirsty, you'll have to drink water.'

'Thanks awfully,' said Jo, with her mouth
full. 'Ripping cake Marie makes, doesn't
she? Are we going for a trot?'

'Just a short one. It's a glorious morning
—going to be boiling later.'

'I'm glad. I love hot weather,' replied
Joey, as she crept downstairs after her sister.

'Cold weather makes me curl up like a dead leaf; but this is gorgeous. The hotter the better, say I! And thim's my sentiments!'

'Be quiet! You'll wake the whole house if you yell like that!' returned Madge, the headmistress completely merged in the elder sister.

Joey gave a subdued giggle, but moderated her tones at once. Madge, glancing at her, felt a throb of joy. The three months in a dry climate had already made a great difference to her. The cough had vanished, and the warm sun and clean mountain air had wiped out the unnatural pallor which her constant illnesses in England had produced. She was getting plumper, too, and her eyes were bright. Pretty she would never be, not even with the elusive prettiness of her elder sister, but she had lost her goblin-like appearance.

'You look pounds better,' decided Miss Bettany. 'Tiern See suits you.'

'Rather!' agreed Jo. 'Suits you too, old thing! You're a bit more freckly, of course, but I'm not sure it isn't an improvement.'

'Freckly! You little horror!' exclaimed her sister. 'It's a mercy the girls don't hear you! And that reminds me, Joey, you really must try to remember not to use my Christian name before them. You did it again last night. Yes, I know it was because you were excited; but you mustn't do it, even if you are thrilled about something.'

'Awfully sorry,' murmured Joey. Then she slipped her hand through Madge's arm. 'Madge, what was in the cablegram from India?'

'Business,' replied Madge briefly. She turned and looked at her small sister thoughtfully. She wasn't very sure how much to tell Joey. She knew quite well that something, at any rate, must be told. The family baby had joined in all their councils ever since she could understand what they were talking about, and she knew Joey well enough to be sure that she would be intensely hurt if she were left out now. Jo was very clannish in feeling. What injured her brother or sister injured her. She would be wondering what had been in Captain Carrick's letter, and the chances were that if she were not told she would guess. Madge decided that it was better to tell her the whole truth rather than leave things to her vivid imagination. Jo's fancies sometimes took rather startling turns.

'Jo,' she said abruptly, 'I'm going to trust you. I don't want any of the others to know, but you've always shared with us, and I'm not going to leave you out now. That letter from Captain Carrick told me that he was leaving Juliet on our hands. He can't afford to keep her, so he says, so he's dropped her on to us. It's very hard luck on her, poor kiddy, because she has no one for the present but us. He did suggest that we might send

her to an institution if we didn't want to keep
her. But that's impossible, of course.'

'Oh, of course!' agreed Joey, her impression-
able little heart filling with pity for the girl
who was looked on as a nuisance by her own
parents. 'Oh, Madge! Poor Juliet! I'll
be as decent to her as I can!'

'Don't let her know you know,' warned the
elder girl. 'She would hate that. Just be
nice to her as you are to Grizel, or Gisela, or
Bernhilda. Remember, Jo, I've trusted you.
Dick's cable was warning me about the
Carricks, but it's too late now. The only
thing we can do is to be as kind as we can to
Juliet, and make the best of it.'

'Rather!' But Joey's bright little face
looked puzzled.

'Well! What now?' demanded Madge.
'What are you thinking, Jo?'

'I was thinking, it seems such a horrid
thing to do, to desert your own child! Mother
and father wouldn't have done it.'

'I should think not!' Madge's thoughts
went back to the long-dead father and
mother who had loved their children so
tenderly. 'I've never heard of any other
parents doing it either. Don't think about
it more than you can help, Joey-Baba. Now
tell me about yesterday.'

'We'd a lovely time,' responded Joey
eagerly. 'You'd have loved it at the Alte
Post. And oh, the mountains! Madge, I
love mountains!'

'Well, you 've certainly got plenty of them here,' said her sister. 'Go on. Tell me what you did. Oh, and about that Berlin woman! What did Grizel say? I imagine she was frightfully rude, though Herr Marani didn't actually say so. But I know what she is by this time. Tell me all about it, Joey.'

Thus encouraged, Jo gave a fairly accurate account of their various encounters with Frau Berlin, leaving Madge divided between laughter at the humour of it all, and horror at Grizel's behaviour.

'Grizel really is dreadful,' she said at last. 'I do hope you didn't join in, Joey?'

'Madge! Is it likely? I 've got a little common sense!' cried Joey, distinctly outraged.

'I should hope so,' returned her sister; 'but one never knows. Now don't get excited. I didn't really suppose you did. Well, it 's time to go back now, so we 'd better turn. Have you got any ideas for Thursday besides the Mondscheinspitze expedition? I 've asked Frau Pfeifen to make some of the cakes for us, and I thought we 'd get some tobacco. Herr Braun says the herdsmen always appreciate it, because, of course, they can't get it up there.'

'Oh, that reminds me, Herr Marani is going to ask his mother to make some cakes for us,' said Jo. 'Gisela says she makes gorgeous cakes—all honey and nuts! The kind that melt in your mouth. Oh, and, Madge, I nearly forgot! He told me to tell you that Frau von Eschenau is coming to see you. He thinks she wants Wanda and Marie to be boarders. Won't it be topping if she does?'

'No, really?' said Madge with quick interest. 'Are you sure, Joey?'

'Well, that's what he said,' replied Jo. 'I say, aren't we growing?'

Madge laughed. 'We are indeed! If we get any more boarders, I shall have to take another châlet for us to live in, or have school in, or something. Here we are! Now, Joey, remember! Not a word of what I have told you to anyone else.'

'Rather not! I say, Madge! You are a sport all right!'

'Pooh! Nonsense! I couldn't turn her out! Now run along and strip your bed while I go and see about breakfast.'

Joey trotted off, and Madge turned into the dining-room, where baskets piled high with brown rolls and glass dishes full of amber honey gave colour to the clothless table. The big, hand-made cups and plates, with their cheerful decoration of unknown flowers painted in vivid colours, which stood at each place had come from Tiern Kirche. The table looked un-English in the extreme, but very pleasant and inviting. Presently Marie came in bearing a huge earthenware jug in which steamed delicious coffee such as one

rarely gets in England. She filled the cups
by the simple method of dipping a mug into
the boiling liquid and pouring its contents
into each cup, while Madge arranged plates
of the sugar oblongs, which were the joy of
Joey, at convenient intervals down the long
table. Her task completed, Marie carried
the jug back to the kitchen, and then rang
the bell which brought them all, fresh and
summery in their white frocks, to the table.

Breakfast on Sunday was always a gay
meal, for rules were then relaxed, and everyone chattered in her native language. Mademoiselle, Simone, and Joey were carrying on
an animated conversation in French, while
Grizel and Margia Stevens argued amiably
in English about the probable ending of some
book they were both reading, and Miss
Maynard and Juliet were describing to the
others the walk they had taken on the
previous day. Juliet, it is true, had little to
say, but Madge noted thankfully that she
looked more natural than she had done last
night. On the whole, the elder girl felt glad
that she had taken her little sister into her
confidence. It would make things easier,
for she hated having any secrets from Jo.
Besides, if anyone should be surprised when
the next term found Juliet helping, Madge
felt certain that her sister would put a stop
to that by her own attitude in the matter.

After breakfast, the girls fled upstairs to
make their beds, and the staff foregathered

in the little sitting-room, where Madge told Miss Maynard that Juliet Carrick was to be a kind of student-teacher next term, as her people had lost money, and had left her at the Châlet School for the present. Miss Maynard was interested, but showed no curiosity. She was a nice but unimaginative girl, and she was quite accustomed to student-teachers, and thought nothing of the arrangement. When Miss Bettany suggested that perhaps she might like to go and write her letters, she went off cheerfully, putting Juliet and her affairs completely out of her mind.

Madge turned to Mademoiselle with a sigh of relief.

'Thank goodness! I wasn't sure whether she would want to ask questions, and it would have been awkward if she had. I've told Jo about it, Elise. If I hadn't, she might have imagined things as being worse than they are. And it's quite safe with her; she won't talk.'

'No, that is true,' agreed Mademoiselle. 'Have you seen Juliette yet?'

'No; I'm going to see her presently and tell her what I've decided. Now I must hunt up my book' She turned to the bookshelves as she spoke, hunting for *The Little Flowers of St. Francis*, which she was reading to the girls. Mademoiselle watched her with a sympathetic smile.

'You are very tender of Juliette's feelings,

chérie. I can but trust that she will repay all your kindness to her! She has not proved an attractive member of the school so far. Have you forgotten the affair of the cinema proprietors?'

Madge shook her head. 'No, I haven't forgotten. But I'm sure Juliet will do her best now, poor child. Ah, here it is! After all, Elise, I'm not so sure that I blame her as much as I did. She has led such an impossible sort of life, you know.'

There was a moment's silence, then Mademoiselle turned to the door with a little nod. 'Perhaps you are right; we shall see! You are not wanting me this morning? Then I will ask Herr Braun to row me across to Buchau for High Mass.'

'Yes, do,' replied her friend absently. 'Elise, why are those children so excited? Look at them!'

Mademoiselle looked out of the open window, to behold Margia, Amy, and Simone racing across the grass with eager faces. At the same moment music was wafted to them on the warm summer air.

'A band! A band!' cried Margia, who had shot ahead of the others. 'Oh, Madame, a band—all violins and flutes and things!'

'Well, but why get excited about that?' asked Madge. 'We've had bands here before—there was one last Sunday.'

'Oh, but not like this! Big, very dark men, with flashing eyes!'

'They wear hankies round their heads,' put in Amy, who had come up, panting, together with Simone. 'Very bright hankies —all blue, and red, and yellow, and green! And huge silver rings in their ears!'

'The Tzigane!' exclaimed Madge, her eyes brightening. 'Why, what fun! I wondered if there would be any of them round here this year. They 're gipsies, children, and their music is often very wonderful. We must go and listen to them this afternoon. I wonder where they will be playing?'

'Gipsies? The people who make gipsy tunes like in Liszt's Hungarian Rhapsodies?' queried Margia, who was intensely musical, and meant to be a pianiste some day.

'Yes, just exactly those tunes. You 'll love them, Margia. They aren't a bit like other music, but something wild and un- tamed like the gipsies themselves. I do hope they 've a good band! If so, we shall have a treat this afternoon.'

At this point the others came to join them, ready for the reading, and as they made their way slowly through the flower-sprinkled grass to the shade of the pines, Madge told them how, in Hungary, the gipsy bands went about playing at the different inns in the villages, spending two or even three nights in the same place, but never longer. She told them, too, of the old superstition that the gipsies were cursed with wandering because one of their race had once denied rest and shelter to our Lord.   The girls were delighted, and seeing this, she repeated the old legend of the attempt to steal the nails which pierced Christ's hands.   'It was a gipsy who did it—or tried to do it,' she said.   'Partly, he wanted the iron; but partly, also, he had pity on Christ.   For that pity, so the gipsies say, thieving is not counted by God as a sin in them, and they think nothing of it.   They are a strange people.   They are to be found in most parts of the world, and the Romany tongue is practically the same the whole world over.   A gipsy from India would talk with a gipsy from our New Forest, and each would be able to understand what the other said.   A true gipsy can never be happy within four walls.   It is misery to them to be imprisoned in any way.   They are very revengeful, too, and never forget a wrong. But then, it is said, they never forget a kindness either.'

By this time they had reached their favourite spot, so they settled down, and, putting the Tzigane out of her mind for the time being, Madge read aloud to them about the gentle 'Brother to all things.'

When the reading was over she got up, closed the book, and strolled away, leaving the girls to chatter eagerly about the visitors. Every now and then bursts of music, sometimes gay and swinging, sometimes sad and wistful, but always with a peculiar haunting wildness in it, came across the meadow to them as they sat talking together, or wandered about among the dark pine trees at the edge of the forest. Joey, who had read *The Romany Rye* and *Lavengro*, told them all she knew, and the fascinating subject had still not been exhausted when the ' tinkle-tinkle ' of Marie's bell summoned them back to dinner. When the meal was over, they were wildly anxious to go to the Kron Prinz Karl at once, but Madge insisted on an hour's rest first.

' And no talking,' she added. ' Run along, all of you, at once.'

When they had gone, she turned to the other two mistresses with a smile.

' Don't they think me unkind ! ' she said gaily.

' It 's extraordinary, though,' replied Miss Maynard. ' Gipsies seem to have a fascination for nearly everyone. As you know, we live near the New Forest, and when I was a little child we were always meeting them or coming on their encampments. I used to know a little of their language, for we always made friends with them, my brothers and I. It is so pretty to hear as some of them say it ; it runs along like a purling brook.'

' I wonder your people weren't afraid you would be stolen ! ' said her headmistress.

' Oh, no ! Nothing would have been more unlikely. Besides, the gipsies all knew us, and my father was always very good to them.'

' I see. Well, I don't know what you two people are going to do, but I 'm going to write

letters. Be ready in about three-quarters of
an hour, if you want to come.'

And Madge turned to her desk, while the
other two, taking the hint, vanished to their
own rooms till it was time to walk to the
Kron Prinz Karl to hear the Tzigane music.

Left to herself, Madge sat down and
scribbled a long letter to Dick, telling him the
full story of the Carricks and the decision she
had made about Juliet. The hour was just
ended as she signed it, so she got up and went
out to the meadow to summon her girls.

They had gone, protesting that they
couldn't settle down to anything; therefore,
great was her amusement to find that, without exception, they were fast asleep, their
books and jigsaw puzzles lying unheeded beside them. Clapping her hands, she cried,
' Wake up, sleepy heads ! Don't you want
to come to hear the Tzigane music ? '

They all sprang up, and surrounded her at
once.

' Are we going now ? '

' Oh, topping ! '

' Shall we run and change ? '

' Well, you can't go in your school-frocks,'
returned their headmistress, ' so you had
better hurry up and change into your white
ones again.'

They collected their possessions in great
haste, and tore off to get into the white
frocks they had discarded before lying down.
Presently they were all ready, and set off

along the lake-shore road, very fresh and cool with their big hats. Marie followed them behind, for Miss Bettany had decided that they should have their tea at the Kron Prinz Karl, so had given her a holiday.

Good Herr Braun, the proprietor of the hotel, met them with a beaming face, and escorted them to three of the tables with their huge scarlet umbrellas nearest the Tzigane. How they all enjoyed that afternoon—even Juliet, and Simone, who was suffering from pangs of jealousy because Joey and Grizel had foregathered at another table! Many of their friends were there—Herr Marani, who brought over Frau von Eschenau for a chat with Madge; the Mensches, who had a table nearby; Monsieur and Madame Mercier with Suzanne and Yvette; and many others.

As Grizel said afterwards, it was so unlike England. There were the gaily dressed Tzigane playing as though they were music-possessed; the merry cosmopolitan crowd seated at the umbrella-shaded tables; the vivid blue lake-waters before them; and, surrounding all, the great mountains, beautiful in the bright July sunshine.

They stayed a couple of hours, and then wandered back for their quiet talk, which was never omitted.

As they were going to bed that night, Grizel spoke what was in the minds of all of them.

' I think this has been a beautiful Sunday,'

she said. 'If things were always like this it wouldn't be half so hard to keep rules.'

'I s'pose it wouldn't really do if things were jolly always,' said Jo. 'It 's because they 're unjolly sometimes that we find other things topping, I think. It would be awfully dull if things were always the same.'

'Yes, but some excitements are horrid, and we could do without them easily,' replied Grizel.

In which she spoke more truly than she then realised.

CHAPTER XVI.

THE MONDSCHEINSPITZE.

IT might have been expected that, after the delightful Sunday described in the foregoing chapter, things would take a contrary turn, and that there would be direful happenings. But for once Fate proved kind, and the week progressed quietly, such small events as Suzanne Mercier pouring ink over herself, and Grizel and Joey having what nearly amounted to a stand-up fight over Simone Lecoutier, not counting at all. The morning of the Head's birthday dawned in a kind of pandemonium, however. Margia Stevens had, the night before, hit on the original idea of serenading Miss Bettany under her window. The idea appealed greatly to them all, and, after a good deal of argument and squabbling, they had decided on ' Who is Sylvia ? '

' Of course, the name is wrong,' said Margia, ' but she 'll know who it 's meant for.'

' I s'pose her second name isn't " Sylvia," is it, Joey ? ' asked Grizel.

' Well, if " Sylvia " began with an " H "—which it doesn't !—it might be,' returned Joey sarcastically. She had had words over the song with Grizel, since her fancy had been ' Golden Slumbers '—a suggestion on which

Grizel poured scorn, and she was feeling ruffled.

' If you 're still feeling mad about that idiotic old " Golden Slumbers," I 'd say so ! ' advised Grizel, smarting under the snub. ' If we intended serenading her at midnight it would be all right, but who wants golden slumbers to kiss their eyes at half-past six in the morning when they 've got to get up in half an hour ?   It 's simply stupid ! '

' Stupid yourself ! ' retorted Joey, and marched off, followed by Simone, the ever-faithful.   However, the quarrel was made up before bedtime, and six o'clock the next morning saw the long dormitory in the throes of getting up.   From behind the yellow curtain which divided off the cubicles came subdued giggles and whispered remarks.

' Joey, is it fine ?   What 's it like over the mountains ? '

' Glorious,' returned Joey, who had stripped her bed and was now sitting on it, waiting for her turn to go to the bathroom.   ' It 's going to be a ripping day.'

' Be quiet ! ' hissed Juliet.   ' You 'll waken Miss Maynard if you shriek so.'

' She 's prob'ly awake already,' returned Joey, not a whit disturbed.   ' Thank goodness !   Here 's Grizel at last !   I thought you 'd drowned yourself ! '

' Rot !   I 've only been six minutes ! ' protested Grizel.   ' Buck up yourself !   Margia and Simone have to come after you.'

'What about my bath?' asked a little voice from the other corner of the room where Amy Stevens slept. It's all cold still, isn't it?'

'Oh, bother! I quite forgot you hadn't to have cold baths!' Grizel paused in the act of putting on one of her stockings. 'Juliet, what shall we do?'

'Marie will be up. Shall I go down and ask her for a kettleful of hot water? I'm just ready,' suggested Juliet.

'Will you? That'd be topping of you. Yes, do go!' urged Grizel. 'Hullo, Joey, old thing! You can't have had much of a bath! You haven't been a minute!'

'Have, though! Tootle on, Margia! You're next, aren't you?'

Margia and Juliet vanished together, and presently Juliet came back with a big jug of warm water supplied by good-natured Marie.

'Come along, Amy,' she said cheerfully. 'I'll tub you this morning. We can't wait till Mademoiselle comes.'

'Oh, thank you, Juliet,' replied Amy shyly; while Grizel stopped in the act of brushing out her curly mop to gape open-mouthed at her curtains. When had Juliet ever offered to help anyone like that before?

Amy herself was very startled. She had never liked Juliet, but was too shy to refuse the older girl's help, so submitted in silence to being bathed with much vigour and good-will, if with some clumsiness. Juliet's whole-hearted rubbing with the towel brought an involuntary 'Ow!' from her, but when the Senior, conscience-stricken, asked, 'Did I hurt you?' she replied hastily, 'No, oh, no, Juliet! And it's very kind of you to bath me. Thank you so much.'

'Call me if you want anything tied or buttoned,' said Juliet, as she returned to her own cubicle. 'Margia will have to dress herself, and I'm practically ready, so I can help you easily.'

Grizel restrained an exclamation of surprise in time. She stripped her bed in an awe-struck silence which lasted until they were all ready to leave the room. Then Joey roused her.

'Aren't you feeling well?' she demanded bluntly.

'Yes, quite well! Why?' queried Grizel somewhat incautiously.

'You're so silent! You've scarcely spoken at all!' grinned Jo. 'I thought something must be the matter!'

'So it is, Joey! Juliet did practically everything for Amy! Did you ever?'

'Well, that's nothing to be wondered at!' returned Joey smartly. 'She's the oldest of us, and someone had to help Amy or she'd never have been ready! You know what a perfect baby she is.'

'Oh, yes, of course!' said Grizel uncertainly. 'I expect you're right, Joey!'

'Course I am! Now come on, and don't stand pow-wowing any more!'

They all slipped down the stairs and out into the glorious sunlight, collecting in a gay little group under Miss Bettany's wide-open windows.

'Let 's start with " Good King Wenceslas," ' giggled Joey.

'Yes; I feel rather like Christmas carols too,' agreed Grizel.

'Stop ragging, you two! We 're waiting for you! This is the note.' And Margia sang 'Loo!' in a very true little treble. 'Now! One, two!'

They all started off, and Madge, who had been sleeping the sleep of the justly weary, was roused by the notes of 'Who is Sylvia?' sung *fortissimo* by the whole band.

She quickly guessed the meaning of the serenade, and sat up in bed with a chuckle. As they finished, she got into her kimono, and ran across to the window.

'Hullo, everybody!' she called. 'What a jolly awakening!'

'It 's to wish you many happy returns, Miss Bettany,' called up Grizel. 'It was Margia's idea, really. Did you like it?'

'Yes; it was delightful. Thank you all very much! Now I 'm going to dress.' She withdrew her head just as a tap at the door heralded Joey's advent.

'Hullo! Many happy returns of your birthday,' she said. 'I 've brought you this.' She presented her parcel, and Madge opened it with delight.

'A picture of the Tiern See! Joey! You gem! It's just what I've wanted,' she cried. 'You couldn't have given me anything better!'

'Glad you like it,' returned Jo, as she turned her cheek for her sister's kiss. 'Herr Marani helped me to choose it last Saturday. I say, can I help you to dress? I'll strip your bed; shall I?'

She suited the action to the word, and presently Madge sauntered downstairs, ready for the day, in her pale green frock and sensible knitted stockings. Marie was scurrying round getting breakfast ready. She stopped to offer her good wishes together with a bouquet of Alpen roses, which she had gathered the evening before.

'*Für* Madame,' she said shyly.

'Oh, Marie! How good of you! And I love Alpen roses so much!'

Marie nodded and smiled as she replied in her own language, 'Madame is so good! I hope it will be a pleasant day for Madame's feast-day.' Then she went on with her task, while Madge performed her usual little duties.

Breakfast was a hilarious meal, followed by a gay rush to put in bedmaking and practice. Nine o'clock brought all the boarders, flower-laden and beaming. Gisela and Bette carried the basket containing the precious china between them, and Maria had another, full of *Grossmutter's* delicious cakes.

'Hurry up! Hurry up!' exclaimed Joey,

dancing with impatience. ' I 've got the tray from Marie, and Mademoiselle is keeping Madame talking in the dining-room till we 're ready! Here you are! Now buck up!'

In the big schoolroom they arranged the dainty coffee-service on the big black tray Joey had produced. Then they formed up in their usual lines, and Amy was sent to ring the bell. She came scampering back, proclaiming in a stage whisper, ' She 's coming! '

The sound of light, rapid footsteps followed, and then Miss Bettany came in and took her place on the dais. As she did so, a chorus of birthday greetings in German, French, and English came from the eighteen girls assembled below her. As they spoke, they all raised their bouquets—the day-girls had brought flowers for the boarders—and the beauty of the flowers, the goodwill and affection in the girlish faces before her, brought a little thrill to the young headmistress, and touched her charming face with rather more colour than usual. Then Gisela and Gertrud came forward, carrying between them the tray with its dainty burden of china.

The Head Girl looked rather flushed and nervous with her responsibilities, but she rose to the occasion bravely, and said in her clear, carrying voice, ' Madame, be pleased to accept from us all this so small token of our feelings for you on this your feast-day.'

' Thank you, girls,' said Madge, a little shyly. ' It is very good of you indeed, and I cannot tell you how much I appreciate your kindness to me. If anything could have made it a happier birthday for me—the first birthday I have spent in the Tyrol—your thought could.'

Then came the business of presenting the bouquets, and soon the table on the dais was heaped with lilies, roses, marguerites, gentians, single dahlias, Alpen roses, and peonies, until that end of the room was glowing with their colour and beauty. When, finally, little Giovanna Rincini had trotted up with her armful of lilies and dahlias, Gisela called for three cheers for 'Our dear Madame!' which were given heartily, and then the serious business of the day was over.

'In half an hour we shall start,' said Madge, smiling at them over the great heap of flowers. 'First, I must place these in water and put them in a cool place. Then we must collect up all our possessions, and then we can set off! Joey, please go and fetch me some big bowls; and Grizel and Juliet, I want some water. Take them into the dining-room; that is the coolest place, I think. Miss Maynard, if you will look after the younger girls, Mademoiselle will see to the food, and the Prefects will help me to arrange the flowers.'

They all flew off to do her bidding, and by ten o'clock a long string of girls was to be seen setting off up the path which led to the Lauterbach Valley, through which they would have to walk in order to reach the mountain-path that led up the Mondscheinspitze. The visitors whom they met looked at them with interest. All had heard the story of the English school which was prospering so finely in the châlet at the lake-side. The fresh, dainty uniform, so different from the uniform of most foreign schools, attracted notice too, and so did the happy faces of the whole party.

As long as they kept to the beaten track—that is, until they reached the white wooden railings that fenced off Briesau from the Lauterbach Valley—they walked in ' croc,' but as soon as the gate had swung behind them, they broke file, and wandered happily along in little groups, chattering gaily among themselves. Gisela, Gertrud, Bette, and Bernhilda attached themselves to Miss Bettany, and were soon eagerly comparing the differences of Cornish picnics and Tyrolean ones. Miss Maynard and Mademoiselle were discussing Paris, which the former knew very well, since she had been at school there. The little ones, needless to state, chased butterflies and gathered flowers; while Joey, Grizel, and Simone, for once in complete accord, strolled along amiably talking about their climb. Presently they came within sight of the Tiernjoch, even in this day of glorious sunshine dark and gloomy, with a hint of menace in its towering crags. Grizel stopped and tilted back her head, looking at it with a determined gleam in her eyes.

' I 'll go up there some day,' she said aloud.

Joey followed her eyes. 'The Tiernjoch? Oh, Grizel, I wish you wouldn't!'

'Don't be silly! It's only a little climb! 'Tisn't even as if there were any glacier to cross!' retorted Grizel. 'Why, there's no snow or anything!'

'It's such a cruel-looking mountain!' said Jo with a little shiver. 'It looks as if it didn't care how many people were killed on it!'

'Joey! Tosh! That's only your silly imaginings!' began Grizel. Then the sudden whiteness of her friend's face made her sorry she had mentioned it, so she added, 'Anyway, I'm not going to-day—or this week either, so keep your hair on!'

'I think you are unkind, Grizel!' broke in Simone unexpectedly. 'Always you tease, tease Joey! And she hates the Tiernjoch!'

'"Tisn't your business!' Grizel was beginning heatedly, when Joey stopped her.

'Oh, shut up quarrelling, you two! An' if you mention that beastly Tiernjoch again, Grizel Cochrane, I'll go away, an' you can walk with someone else! So there!' And she marched ahead, leaving Grizel and Simone to follow meekly after her.

Luckily, at that moment, loud screams from Amy Stevens distracted everyone's attention to her, as she came flying down the slope, yelling at the full pitch of her lungs, 'Ooh! Ooh! A snake! A snake!'

'What!' exclaimed Madge. She started

forward, catching up the frightened child.
'Amy! Are you hurt? Stop crying, dear,
and tell me!'

'No, she isn't!' Margia supplied the
information disgustedly. 'She saw a little
greeny snake curled up asleep by that stone,
and so she howled! It never came near
her!'

'Thank Heaven!' Madge set the child on
her feet again with a sigh of relief. There
were very few snakes found round the
Tiern See, and, so far as she knew, the only
venomous ones were vipers, which were even
more rarely seen than the harmless green
variety; but Amy's shrieks had scared her for
the moment. 'There's nothing to cry about,
Amy,' she added. 'If you scream when you
only see a snake, you aren't a very plucky
person, are you? Now dry your eyes and
stop crying. And, girls, don't go into the
long grass, please.'

'It will be all right, Madame,' said Gisela
seriously. 'Snakes prefer the sun, and that
grass is in the shadow, and is cold.'

'Nevertheless, I shall feel safer if you keep
more to the path,' returned her headmistress
decidedly. 'Frieda, I'm sure you've carried
that basket long enough. Give it to Joey.
And Grizel, take Juliet's for a while.'

They went on again, Madge keeping a rather
nervous eye on the Juniors. However, they
soon had to leave the track, and strike across
the valley to get to the mountain-path.

'Do we cross here?' demanded Miss Bettany, eyeing what looked like the stony bed of a dried-up river somewhat doubtfully. 'Isn't there a bridge?'

'Only a log further down,' said Bernhilda. 'You see, Madame, when the storms of autumn come, this is a torrent, and already three bridges have been swept away. The water comes suddenly, and there is nothing to break its strength. It is easy to reach, though. See; down here.' And she pointed to some rough, natural steps which led down to the stony bed.

Already more than half the girls were struggling across, the unfortunate bearers of baskets uttering wild shrieks as the stones slipped under their feet, and they more than once nearly went headlong. At length they were all safely at the other side, and once more on the beaten path which led through grass and wild flowers to the foot of the mountain, where they all paused for a rest.

'Ouf! Isn't it hot!' panted Margia, as she mopped her crimson face.

'I'm just comfortable,' said Joey with an exasperatingly superior air, 'but I'm awfully hungry! What's the time, anyone?'

'It is half after eleven,' said Gisela, glancing at her pretty little watch.

'You must be slow, Gisela,' laughed Juliet, showing hers. 'I make it ten past twelve.'

'So do I,' said Madge, 'and mine was right

this morning. Miss Maynard, what does yours say ? '

'Nearly quarter past,' replied Miss Maynard, ' but I may be a little fast.'

'Well, anyhow, it's time for lunch,' said Joey. 'Do let's have it here !'

'Oh, yes !' agreed several voices at once. 'I am hungry !'

Madge laughed and gave way. 'Very well. I'm rather hungry myself; and it would certainly lighten the baskets !'

Accordingly they all sat down, and in a very few minutes the baskets were considerably lighter than they had been.

'It's funny how much hungrier one is out of doors than in,' said Grizel presently, as she tackled her sixth sandwich.

'It is !' agreed Joey. 'But I'm not so hungry as I was,' she added pensively.

'After having only five sandwiches and six biscuits and two apples !' jeered Grizel. 'There must be something up with you, Joey, old thing !'

'You can't talk !' said Joey contentedly. 'You've had just as much. I say,' she added in rather changed tones, 'where's the lemonade ? '

'Bette has it,' said Gisela.

'I haven't,' replied Bette. 'I thought you had it !'

'No; I was carrying the apples. I was certain you had it !'

'Oh, no ! I never had it !'

Madge began to gurgle with laughter. It was only too plain what had occurred to that lemonade.

'Sitting in the passage at home,' she choked. '*Oh!* And I'm dying of thirst!'

'And I!' 'And I!' rose on all sides. 'What are we to do?'

'Wait until we reach the Alpe. We can get plenty of milk from the herdsmen,' said Miss Bettany somewhat unfeelingly. 'I'm sorry, but it's your own faults.'

'Then,' said Jo, scrambling to her feet, 'there's only one thing to be done—get up to the Alpe as soon as we can. Come on!'

There was common sense in her statement, so with loud groans the girls repacked the baskets and set off.

The climb up the Mondscheinspitze is remarkably easy. There is a well-defined path, which winds in and out among the dark pine trees, every now and then coming out into narrow—very narrow—grassy ledges. Presently, however, it left the woods, and they climbed up the bare limestone face of the mountain beneath the glare of the July sun. Tufts of grass, with wild scabious and white marguerites, punctuated the way, and gorgeous butterflies, brown and orange and scarlet and yellow, fluttered round them, so little afraid, that often they settled on hat or frock, and little Amy Stevens cried out in delight when one balanced itself on her outstretched fingers, resting there for a moment before it fluttered off.

Madge was thankful for the distraction the dainty creatures afforded the girls; otherwise, the Juniors at any rate would have found the path more difficult than they did. As it was, she was very thankful when a triumphant cry from Joey, Simone, and Frieda Mensch, who had raced on, announced that they had reached the Alpe.

'Isn't it a gorgeous view?' demanded Jo, when they were all standing on the short, sweet grass. 'Just look!'

They looked. At their feet lay the valley they had crossed that morning, cool and green, with the empty river-bed stretching like a white ribbon down its length. In the distance they could see Briesau, lying like a toy village some giant child had set out; and beyond it, blue—blue—blue, the Tiern See, a living sapphire, gleamed beneath the sun.

'Oh, wonderful!' breathed Madge softly.

They did not gaze long, however; they were all too thirsty. With one accord, presently, they turned, and made for the herdsmen's hut—and milk.

CHAPTER XVII.

ON THE ALPE.

ALTHOUGH both Joey and Grizel had been up the Bärenbad Alpe many times since their arrival at Briesau, and had partaken, in the châlet, of whipped cream, wild strawberries, and bread-and-butter, they had never been inside a herdsman's hut, and great was their interest in it. The same applied to Simone and the two little Stevens, but they were younger and less curious about the way the herdsmen lived than the other two.

Only one man was there when they reached the place—a tall, lanky young fellow, in weather-stained green breeches and ragged shirt, open at the throat. His black hair was rough and long, and his face burnt brown with the weather. He wore the little green Tyrolese hat with its cock-feather, and was sitting contentedly smoking a long china-bowled pipe, such as most men smoke in the Tyrol. On seeing them coming, he rose to his feet with a smile of welcome and a hoarse-voiced 'Grüss' Gott!'

'Grüss' Gott!' replied Madge briskly. 'Can you sell us some milk and cheese?'

'Yes, gracious lady. Will the gracious lady and the young ladies come in?'

Only the English girls availed themselves of this offer, so that they might look round at the little bare room, with its huge well in one corner, where a wood fire was burning although the day was so hot. A broad shelf ran round the room, well above their heads, and on this stood enormous earthenware pans for the milk and big cream-coloured cheeses. The one window was about two feet square, and set high up in the wall; a long wooden bench stood at one side, and next to it a huge cheese press; a door opened into another room beyond, where trusses of hay were to be seen. The atmosphere of the place was indescribable—a mixture of cheese, garlic, tobacco, and burning wood. The visitors soon left the hut for the sweeter atmosphere of the Alpe, where the others were gravely taking it in turn to drink out of an enormous bowl, full of rich, creamy milk, while their host stood nearby, still smoking, and gazing vacantly across to the mighty peaks on the other side of the lake.

When Miss Bettany presently brought back the empty bowl, together with the tobacco she had brought, and some *Kroner* notes to pay for the milk, he smiled again, and answered her questions in his curiously hoarse tones.

Yes, he and four others were there for the summer. They had come up early in May, and would stay there till the end of September if the weather was good. Then the cattle must be brought down to the valley before the autumn storms began.

'But aren't you ever lonely?' queried Joey, who had accompanied her sister to the hut. 'Don't you ever want to go down to Briesau?'

He turned indifferent dark eyes on her. 'No, gnädige Fräulein. There are the cows and the mountains. We are five, and I have my pipe.'

'What do the cows do in the winter?' asked Madge, a fine instinct preventing her from asking what he did, though she felt curious about it.

'They live in the sheds in the winter,' he replied, 'and I go to my home in Scholastika. They do not need us in the winter, so we all go to our homes, and pray to *der lieber Gott* and the blessed Saints for an early spring. Last winter it did not come, and some of us went hungry for a time.'

'How dreadful!' said Joey with whole-hearted sympathy. 'I hope it's a good autumn.'

'It will be as *der lieber Gott* wills,' he replied, with the curious fatalism of his race.

'Is it very terrible up here in the winter?' asked Madge.

'I do not know. I have never been,' he replied.

Seeing that his interest in the conversation seemed to be dying, Madge made arrangements for milk and cheese for the tea, and then went back to her flock. She found them all lying about in exhausted attitudes, and promptly proposed that they should have a rest before exploring the Alpe any further.

' It will be easier going down than coming up,' she said. ' We climbed in the noon-day heat, but by then it will be cool, so we shall go twice as quickly. Lie down, everyone, for half an hour or so, and then we shall all be fresh, and ready for anything.'

' Good scheme ! ' said Joey approvingly. ' I 'm awfully sleepy—I s'pose it 's the heat. Hai-yah ! ' She ended with a yawn.

' It 's being up so early, too,' said Juliet.

' Yes, that too,' agreed her headmistress. ' Half an hour, or even an hour's sleep won't do any of you any harm. I 've got a book in my pocket, so I 'll read and keep an eye on the time.'

They promptly curled up in various attitudes, Mademoiselle and Miss Maynard among them. At first there were sundry murmurs, but by degrees they all dropped off, and Madge was soon the only one awake. She glanced at her watch with a smile.

' A quarter past three,' she thought. ' I 'll let them sleep for another half-hour, and then we must have tea.'

She turned back to her book. It was terribly hot—almost oppressively so, although the sun was not shining so brilliantly as it had done earlier in the day. The German print looked all funny and jumbled up ; the page wasn't there any more. Madge was asleep.

The lonely herd came past them later on, on his way to the spring which bubbled up out of the earth at the other side of the Alpe. He looked at them curiously, but it was no business of his, so he left them. Meanwhile, the sunlight faded away, hidden by the huge black clouds that began to marshal themselves in terrifying squadrons in the northwest. Even the faint breeze which had stirred the Alpine flowers in the short grass had died away. There was a waiting stillness, broken only by the occasional cry of a wild bird, frightened at what it felt was coming.

Joey was the first to feel it. She woke up with a sensation that something was wrong. The next minute she knew what it was. The electricity in the air was tingling through and through her. She sprang to her feet with a little cry, gazing wildly round her. The sunshine was gone; the whole place was wrapped in gloom. At the other side of the valley the mountains reared ghastly white heads against the blackness of the sky, and every now and then the lightning flashed across the awful inkiness, seeming to rip it open for a moment. There was no thunder yet, which made it all the more terrifying. For a moment Joey nearly lost her head. Dashing to her sister's side, she shook her vigorously.

'Madge! Madge! Wake up! Wake up! Madge! I'm frightened!'

In a moment Madge sat up and regarded

the awesome scene with horror in her eyes. The next instant she was on her feet.

'Thunder! What a fool I was not to think of it! Joey, be a man! You must! We must get down at once! Girls! Wake up!'

They woke up at her urgent cries, and Simone and Amy promptly burst into tears. The Tyroleans were too accustomed to the terrible thunderstorms which come up with such terrifying suddenness to be scared, although the elder girls looked serious. They knew what thunder from the north-west meant.

Meanwhile, the three elders were taking rapid counsel, while Juliet and Gisela tried to console the two weepers. Joey was watching her sister's face anxiously, and Grizel was too excited to feel afraid.

Then, even as Miss Bettany turned to bid the girls hurry to the mountain-path, there was a vivid glare, that seemed to rend the very clouds asunder, followed by a terrific crash, which scared what few wits Simone had left completely from her. She clung to Mademoiselle, screaming hysterically, and Madge realised that if they were to get her down the path at all they would have to carry her.

A sudden shout coming out of the gloom which had descended so rapidly made her turn, and there was the herdsman running towards them, beckoning to them as he did so. In a

flash she realised that he meant them to
come to the hut.   The next moment the darkness descended completely, and overhead the
lightning flickered and the thunder crashed
almost incessantly.   There was no question
of going down yet.   Even if Simone had kept
her head it would have been impossible.
The path was easy enough in daylight, but
there were great tree roots sprawling across
it at intervals, as well as occasional boulders
which had worked loose and rolled into it.
Any attempt to descend it now was more
than likely to end in sprained ankles, if nothing
worse.   She made a swift decision.   Even as
the panting herd reached them, she spoke.

'Come! We must go to the hut! It is
the only thing to do, and we can stay there
till it is over——'

The rest of her sentence was drowned in a
mighty peal of thunder.   The girls, luckily,
were trained to an instant obedience.   Gisela,
Bette, and Bernhilda had already collected
the baskets together, and now they all turned
and followed the man, who had picked up
Simone with as much ceremony as if she were
a bundle of hay, and was now leading them
across the little plateau to the hut.

It was really quite a short distance, but to
Madge it seemed never-ending, that strange
walk—half walk, half run—in almost pitchy
blackness, lightened only by the fearful glare
of the lightning, while all round them the
thunder roared frighteningly.   Little Amy

Stevens was between her and Miss Maynard, while the elder girls looked after the other Juniors, and Mademoiselle hurried gaspingly after them, with an arm round Margia Stevens. At last they reached the hut, and oh, what a haven of refuge it seemed to them, with the cheerful glow of the wood fire lessening the gloom a little!

Once they were all safely inside, the herd shut the door and set Simone down on the bench. She had stopped screaming now, but little heart-rending moans came from her lips every now and then. Leaving Amy to Miss Maynard's care, Madge went over to her.

'Simone,' she said sternly, 'you must stop crying at once—at once! Do you hear?'

'I—I have such fear!' sobbed Simone in her own language.

'So have the others,' replied her headmistress, 'but you are the only one who is behaving like a baby. Come! You must stop at once or I shall slap you!'

She nearly burst out laughing when she finished, for, as she glanced up, she had happened to catch sight of Joey's face, with eyes and mouth round O's of wonder. However, her dramatic speech had its effect on Simone, who gradually began to recover her self-control, and presently was able to sit up and drink the milk Gisela brought her.

Meanwhile, the herdsman had drawn the young headmistress aside.

'The gracious lady must stay here to-night,'

he said. 'There is hay, and we can give bread and milk and cheese. To go down the path would be dangerous while the storm rages.'

'But surely it cannot go on long?' said Madge in startled tones. 'It is too heavy to last.'

'It is from the north-west,' he replied. 'It will last many hours yet—four, or perhaps five; and then it will be night.'

'Good heavens! How awful!'

She stood silent for a few moments, going over the state of affairs in her mind. Then she turned to the Seniors. 'Gisela! Bette! Is this true? Are we storm-stayed here for the night?'

'I am afraid so,' replied Gisela. 'When a storm comes from the north-west it does not die quickly.'

'But how appalling! What will your parents think?'

'They will know we took refuge here,' said Bette. 'Everyone at Tiern See knows of the hut, and they will know that we should stay here. These storms come so quickly; often there is no time to do anything. Don't worry, Madame. They will be sure we shall be here, and quite safe.'

'I wish I could think so!' murmured her headmistress. 'Well, I suppose there is nothing else for it.'

'Do you mean we 're going to stay here all night?' gasped Grizel, who had been standing near. 'How simply thrilling!'

'I'm glad you think so!' returned Madge dryly. 'I'd be thankful to know we were all safe in our beds.'

'It's an adventure, though,' said Joey, who had quite recovered her self-control, although her jaunty air was rather overdone. She did not like thunderstorms, and this one was really alarming. 'It'll be something to tell Dick when we write next.'

Madge laughed rather ruefully, and moved away. She felt tired, for it was no joke talking against the thunder. You had to shriek to make yourself heard, and even then it sometimes meant repeating what you said.

The herdsman, having given his opinion, was now busily engaged in carrying in great armfuls of fresh, sweet hay from a little shed which stood nearby. The rain had not yet come, and he had evidently made up his mind to prepare for the night before it did.

Grizel sprang forward. 'Let me help!' she said in her pretty broken German. 'Yes, do! I'd like it!'

'Oh, so would I!' exclaimed Margia. 'I'll come too!'

The man made no attempt to stop them, so they followed him out; and very soon one end of the room was thickly littered with the hay, which the elder girls shook up and covered with their raincoats. When that was done, he shut the door once more, cast a couple of logs on the fire, and then sat down on the bench and lighted his pipe. He had done all he could, and now he was prepared to sit and smoke contentedly until he was sleepy, when he would go to bed in the next room.

A little silence fell on them all, which was suddenly broken by a ' swish-swish ! ' and the rain had come. Such rain ! Joey, opening the door to see, had to shut it again in a hurry or they would have been flooded out.

' Gracious Peter ! ' she remarked, as she came back to the others. ' It 's like the Flood ! This is Mount Ararat, I shouldn't wonder ! '

' Tosh ! ' retorted Grizel. ' Mount Ararat has snow on it—I think ! '

She finished rather doubtfully.

' Well, *this* has in winter,' argued Jo amiably. ' Anyhow, it 's some rain ! '

' Not unlike the rainy season in India,' laughed Madge—the thunder had died away for the moment. ' Do you remember how I told you about the time when we were flooded out the year before we came home ? '

' Rather ! Tell the others now ! ' said Joey. ' It 's like a story in a book ! '

' It will take too long,' replied her sister. ' Ask me about it some time when there isn't a thunderstorm going on. Just listen to it ! ' as a fresh rumble forced her to shriek the last words.

' It often does that,' said Gisela. ' It travels round and round the lake till it dies away. It will come back again and again before it is over to-night.'

' How dreadful ! ' shuddered Simone.

' I call it jolly thrilling ! ' laughed Grizel.
' I 've never been in such a storm in my life
before ! '

' Where are we going to sleep ? ' asked Amy
with interest. ' And oh, Miss Bettany, what
is that funny thing on the wall ? '

She pointed as she spoke to a zither which
was hung up by a loop of soiled ribbons.
The herdsman, seeing her point to it, got up
from his seat and, taking it down, produced a
little twist of wire attached to a silver ring
which he fitted on his thumb, and then ran
it across the string, producing a shower of
silvery sounds.

' A zither ! ' cried Miss Maynard. ' And I
never noticed it ! '

' Gnädiges Fräulein plays the zither ? '
queried the man, holding it to her.

' Yes ; but you play first,' she said, smiling
at him.

He bowed somewhat clumsily, and then
played them a simple little air, whose notes
rippled through the hut like bird-notes.
When he had finished, he handed it to Miss
Maynard, and she played a song which, she
told them, she had learnt from the New
Forest gipsies. Every now and then the
thunder roared above the tinkling music, and
made the nervous people start. The first
awful gloom was wearing off, but the lightning
flashes were as vivid as ever, and the rain
still poured down ceaselessly.

Presently the herd produced a huge pot, which he slung on a hook hung over the fire by an iron chain.   Into this he poured a panful of milk, and, when it was heated, he invited them to dip big earthenware mugs, which he had brought from the inner room, into it, and drink.   It proved very good if it did have a smoky flavour.   Certainly, drunk in that room as an accompaniment to black bread and milk-cheese, it had a taste all its own.

When they had finished it, there was silence for a little.   The close atmosphere and the warmth were doing their work.   It was barely seven o'clock, but most of the Juniors were already nodding sleepily, and presently Amy turned to Miss Bettany with a request for bed.

' Please may I go to bed ?   I 'm so sleepy ! ' she pleaded.

' I think most of you would be better in bed,' said the young headmistress.   ' Come along, you people !   You can slip off your frocks and lie down in the hay, and then we 'll cover you up.'

' In the hay ? '   Amy wasn't sure whether to laugh or cry.

Luckily, Maria Marani settled it for her. ' It is topping ! ' she said cheerfully.

' Just like camping out ! ' added Grizel approvingly.   ' Oh, this is something like an adventure ! '

The herdsman, seeing that bed seemed to be the order of the day, got up, lit two lanterns, hanging one on a nail near the door, and, taking the other, slouched into the inner room with a muttered 'Gute Nacht!'

'And that's that!' observed Joey, wriggling out of her frock. 'I say, supposing the others come back, what a shock they will get if they walk in and see us lying round!'

'I hadn't thought of that!' Madge looked disturbed.

'I do not think they will come,' said Gisela consolingly. 'See, the door is barred. I think there is another hut at the other side, and they will spend the night there.'

'Do you? Shunt along, Grizel! You've got three times your share of the hay—I mean bed! Righto, Simone! You can come next me—if you can keep your arms to yourself, that is!'

Thus Joey, as she slipped off her shoes and curled herself up. She suddenly sat up again to ask, 'I say, does anyone snore?'

'Not unless it's yourself!' retorted Grizel promptly.

'Girls! Girls! Be quiet!' put in Madge, laughing. 'You really must settle down and get to sleep! We shall have to be up at six, to get down before Briesau is awake to see what scarecrows we are!'

Joey lay down, and presently they were all settled. Madge put out the lantern and lay down in her own place. It took her a little time to drop off, though everyone else quickly fell asleep—or so it seemed. But just as she was getting drowsy, a low voice said, 'Madge!'

'Well?' she asked sleepily.

'We 'll have a holiday to-morrow after this, shan't we?'

Madge sat up, fully awake.

'Joey Bettany, lie down at once and go to sleep, and don't let me hear you again till the morning!' she said severely.

There was a rustle in the hay and a little chuckle. Then silence.

CHAPTER XVIII.

THE CHÂLET MAGAZINE.

'OH, it was priceless!' Grizel gave a little chuckle. 'There we were, all grubby and untidy, and our hair full of hayseed, and all that walk to take! You'd have screamed if you had seen us!'

She laughed again at the memory, and Wanda von Eschenau joined her. Arrangements had been made for the next term, and Wanda and Marie were to join the Châlet School as boarders. In the meantime, they were to be with the girls as much as possible, partly with a view to learning English, so that they should be able to follow the lessons easily. Wanda already spoke fairly well, but Marie made funny mistakes at times. She and Joey and Simone were sitting in the grass some little distance away, revelling in the warmth of the sun, while Wanda and Grizel were perched on the railings which cut off the path to Geisalm. Farther along, Juliet was lying on the bank reading, while Margia, Amy, and the two little Merciers were making wreaths of the big white marguerites which grew everywhere.

It was a Saturday morning; practice was finished, and the boarders were free to amuse themselves. Grizel was telling Wanda about the birthday expedition with its unexpected ending. The young Viennese, who led the sheltered life of most girls of her class, was deeply thrilled, for Grizel told the tale well.

'It must have been full of terror up there on the Alpe,' she said in her slow, careful English. 'The storm was terrible, even here!'

'It was ghastly,' agreed Grizel. 'Simone shrieked like mad and Amy cried, and I'm sure I don't wonder! It must be awful if you are afraid of thunder! I'm not! But then, I'm not afraid of anything much!'

'You must be very courageous,' replied Wanda simply.

Grizel coloured to the roots of her hair. She had not meant to boast, but she had to admit that her last speech sounded uncommonly like boasting.

'Sorry! I'm afraid that was swank,' she said.

'Swank? *Was ist denn* "swank"?' queried Wanda.

'Oh, bucking — er — boasting,' returned Grizel hastily. 'Er—I wouldn't use it if I were you, Wanda. It isn't good English—not proper, you know.'

'What you call "slang." I see,' replied the other girl. 'But go on, Grizel. Did you meet with anybody?'

'Only cowherds,' said Grizel. 'Oh, but it was lovely, so early in the morning! Everything looked so new and well-washed after

the rain !—except us, of course ! I don't know
about the others, but all us boarders had a hot
bath and washed our hair. We had to, to get
the hay-seed out ! Then we all went to bed
and to sleep. I never knew bed could be so
nice before,' she added meditatively. 'Sleeping on hay is fun all right, but you don't get
much sleep ! First of all, a beetle walked
across Joey's face, and she yelled and hung
on to my hair—suppose it was the handiest
thing there was to hang on to ! Then, when
we had got over that excitement Amy began
to cry because the hay-seed had gone down
her neck and was tickling her. Then, just
before dawn, an owl of sorts started to
screech, and so did some of the little ones ! '

'But how could you enjoy such happenings ? ' asked Wanda, wide-eyed.

'Oh, I don't know ! You do, you know !
It 's something fresh—I s'pose that 's it.'

'Perhaps,' said Wanda doubtfully. 'But
I should not like it.'

'Oh, you will when you 've been with us
a while,' said Grizel confidently. 'Only, of
course, there won't be any mountain expeditions next term.'

'No, not with the snow here,' agreed the
young Austrian. 'How shall we amuse ourselves then, my Grizel ? '

'Oh, I don't know ! Dancing and games, I
suppose. P'r'aps we shall get up a play. Just
the usual things one does do in the winter.
I 'm tired of these old railings now—they 're

so jolly hard! Let's walk along to the other end. Gisela may be coming. She often does on Saturdays, and so do Bernhilda and Frieda Mensch. It makes it jollier for Juliet and me. Most of the others are rather babies, you see. Coming, Juliet?'

Juliet raised her head. 'Where to? Oh, the other gate? No, thanks, Grizel. I want to get on with my book; and anyway, it's too hot to move.'

'Lazy old object!' laughed Grizel. 'All right! Come on, Wanda! Let's leave her to it!'

They went off, laughing and talking gaily, while Juliet, uncurling herself from the little heap in which she had been lying, gazed after them thoughtfully.

She was not jealous, although Grizel had very little to say to her nowadays. In Grizel's eyes, Juliet had become suddenly and tiresomely 'good'; Wanda was fresh, and the English girl was rather given to running after fresh things. One thing, thought Juliet, as she sat hugging her knees in a brown study, Grizel could come to no harm with Wanda, who had been trained on the most conventional lines, and was often horrified at her new friend's tomboyish ways. It was rather a relief to the elder girl to know this, for she could not forget Grizel's declaration of a fortnight or so ago that she would be off up the Tiernjoch the first chance she got, and she didn't care who said what! City-bred Wanda was most unlikely to attempt such an expedition. The

Bärenbad Alpe was as much as she could manage, though Marie and Wolfram were ready for anything, and Kurt, the elder boy, went on climbing and hunting expeditions with his father every day.

Satisfied that Grizel was safe at present, Juliet returned to her book, and was soon lost to the world.

Meanwhile, the younger children had grown tired of their wreaths, and were making their way slowly towards the boat-landing to watch the steamer come in. As they went, Marie raised a tuneful little voice in ' *Röslein auf der Heider*,' in which the others joined, for they all knew it. As they strolled along, they saw a couple of big boys come racing down the path towards them, followed by a little girl of about nine. Instinctively the children moved to one side, and the two lads tore past them without giving them a glance. The little girl turned and looked at them, however, with a look of friendly curiosity, before she galloped after the others.

' Wonder who they are ? ' commented Jo in German, which language she now spoke as fluently as she did English. ' They looked rather jolly, didn't they ? '

' I think they are English,' said Simone gravely.

' Das Mädchen was not,' corrected Marie. ' She hadn't the English view.'

' Appearance, you mean,' observed Margia. ' Amy, come back ! You 'll fall in.'

'It wouldn't matter if I did—'cept for having to change,' replied Amy.

'Well, that would be bother enough,' said Margia, as she hauled her little sister back into safety.

'It wouldn't be yours anyhow!' snapped Amy.

Margia released her little sister in sheer amazement. It was the first time that Amy had ever attempted to have an opinion apart from her, and she gasped with wonder.

Joey laughed at her startled face. 'Margia, if you open your mouth like that the mosquitoes will dash in to their doom. "Be always kind to animals, wherever you may be." If a mosquito *is* an animal!'

'Oh, don't talk rubbish!' burst out Margia. 'Amy, you must be ill!'

'No, I'm not!' returned Amy pettishly. 'But I'm not going to be pulled about.'

'Oh, say no more, Margia!' interposed Simone. 'It is but that Amy grows up.'

'Well—but——' If her gentle little sister had slapped her in the face, Margia could not have been more surprised.

'Never mind now,' said Joey tactfully. 'I want to talk about my idea—at least, it's Gisela's really,' she added truthfully; 'but don't you think it would be topping to have a school mag. ?'

'Gorgeous!' said Simone, who had picked up this expression from Jo.

'It would be like the school tales,' said

Marie thoughtfully. 'But we play no—no matches of the cricket and the tennis wit' ozzer schools.'

' " Other," ' corrected Joey. ' Nor we do, but we do other things. There 's the Mondscheinspitze for one. That would be a topping thing for a mag. ! '

'And your day at Innsbrück and Frau Berlin,' added Margia; for all the school knew of that episode by this time.

'Yes; and the day we went boating and the storm came on. And we do play cricket and tennis with ourselves,' said Jo thoughtfully.

'Then let us ask Gisela, shall we not?' suggested Marie.

'An'—an' I 'll write a poem for you,' proposed Amy cheerfully.

They all stopped still with one accord and stared at her. She blushed crimson, but stood her ground.

Joey was the first to speak. 'I say!' she said, and whistled loudly.

'Amy!' cried Margia. 'What do you mean? You know you can't write poetry.'

'I can, then!' retorted Amy. 'I writed some last night!'

'Let 's see it, then!'

'Can't! It 's in my cubey under my pillow!'

'What is it about?' demanded Marie.

'A river. The one beside the Kron Prinz Karl.'

'That's not a river; it's not big enough,' declared Margia.

'Well, I've called it a little river,' returned Amy defiantly.

'Oh, Amy, do let us see it!' pleaded Simone. 'I think you are awfullee clevaire! I could not do it. I! No, truly!'

'I tell you it's in my cubey,' said Amy, nevertheless softening before Simone's compliments. 'I'll get it when I go to wash my hands for *Mittagessen.*'

'There's Gisela, with Wanda and Grizel,' put in Joey. 'Let's scoot and ask her.'

But Amy had caught at her arm. 'Joey, don't let Grizel know!'

'Why ever not?' demanded Joey in surprise.

'She'll laugh if you do! Don't tell her, Joey! Not yet, anyhow!'

'Grizel Cochrane sha'n't laugh at you!' said Margia determinedly. 'Why should she?'

But all Amy could be got to say was, 'She will! I know she will!'

'Oh, all right, then! But we can ask Gisela about the mag.,' said Joey. 'Come on, everybody! Gisela! Gi—se—la!'

Gisela, who had been chattering gaily with Wanda and Grizel, lifted her head.

'Yes! I come!' she called back, and set off at a run, heedless of Grizel's impatient 'Oh, don't bother with the kids just now, Gisela!'

'What is it?' asked the big girl, as she

reached the Juniors. 'Is there anything wrong ?'

'No, nothing. Only, do you remember what we were talking about the day we decided to get my sister's birthday present ? Gisela, let 's have a school mag. ! '

'Yes ; and you be editor,' added Margia.

Gisela looked thoughtful, and at this moment Wanda and Grizel came up with them.

'Well ! What 's the worry ? ' demanded Grizel. 'Anyone dead yet ? '

Joey turned on her like a flash. 'Grizel ! I hate that horrid sneery way of talking you 've got lately ! You 're always making fun of us ! It 's horrid of you ! '

'Keep your hair on ! ' said Grizel easily. 'No need to get hot about nothing ! '

'I 'm not ! ' retorted Joey. 'And anyhow,' as an unholy memory came to her, ' anyhow, I didn't ask to have my hair rinsed in holy water ! '

'Joey ! What do you mean ? ' cried Wanda, astounded.

'Ask Grizel ! She knows ! ' said Joey with somewhat malicious delight.

Grizel, crimson and furious, glared at her tormentor. 'You little pig, Joey ! '

'Well, you did—didn't you ? ' Then Joey's malice vanished in a chuckle. 'I say ! Do you remember the man's face when he heard you ? Oh, wasn't it funny ? '

'It was only a mistake,' said Grizel with an unwilling laugh.

'But what was it?' asked Gisela, bewildered. 'Please tell us, Grizel.'

'Oh, it was only that I mixed up *heisses* and *heiliges*,' explained Grizel. 'Jo's a horror to drag it up like that! What about the time you threw flowers at a guide?'

'That was years ago,' returned Jo, not one whit abashed. 'He looked about as horrified as Herr Alphen did when you asked for a rinse of holy water.'

'But I still do not understand,' said Gisela. 'Let us sit down, and you will tell us.'

So they sat down beside Amy's 'little river,' and between them, Joey and Grizel explained what they meant. Gisela and Wanda rocked with laughter at the stories, especially the holy-water one.

'But it must have been very funny!' laughed Gisela.

'Oh, it was!' Joey chuckled ecstatically. 'If you'd seen the man's face!'

'Oh, well, let it alone now, and let's get on to the magazine,' suggested Grizel.

'It is an English institution,' observed Wanda. 'I have read of it in my story-books. Papa has given me several, you know, as he wished Marie and I should know something about life in the English schools.'

'But you can't always go by stories,' said Joey. 'Some of them are awful tosh—like that *Denise of the Fourth* one you showed me, Gisela.'

'There is one about a girl who was a Guide,' began Gisela doubtfully, 'but I did not quite understand it. It is not the kind of guide we know here.'

'Girl Guides, was it?' asked Joey with interest. 'I always wanted to be one, but my sister would never let me, because in England I caught cold over everything. I'm heaps better now, though.'

'It was a Girl Guide,' said Wanda. 'Her name was the same as yours, Gisela, but they called her "Gilly." I liked the book very good.'

'You should say "very much,"' Grizel corrected her. 'Well, we can't do anything about the Guides just now, though it's jolly well worth thinking about. Let's get on to the magazine. And this afternoon, I vote we play cricket. Wanda is keen to learn; aren't you, old thing?'

'I should love it,' said Wanda, 'but it sounds to me a painful game.'

The English girls went off into fits of laughter over this; and even Gisela smiled. But Simone nodded sympathetically. She had been badly bruised only three days before by a ball flung in carelessly by Bette when fielding, and she much preferred tennis. Joey played cricket, however, so Simone must too.

'It is a tophole game,' said Grizel. 'You'll soon learn it. Now, about the magazine.'

'I have never seen an English school magazine,' began Gisela, 'but I have read of them. We must have for editor one who can write the—the—editorial, and also arrange. Then we must have articles upon our games and the happenings of this term. There should be stories and poetry, and a letter from our Head. There are only eighteen of us, but I think we might do it. It is an English custom, as Wanda says, and we are an English school, and I should like to do it. Bette and Gertrud and Bernhilda wish it too. What do you think, Joey? Would Madame allow it?'

'Rather!' said Joey enthusiastically. 'She'd be awfully keen, I know.'

'Then what do you say? Shall we see what we can do about it?'

'Yes, let's!'

'It's a ripping scheme, Gisela!'

'But we—we, too, Gisela! We shall be members of the school soon. May we not write for it?'

'Well, I—I—I'll let you have some poetry!'

This last was Amy, of course. The Seniors looked at her with much the same surprise as the others had done.

'Poetry, Amy? Why, you don't even know what poetry is, do you?' teased Grizel.

'Yes, I do! It's lines that rhyme! So there, Grizel Cochrane!' flashed Amy, her fair little face burning with a mixture of shyness and indignation.

'Oh my hat! There is a cat! On the

mat !' mocked Grizel. 'Your poetry anything like that, Amy ?'

'It's a jolly sight better than anything you
could do, anyway !' declared Margia, coming
valiantly to Amy's assistance. She might sit
on her little sister for her own good, but she
wasn't going to have Grizel Cochrane doing
it if she could help it.

Grizel tilted back her pretty head and
laughed aggravatingly. But Joey now took
up the cudgels.

'You're horrid just now, Grizel ! I don't
know what's the matter with you !' she said
with more vehemence than politeness.

'Don't get excited, babies——'

'Grizel !'

At the sound of their headmistress's voice
they all turned round.

'What is the matter with you, girls ?'
asked Miss Bettany, as they faced her.

Gisela rushed into the breach. 'Madame,
it was just a little argument. And please may
we have a magazine for the school ?'

'A school magazine ?' She looked at them
with twinkling eyes. 'Yes, if you will promise
not to quarrel over it, and not to leave all the
work to one person, I think you may.'

And so was the idea of *The Châletian* book.

CHAPTER XIX.

SOME PRANKS.

'ONLY three weeks till the end of term! Nothing much can happen in three weeks!' Thus Madge Bettany, as she sat in her bedroom, talking things over with Mademoiselle La Pâttre. 'Our first term,' she went on dreamily. 'Well, it hasn't been a bit what I thought it would. For one thing, I never expected we should get such a large school together so quickly. Eight or ten was the most I had hoped for. But here we are with eighteen, and at least seven more for next term! It isn't bad, is it?'

Mademoiselle nodded her head slowly. 'It has gone well, *ma chérie*,' she said gravely.

'The girls are so keen on being really English,' went on the young headmistress. 'Even the Juniors are infected with the desire. The other day I heard Suzanne Mercier and Berta Hamel discussing some prank or other, and Suzanne asked very seriously, "Are you sure it's English?" Berta wasn't certain, so they went off to discuss it with Joey.'

'Has it occurred yet?' asked Mademoiselle with a smile.

'I haven't heard anything, so I don't suppose it has.'

'I wonder what it is?' ruminated the elder woman. 'They think of things so extraordinary, these little ones. I am sure Simone would never have thought of cutting off her hair a year ago.'

'It's far better for her,' said Madge decidedly. 'She really had too much. She's much better in every way, I think; and she's losing that tragic look she used to have, and she does things—well—off her own bat!'

'My dear!' Mademoiselle was genuinely horrified at the slang, but Madge only laughed.

'Awful, isn't it?' she said gaily. 'Mercifully none of the girls heard me. Do remember, Elise, that I've not been a Head for three months yet! You must allow me a little slang just very occasionally.'

Mademoiselle joined in her laughter, which was cut short by a piercing shriek.

'Mercy!' gasped Madge. 'What on earth has happened?'

She fled to the door, tore it open, and ran down the stairs, to meet a scared and horrified Bette and Bernhilda, who both exclaimed, 'Oh, Madame! Come quickly! Come at once!'

'What is it? An accident?' she gasped with whitening face.

'No—no! It is much worse! It is witchcraft!' wailed Bette.

'Witchcraft! Nonsense! There is no such thing as witchcraft!' she said sharply, nevertheless following them along the narrow passage to the little boarded-off compartment where the 'splasheries' were. Arrived there, she gasped at what she saw. Then, realising what had happened, she burst into laughter. Each of the two basins was full to the brim of sparkling, sizzling bubbles! Even as they looked, the foaming began to subside, and in another minute or two the bowls held only ordinary water—or what looked like ordinary water.

'Oh, Madame, what is it?' sobbed Bette in German. 'I did nothing! I only poured in the water, and Bernhilda also, and it foamed up at once! Oh, is it witchcraft?'

A sudden gurgle outside the window, followed by a 'Hush!' drew the Head's attention for a second, but she took no further notice.

'Oh, Bette! You silly child!' she said rather impatiently. 'Of course it isn't! Haven't I told you there is no such thing as witchcraft? All that has happened is that those young monkeys have powdered the bowls with sherbet or salts or some fizzy stuff! Of course it bubbled up when you poured the water in! But that's all it is!'

Had she been able to see through the bushes which grew against the side of the house, she would have seen four faces grow rather blank at her omniscience.

'I say!' murmured Joey. 'I forgot they would probably fetch my sister, and it's a trick my brother told us of. He did it at his school.'

'Will she be angry?' asked Berta, a trifle apprehensively.

Joey considered, her head on one side. 'Shouldn't think so,' she said finally. 'There's nothing wrong in it—it's only a lark, and it doesn't hurt anyone. That idiot, Bette! Fancy believing in witchcraft at her age!'

'But lots of them do,' argued Simone, with somewhat incautious loudness. 'You remember, Joey, you told us of the little boy who made the "horns" at you!'

'Shut up, idiot!' hissed Joey. 'D' you want them to come and catch us? Come along! We'd better clear out now!' And they promptly vacated their position and decamped to the ferry-landing.

Meanwhile, Madge was busy soothing the injured feelings of the Seniors. Bette was furiously angry at having been so taken in, and even Bernhilda the gentle was inclined to be indignant.

'It is an impertinence,' she said in her soft, careful English. 'Is it not, Madame?'

Madge nodded. 'Oh, yes! But it is the kind of thing that often happens with Juniors, and I advise you to take no notice this time. If they do it again, of course, the Prefects should take it up. It's not bad mischief. You people must learn to distinguish between bad mischief and nonsense like this.'

With this she left them, to go and relate
the occurrence to their compeers, while she
herself chuckled over it with Mademoiselle
and Miss Maynard, who had just come in.

' It 's healthy mischief anyhow,' she said,
' so I sha'n't interfere.   There 's *Mittagessen*.'

At *Mittagessen* the four Juniors kept giggling
together, and many were the meaning glances
shot at Bette, who held her head very high,
and was remarkably chilly in her behaviour
to them.   Bernhilda had cooled down, and
was able to laugh at the affair, but Bette was
half Italian, and her indignation still ran hot.
Gisela and the others had enjoyed the joke,
even while they admitted that it was ' an
impertinence,' and, as the Head Girl said, it
was better than the defiance of Grizel and
Juliet of the previous week.

For the rest of the day, however, she
kept a sharp look-out on them; but their
conduct was most exemplary, and the day-
girls went off, satisfied that it was only a
sudden spurt and there would be no more
of it.

There were three bedtimes during the week
at the Châlet.   Amy and Margia Stevens, and
the two little Merciers, who were boarders till
the end of term, as their parents had been
obliged to go to Paris owing to the sudden
illness of Madame Mercier's mother, went at
seven, Joey and Simone at eight, and Juliet
and Grizel at nine.   On Saturdays and
Sundays they all went at the same time—

half-past eight on Saturdays and eight on
Sundays. When seven o'clock came that
evening, the four Juniors trotted off quite
happily. Miss Maynard went up to brush
hair at half-past seven, and see that they were
all safely in bed. She found them, as she
afterwards said, 'rather gigglesome,' but as
the story of the powdered basins—they had
used sherbet, as Madge had surmised—had
gone round the school by that time, she set
it down to that. At eight o'clock punctually
Joey and Simone said good-night and retired
in their turn. It was Mademoiselle's duty
to go up half an hour later to see that
they were all right. Juliet and Grizel were
considered old enough to be responsible for
themselves.

When half-past eight came, Mademoiselle
was in the middle of writing a letter, so Miss
Maynard good-naturedly offered to run up for
her. The Frenchwoman accepted the offer,
and the mathematics mistress ascended the
stairs lightly. She expected to find the two
in bed, ready to bid her 'good-night,' so she
was considerably startled to find Joey in her
dressing-gown, grimly unpicking the top of
her pyjama legs, while Simone was wrestling
with a sleeve of her nightdress.

'Girls!' exclaimed the mistress. 'What
is the meaning of this?'

'All our night garments are sewn up,' said
Simone mournfully.

'Some joke!' remarked Joey. 'Look,

Miss Maynard! Stitched top and bottom of legs and sleeves, and the top of my trousers too!'

Miss Maynard's eyes twinkled, and she bit her lips. 'H'm! So the biters were bitten,' she said softly. 'Well, I will give you five minutes longer. Be quick!'

She knew better than to look through the other curtains to see if the Juniors were asleep. Certain little rustles and snorts made it quite evident that they were not. She took no notice of the suspicious sounds, but simply waited by the window until the other two were safely in bed, and then withdrew, remarking that she hoped they would all—with an emphasis on the ' all '—get off to sleep quickly.

'Pigs!' remarked Joey, as soon as she was well out of the way. 'Little horrors!'

Four separate giggles answered her, but no one spoke. She gave a snort and turned over, burying herself beneath the sheets. Simone had done the same.

'An' the worst of it is that it completely put the lid on our stunt!' she groaned next morning when she and Simone had finished telling the other four what they thought of them. 'We'd intended ragging the Senior cubicles, but I thought we'd better get ready for bed first, and then we found what you'd done! An' Maynie came up before we were half ready.'

'Well, why didn't you tell us?' demanded

Margia. 'Then we'd have helped, and left you till to-night!'

'Well! Of all the cool cheek!' gasped Joey. 'Margia, you're the limit!'

'It's your own fault!' retorted Margia. 'You said we hadn't had any rags yet, and it would be a pity to finish the term without.'

'Yes; but I never meant you to rag us! An' that reminds me. Is the piano done?'

'Uh-huh! Amy did it when she had finished her practice.'

'Good enoughsky! No one saw you, did they, Amy?'

Little Amy shook her head till all her curls danced. 'No one! It will be fun!'

'Well, it's Grizel's practice first! Won't she be mad?'

'Hopping mad,' agreed Margia. 'There's the bell! Come on!'

The conspirators scurried in to lessons, and only saved themselves from complete disgrace by the most valiant efforts. Amy, her mind wandering to the latest joke, when asked to explain what a delta was, said dreamily, 'It's another name for the keyboard of the piano—the white keys!'

Miss Bettany dropped the blackboard chalk in her surprise. 'Amy!'

'I beg your pardon, Madame,' she faltered. 'I—I——' She stopped, unable to go on.

'I see,' said Madge dryly. 'Will you kindly pay attention to the lesson? What is a delta?'

Amy managed to stumble through a fairly accurate if somewhat lengthy explanation. ' It 's all the stuff brought down by the river and left in a heap at the bottom—I mean the end—in a funny shape, sort of three-cornered, you know.'

Joey and Simone, doing algebra, came off little better. Joey's simple equations were a hopeless muddle, while Simone's had neither beginning nor ending.

Frieda, Anita, and Sophie stared at them in amazement, while Miss Maynard scolded them sharply for carelessness and inattention.

Much they cared, however! They were only longing for two o'clock and the beginning of practice-time. They had not dared to meddle with the music-room piano, for this was one of the days on which Herr Anserl came up from Spärtz to give music lessons. He was a magnificent teacher, and a musician to his finger-tips, but he was terribly short-tempered, and any pranks would have sent him storming off to Miss Bettany. His pupils all regarded his lessons with a mixture of terror and amusement. He told Grizel that she had the fingers of a machine, and the soul of one too, which offended her dreadfully, but she dared not show it. Joey he raved at for her lack of a sense of time, while Juliet's stumbling performances brought German phrases and epithets rumbling from his very boots. On the other hand, he had once told Margia Stevens that if she worked hard and thoroughly for the next six years, she might make a performer who would not disgrace him. Margia was the only one of the younger girls to go to him, the others being taken by Mademoiselle.

Simone learnt the violin, and so did Gisela Marani and Gertrud Steinbrücke, so they three went down to Spärtz on one afternoon in the week for their lesson.

After *Mittagessen*, they were allowed to do as they liked until two o'clock, when preparation and practice were the order of the afternoon. The schoolroom piano stood in the Senior classroom, and while the Juniors did prep. under Miss Maynard, the Seniors had an English literature lesson with Miss Bettany, and Grizel practised under Mademoiselle's eye, so that she should work as accurately as possible. The partition between the preparation-room and the Senior room was of light matchboarding only; the windows were wide open, and it was possible to hear everything that went on in the next room. The Juniors listened eagerly. They heard Grizel settle herself down and touch the notes tentatively before she began. Then Joey stood up.

'Please, Miss Maynard, may I take my French to Mademoiselle?' she said. 'I don't quite understand her corrections.'

'Yes, Joey, if you must,' said Miss Maynard, glancing up from her work.

Joey escaped, and hastened into the other room. It was no part of their plan to let Mademoiselle find out what they had done.

She would probably be angry, and report them
to the Head, and they did not want that.

'*Eh bien*, Joey, what is it ? ' asked Mademoiselle, as she made her appearance.

' It 's this exercise, Mademoiselle,' replied
Joey meekly. ' I don't quite see where I 've
gone wrong.   Should I have used the sub-
junctive mood ? '

Unsuspectingly, Mademoiselle took the book
from her and looked it over.

' Yes, my child, it is here,' she said. ' If
you use '' *est-ce que*,'' you must follow it with
the *subjonctif*, which you have not done.
Grizel !   What, then, are you doing ? '

She might well ask !   Grizel was supposed
to be practising modulatory exercises, but
even they were no excuse for the hideous
noise she was producing.

' I—it 's the keys, Mademoiselle,' said
Grizel. ' They are so slippery.'

' Slippery ?   Bah !   It is your own abomin-
able carelessness !   Begin again, and with
more care, I pray you ! '

Hunching her shoulders and compressing
her lips, Grizel started again, with much the
same results.   For once, it was a cool day, and
chilly fingers combined with slippery keys
proved too much for her.   Suddenly it
dawned on her to look at her finger-tips.
They were powdered with white !   In a flash
she realised what had happened : the Juniors
had covered the keys with French chalk !
Nearly choking with anger, Grizel took out

her handkerchief and dusted the keyboard as
unobtrusively as she could. Furious though
she was, she could not give them away to
Mademoiselle, who was busy instructing an
extraordinarily stupid Jo.

As for Jo herself, it was all she could do to
keep a straight face. She was unable to see
Grizel's expression, but a back can be very
expressive at times, and Grizel's looked as if
she had swallowed a poker whole. When,
presently, she had apparently listened to all
Mademoiselle's explanations, and was dismissed, the Middle girl literally fled out of the
room, and, collapsing at the foot of the stairs,
rocked backwards and forwards with laughter.
The sound of footsteps overhead made her pull
herself together with a mighty effort, and
getting up, she went back to the prep.-room,
where, for all the amount of work she did,
she might just as well not have been.

Never had the afternoon seemed so long to
the Juniors. When at length Miss Maynard
said, ' Five minutes to four ! Pack up your
books and get ready for tea ! ' they all sighed
audibly with relief, much to her astonishment.
She had barely taken her departure before a
righteously indignant Grizel dashed in.

' Where 's Joey Bettany ? ' she cried. ' Jo,
you little horror, how dared you mess up the
keys like that ? '

' I didn't ! '

' She didn't ! ' ' It wasn't Jo ! ' exclaimed
several voices at once.

'But she knew all about it! I know that!'

'Jolly well I did! But I didn't do it,' returned Jo stoutly.

'Then who did? I never heard of such nerve in my life! Who did it?'

'Me,' said a small voice, and Grizel turned to stare incredulously at the baby of the school.

'Amy! You!'

Amy raised angelic blue eyes to the startled face above her. 'Yes. It was a joke!'

'Well! I—I'm—I'm jiggered!' declared Grizel flatly.

She went slowly out of the room to her own quarters, where all the coaxing and teasing of the other Seniors could not get out of her what was wrong with her, and it was only after Gisela and Bette had heard from the delighted Juniors what had occurred that they understood. Then they were almost as startled as Grizel herself. Amy was the last person they would have suspected of such a trick. Margia, Joey, Maria, even Suzanne might have done it. But Amy! The Seniors were completely flabbergasted.

As for Amy herself, she was in high glee over it, and cut capers to such an extent that she called down upon herself a sharp reprimand from Miss Maynard, who coached them for tennis, and who, of course, had no idea why Amy Stevens was behaving with such sudden wildness.

On their way home after tennis in the

evening, Gisela summed up the state of affairs rather neatly to Bette.

'Amy is becoming a schoolgirl and ceasing to be a baby,' she said. 'But one doesn't expect it so suddenly.'

'No,' agreed Bette—they were talking in their own language—'but I think you are right.'

'I know I am,' said the Head Girl with finality.

CHAPTER XX.

AND STILL MORE !

THE Juniors, having begun to play pranks —all, it must be admitted, of fairly harmless character—found it too pleasant a pastime to give up. The night after the affair of the French-chalked piano-keys, Juliet, on going to bed, barely suppressed a wild yell when she entered her cubicle, for there, sitting up in her bed, was a figure that looked curiously lifelike in the half light. A closer inspection informed her that the creature was made of her own pillow, decked in her own pyjama jacket, with a boudoir cap, hastily manufactured out of two handkerchiefs, stuck on top, while beneath this an amiably smiling face drawn in coloured chalks on a sheet of white paper made the thing natural enough to have scared her badly for the moment.

Grasping the ridiculous object, she marched into the cubicle where Joey Bettany, who had caught the extraordinary sound she had made, was choking her laughter with the sheet.

' Joey ! ' said Juliet indignantly, ' did you do this ? '

' I—I—— ' Joey was incapable of uttering more at the moment. The sight of the weird object completely upset her.

Dropping it, Juliet took her by the shoulders and shook her. 'Joey! Stop giggling, and tell me if you were so stupid!'

'Well, stop shaking me then!' retorted Joey, as well as she could for lack of breath.

'You deserve more than shaking, you little horror!' declared Juliet, releasing her as she spoke.

'If anyone hears you, there'll be a row,' said Joey calmly. 'It's "lights-out" for me, and you're not supposed to talk to me now.'

Juliet was rendered speechless by her virtuous air, but she soon recovered herself.

'Well, upon my word!' she said. 'For cool cheek, that beats everything! It would serve you right if I took this thing to Madame!'

'You won't, though,' returned Joey with confidence. She was leaning back against her pillow, smiling up at the older girl as she spoke.

Juliet suddenly laughed back at her. 'No; you're quite right—I won't! But be careful, my child! I'll have my r—r—revenge, so don't forget!'

'I won't,' replied Jo cheerfully. 'What! Must you go? So sorry! Good-night!'

She turned over on her side and snuggled down, and Juliet, with rather a grim smile, left her. All the time she was preparing for bed she was turning ideas over in her mind. Just as she was kneeling down to say her prayers, a smothered shriek from Grizel brought her to her feet with a bound.

'Grizel! What on earth's the matter?
Are you hurt? Oh——'

'Those little beasts!' spluttered Grizel, as
she drew her curtain back. 'Look at that!
Two brushes in my bed!' She held them out
as she spoke.

'Little horrors!' laughed Juliet. 'I had
an effigy in mine!'

'They must have gone mad!' declared
Grizel. 'It's all Joey, of course! She
thinks of the things, even if she doesn't do
them.'

'She does not!' said a third voice indignantly. ''Twas me did that!'

'Girls! What are you thinking of?
Juliet! Grizel! Why are you not in bed?'

They all jumped, as the outer curtains parted
to show Miss Bettany.

'Why are you not in bed?' she repeated.
'And why have you drawn back the curtains
between your cubicle and Juliet's, Grizel?
You know it is against the rules?'

Silence answered her. On hearing her
voice, Grizel had dropped the brushes, so she
did not see them. As no one seemed to have
an answer ready, she bade the two Seniors
hurry into bed.

'I will see you in the morning,' she said
coldly. 'I am very disappointed in both of
you. I thought you could be trusted to keep
rules!'

With this she left the room, while two
unhappy people stared at each other. Then

Grizel drew the curtain again and retired to her bed, after she had pushed the brushes underneath it. Juliet followed suit, and a deadly silence filled the room. It continued next morning, and, when Grizel met Simone on the stairs, she drew to one side. Simone lifted her dark eyes to the Senior's face with the glimmer of a smile, but Grizel tilted her head and stalked downstairs with an offended dignity, that was rather marred by her missing the last step and staggering somewhat ignominiously across the hall.

'Grizel is furious!' reported Simone to the others. 'She would not regard me.'

'If you mean "look at," I'd say so,' murmured Joey. 'When are you going to my sister to say it's your fault?'

Simone's eyes fell, and she began to play nervously with the end of her girdle. 'I—I don't know,' she stammered.

'Why not? I should go after breakfast an' get it over.'

'Ye—yes!'

Joey turned and looked at her incredulously. 'You surely don't mean you're goin' to funk it?' she demanded.

'N—no! No! Of course I will go! Will—will Madame be very angry?'

'Couldn't say! Shouldn't think so,' was the laconic response.

'Oh, Joey, do not be angry with me!' pleaded Simone, half crying. 'I will go certainly, and say it was my fault.'

'Righto!' said Joey.   'Come on to break-fast—there's the bell!'

Simone would have made only a poor breakfast had Joey not kept a watchful eye on her. As it was, she was persuaded to eat her usual meal. And then Joey went with her as far as the study door.

'Buck up, old thing!' she said cheerfully. 'She can't eat you, an' I'll wait for you here.'

Thus adjured, Simone went in after tapping at the door. Miss Bettany looked up in surprise when she saw her; she had been expecting Grizel and Juliet.

'Well, Simone,' she said, 'what is it, dear?'

'Please, Madame, I am come to say that it was my fault,' said Simone.

'Your fault? What is your fault? I don't understand.'

Simone took hold of her rapidly departing courage with both hands and said, 'The—the disturbance last night—I did it!'

'You did it? But it had nothing to do with you!'

'Yes, Madame. I had put two brushes in Grizel's bed.'

For a moment Madge's lips twitched, Simone's expression was so serious. Then she pulled herself together. 'That was very silly,' she said gravely.

'Yes, Madame. I know it was,' agreed Simone. 'But you will forgive them, since the fault is to me?'

'"The fault is mine,"' corrected her head-

mistress. 'I will see Grizel and Juliet,
Simone. And please don't do such a silly
thing again. Run away, now.'

Greatly relieved, Simone trotted off, after
making her little regulation curtsy, and a
minute or so later Grizel and Juliet presented
themselves, inwardly quaking a little. They
met with an agreeable surprise.

'Simone has been to me,' said Miss Bettany
soberly, ' and she tells me that it was her fault
that there was a disturbance in the dormitory
last night, so we will say no more about it.
But remember that for the future even brushes
in your bed will not be accepted as an excuse
for breaking rules. You may go now.'

They bobbed their curtsies and went. Outside, they turned and looked at each other.

'Jolly good for Simone,' said Grizel. 'I
didn't think she had it in her.'

'Joey would make her,' responded Juliet.
'But it was plucky for her.'

'Rather! Joey's a sporting kid all round;
she's awfully good for the others.'

'Yes; she just sees the straight thing to do,
and does it. Hullo! There's Wanda! Let's
trot out and talk to her!'

The next joke was a harmless one, that
nobody minded except the perpetrators, but
which had far-reaching consequences. Two
days after Simone's confession, Joey and
Grizel came up to Gisela and solemnly
informed her that on the fifteenth of July,
which was St Swithin's Day, it was the custom

in all good English schools to sip a cup of water, which was passed round, and wish as one did so.

'But first you must take it to any foreign mistress in the school,' said Grizel impressively, meaning, of course, that the water should be offered to Mademoiselle.

As the two practical jokers had already played tricks of a similar nature on her, Gisela looked at them sharply. Neither had the ghost of a smile on her face, and Joey's expression was super-angelic—a bad sign, which her sister would have recognised at once. Gisela, however, was not so experienced, and she was completely taken in.

'The fifteenth—that is to-morrow,' she said seriously. 'I will remember!'

'What a lark! Didn't think she'd be had so easily!' chuckled Joey.

'Neither did I,' replied Grizel. 'Sha'n't we crow over them to-morrow!'

Unfortunately, Gisela had misinterpreted one part of Grizel's speech. In her eyes, of course, all three mistresses were foreigners, and both Joey and Grizel were thunderstruck when, just before prayers, the Head Girl advanced to the little dais where the staff was, and offering the cup of water, murmured in her pretty English, 'The cup of water for a wish, as is the custom in all English schools on St Swithin's Day.'

There was a moment's silence. Miss Bettany looked puzzled, Miss Maynard choked audibly, and Mademoiselle wore an outraged expression. Then the headmistress, with one rapid glance round the room, took in the affair at once. Quietly she accepted the cup, and drank from it.

'Thank you, Gisela,' she said, as she returned it. 'And now we will have prayers.'

The ensuing events were lost on Joey and Grizel, who were almost petrified with horror. They were more horrified when, after she had given out the notices for the day, Miss Bettany added, 'I should like to see Josephine and Grizel in my study now, before lessons.' Then she dismissed the school and went to her own room.

The culprits presently appeared. She waited till they had shut the door.

'Now,' she said, 'I want to know what Gisela meant.'

'It—it was only a lark,' mumbled Joey at last.

'Please speak correct English, Josephine. Repeat your sentence.'

'It—it was only a joke,' repeated her small sister rather faintly.

Miss Bettany's eyebrows went up at the statement.

'A joke ? I'm afraid your sense of fun is too elemental to appeal to me. I see nothing humorous in a silly trick like that. Who suggested it ? '

Joey went scarlet ; Grizel hung her head and said nothing. Truth to tell, she was rather scared. She had never encountered her headmistress in this mood.

'Who suggested it?' repeated Miss Bettany, in a voice that intimated that she meant to know sooner or later.

'It was me,' said Grizel at last, as sulkily as she dared.

'Indeed? Your grammar seems to stand in as much need of correction as your idea of humour. Well, I am going to send for Gisela, and you will both apologise to her before me for your silly impertinence towards her.' She rang her little bell as she spoke, and presently Marie appeared and was dispatched for Gisela.

The two sinners, meanwhile, were left to their own thoughts, as Miss Bettany occupied herself with her letters. Presently Gisela appeared, wearing a rather startled expression.

'You have sent for me, Madame?' she said.

'Yes, Gisela. Josephine and Grizel wish to express their regret for being impertinent enough to play a silly trick on you about St Swithin's Day observances.'

Gisela's face cleared at that. 'But it is all right,' she said. 'I knew when I had offered you the water that it was a—a take-in!'

'Nevertheless, it was very impertinent of them,' replied Miss Bettany. 'Girls!'

'I'm sorry,' said Joey, 'I suppose it was cheek, Gisela, but I didn't think of it; honest Injun!'

'It is all right,' repeated Gisela, bending and kissing her, much to Jo's discomfort.

'Now, Grizel,' said the headmistress.

'I'm sorry,' mumbled Grizel, and she ducked to avoid the kiss.

Miss Bettany was wise enough not to insist on anything more. After dismissing the Head Girl, she said a few more words on practical joking, and then sent them to their form-rooms, where Jo, at any rate, was soon immersed in her history. Not so Grizel. She was intensely proud, and hated apologising to anyone. Besides this, her headmistress's strictures on her sense of humour had offended her dreadfully. She sulked till half-way through the morning, then the sudden memory of a joke she had once heard of as being played on a master at her cousin's school came to her.

'I'll do that!' she thought. 'Perhaps that may not seem kiddish! At any rate it'll be something to rag me for! That idiot of a Gisela!'

The joke in question required careful preparation, and Grizel was rather doubtful as to whether she could get the materials she required. Fortune, however, favoured her. On the landing near the big dormitory stood an old armoire in which Mademoiselle kept such simple medicines as they were likely to need. As a rule it was kept locked, but Amy had fallen down and bumped her head, so Mademoiselle went to fetch some cold cream for the lump. She left the cupboard open,

and Grizel, passing at the time, saw her
chance—and took it. After tea that day she
vanished, and none of them could find her.

'Never mind,' said Joey, who had quite
recovered her usual spirits. 'She's only sulk-
ing over this morning's row—silly ass! Come
on to cricket! She'll turn up when she feels
like it. Bags me first innings, everyone!'

They settled down to their cricket practice,
and no one noticed that she never came near
them till the bell called them all in to supper.
Then she was already at the table, in a clean
frock, looking almost aggressively tidy.

The fun started next morning when
Mademoiselle came to give B division their
German lessons. Both Grizel and Jo came
for this. Jo's German was fluent enough,
but her written composition was weak, so
Madge had ordained that she must attend
the lessons of B division as well as those
of A. Happy-go-lucky Jo accepted her lot
quite calmly, and rejoiced in the fact that,
at any rate, she was missing hated geometry,
and might have been much worse off.

The first half of the lesson was devoted
to the correction of a previous composition;
then Mademoiselle turned to the blackboard.

'We will now do some oral composition,'
she said in German. 'I will write the title on
the board, and then we will all make sentences.
We will, to-day, talk of the mountains.
Margia, give me the German for "the mountains."'

'*Gebirge*,' said Margia promptly.

'The article?' said Mademoiselle, waiting, chalk in hand.

'Oh—"*die*," I think,' said Margia, somewhat doubtfully this time.

Mademoiselle beamed approval on her, and turned to write it up. In vain she struggled with the chalk. Not one mark could she make.

'I do not understand,' she said, lapsing into her own language in the stress of the moment.

'P'r'aps the chalk is wet,' suggested Joey. 'If it is, it doesn't write, I know.'

'Perhaps that is the reason,' agreed Mademoiselle, looking at the chalk dubiously. 'Margia, my child, go to the stationery cupboard and fetch me a fresh piece, if you please. There is no more in the desk.'

Margia darted away, and presently returned with a new stick. But for all the impression it made, she might just as well never have fetched it.

'But this is an extraordinary occurrence,' Mademoiselle was beginning, when the door opened and the headmistress entered, white with anger.

At the sight of her, sundry people hastily searched their memories for past sins, but most of them could recall nothing that would make Miss Bettany look like that. Mademoiselle was too full of the unusual behaviour of the chalk to notice anything wrong.

'Madame,' she began eagerly, 'the chalk will not write!'

' I know,' said her Head in low tones. She advanced to the board and drew her hand down it in one sweep. Then she looked at her palm. ' As I thought,' she said. ' Which of you has vaselined all the blackboards ? '

There was a deathly silence, broken suddenly by Amy Stevens.

' Please, it wasn't me ! ' she wailed, bursting into tears. ' And—and I 've l—lost my hanky ! '

No one took any notice of her. Everyone was staring with fascinated eyes at the head-mistress, whom they seemed to be seeing for the first time. Miss Bettany suddenly struck the desk with her hand. Everyone jumped.

' Who did it ? ' she demanded. ' Is there a coward in the school ? '

On the word, Grizel sprang to her feet, head up, eyes blazing defiance.

' I did it ! ' she said, as insolently as she dared. ' I—— '

' Hush ! ' There was that in the one word which checked the rush of speech to her lips. ' You say you did it, Grizel Cochrane ? '

' Yes.'

' Go to your room,' said Miss Bettany quietly, ' and wait there till I come to you. I am ashamed to think a girl I had counted as a Senior should cause so much trouble by her childishness and impertinence. Go at once ! '

Grizel went.

CHAPTER XXI.

PLANS.

JUDGMENT had gone forth. Grizel was to be left severely alone by the rest of the school. No one was to speak to her, and she was to speak to nobody. She was to sit by herself in classes, and her meals would be brought to her in the schoolroom. When the others were at games, she was to go for a walk with whichever member of the staff could take her. This was to last for two days, and it was the severest punishment that had ever been given at the Châlet School.

In vain did Joey plead that the fault was largely hers, since it was she who had suggested that it would be a pity to let the term go by without some practical jokes. In vain did Mademoiselle, who was fond of the troublesome child, appeal against the sentence. Not even could Gisela, speaking for the school, avail anything. Miss Bettany had made up her mind that punished Grizel was going to be, and nothing would save her.

In the interview she had had with the girl, Grizel had proved herself defiant in the extreme. She possessed a temper which, once aroused, took some time to cool off. She had hated having to apologise to Gisela the day before, and the two affairs together had roused all the worst in her. Finally, Miss Bettany had given up trying to make her see reason, had named her punishment, and left her to herself, hoping that a little solitude would bring her to her senses.

By this time the boards had been cleaned and school was in full swing; but there was an atmosphere entirely strange to it. The girls worked with a will on most occasions, but to-day nobody attempted to dream, much less play. They were all far too subdued by events to do anything but work.

' Oh dear ! ' sighed Joey in the dinner-hour, when they were all wandering about doing nothing in particular. ' I wish I 'd never heard of the word " joke " ! '

' Is Madame very angry ? ' asked Gisela, slipping an arm through hers.

' She 's rather mad,' acknowledged Joey. ' I think Grizel cheeked her.'

She threw a wistful glance at the window of the little room where Grizel was, presumably, confined. Then, turning to the elder girl, she went on : ' Grizel's got such a beast of a temper. When she gets her monkey up, she doesn't much care what she does.'

' " Gets her monkey up " ? ' repeated Gisela with a puzzled frown. ' I do not understand.'

' Sorry ! That 's slang, I 'm 'fraid,' apologised Joey. ' Loses her temper, you know.'

' Your English slang is sometimes so incomprehensible,' complained the Head Girl.

'Yes, I s'pose it is. But it's jolly expressive. Hullo! Here's the postman! He is late to-day. Grüss' Gott, Herr Sneider!'

The postman returned her greeting amiably, handed her the letters, and departed.

'One from Dick—that's my brother— for Madame,' commented Joey, 'two for Maynie, and one for Margia and Amy. None for me. What a swizz!'

'There is the bell for *Mittagessen*,' said Gisela. 'Come! Let us go in!'

They went in, Joey leaving the Tyrolean in order to take the letters to her sister. Madge was standing by the window, her lips set and her eyes thoughtful.

'Hullo,' she said, when she saw her small sister, 'what is it? Oh, letters!'

'Letter from Dick,' said Joey, 'and it's *Mittagessen* now!'

Madge's face relaxed as she took the letters. 'All right. You can come here after, and we'll read it together. Take the others to their owners, will you?'

Mittagessen seemed never-ending to Joey. She bolted her own food, and when Simone accepted a second helping of *Pflaumekuchen*, cast a look of deep reproach at her.

However, everything comes to an end sooner or later, and at last they all rose, and grace was said. To Madge, two minutes later, appeared a flushed and excited Joey, who could scarcely be induced to sit down.

' Then you can wait till tea-time,' remarked her sister conclusively.

The recalcitrant subsided at that on to a little stool by her sister's side, and, planting her elbows on that young lady's knee, proclaimed herself ready.

' Buck up and get on ! Do !'' she urged. ' I 'm dying to hear what Dick says.'

Madge laughed. ' Here goes, then ! ' she said, as she smoothed out the thin foreign paper.

' DEAR KIDS,' Dick had written,—' Thanks awfully for your last letters, though it took me all my time to read Joey's. What on earth she wrote with I suppose she knows ! Some of the words looked as though a good-sized black beetle had fallen into the inkpot and then staggered about on the paper. They don't seem to teach the young to write nowadays.'

' Cheek ! ' interjected Joey swiftly. ' He needn't talk; his own fist 's bad enough for anything ! '

' I 'm glad the school 's going so well ; but, my dear kid, have nothing to do with Carrick. He 's an awfully bad hat. They do say that he was practically kicked out of here—had made the place too hot to hold him. But it's only gossip so far, and there may be no foundation for it. All the same, a chap from the Hills told me that they 'd sent that unfortunate kid of theirs to some school up there,

and then tried to clear out and leave her on
the Head's hands. Luckily, the old lady
contrived to track them, and they were
obliged to stump up what they owed and take
the girl with them. One's awfully sorry for
her. She seems to have a rotten time from all
I can gather. Mrs C. has a vile temper, they
say, and he isn't much better. It's an awful
life for a girl to go dragging about like that!
If Carrick wants you to have Juliet—isn't
that her name ?—as a boarder, don't you do
it! I wish to goodness you had someone
more reliable to look after you than Mlle La
Pâttre. I know she's a jolly good sort, but
women are so helpless! They ought to have
a man to look after them.

'I'm awfully glad to hear that the picca-
ninny is going strong and getting fat. Austria
seems to suit her. That cinema stunt was
rather cheek, I thought. I'm thankful it got
no further. I certainly don't want my sisters
stuck up in every cinema for any idiot to see!

'There's precious little news to tell you.
We are busy with some experiments at
present. The Gobbler (Dick's superior) has
some wild notion of growing European fruit-
trees here, so we're mucking about in a
fair-sized clearing growing good old plum
and apple. This, of course, is in addition to
our ordinary work. I blessed him the other
day, I can tell you. He had us pruning and
planting the whole day, and the mercury
doing the high jump for all it was worth.

'The rains are going well, and there's a chorus of frogs outside my bungalow at the moment. This is beastly weather. The one consolation is, that anyhow the snakes are lying pretty low. My bearer caught a whacker the other night—a king cobra—so he's introduced a mongoose to the household in case the mate is anywhere round. We've called the little lad "Binjamin," after "Stalky's" Binjamin. Remember? Well, there's nothing more to tell you, and I'm dead tired, and just going to turn in when I've finished this screel. Remember what I say, and leave Carrick alone. Salaams.—DICK.'

There was a little silence when Madge had finished. Then Joey broke it.

'Dick's too late,' she said. 'We've been and gone and done it! Poor Juliet!'

'Poor Juliet indeed!' sighed Madge. 'Oh, Joey Bettany, you've a lot to be thankful for, let me tell you!'

'I know,' said Joey soberly. 'You're a sport to me, Madge! And Dick's another!'

'We're all you've got,' said Madge briefly.

'Some people haven't as much,' replied Joey, leaning her head against her sister. 'Look at Juliet! And then Grizel hasn't anyone much. You can't say her father's up to much, can you? Poor old Grizel!'

Madge slipped an arm round her little sister. 'You're right there, old lady. But Grizel must come into line with the rest of you.

You 're up to monkey tricks as well, I know, but you haven't been impertinent too. I know you think I 'm being a perfect beast to her, but she can't be left to go on like that, can she ? '

Joey acknowledged the truth of this. 'No; I see your point. But, Madge, old thing, I do think she 's sorry by this time ! Can't you go and see ? '

Madge shook her head. 'No, Joey ! She won't be sorry yet. Now it 's time for prep., and you must toddle off. Come along early to-morrow morning and we 'll have a palaver. It 's only a fortnight to the holidays now, and then we 'll have a good time together.' She gave her sister a little squeeze and then sent her off to her preparation.

Left to herself, she faced the Grizel problem once more. She knew that it would take a lot to make that young lady say she was sorry, and yet she had determined that apologise Grizel must and should. The point was, how was she to be brought to it ? She recognised the truth of Joey's statement that Grizel hadn't 'anyone much.' In some ways she was more to be pitied than Juliet. From all accounts, the latter had been accustomed to little different treatment from what she had received ; but Grizel for five years of her life had been the spoilt darling of her grand-mother, the next few years had been a hard discipline for a wilful, petted child ; and apparently too much freedom from such

discipline had gone to Grizel's head.   Nothing
else could explain her present defiance.

' Oh dear ! ' thought Miss Bettany.   ' Running a school isn't the easiest thing in the
world—especially when there are two such
girls as Grizel and Juliet in it !   I wish I knew
what to do ! '

Later in the day she went to see Grizel
again, but found her stonily silent and
absolutely unrepentant.   The interview did
no good, and she left the girl with a hopeless
feeling that something was all wrong here.
Grizel herself was still too miserably angry to
care what happened.

' I hate her—I hate them all ! ' she thought
to herself.   ' I 'd run away if I 'd anywhere
to run to !   Oh, I wish I was dead, I do ! '

She leant her forehead against the edge of
the window-frame, staring miserably out at
the dark pinewoods and the slopes of the
Bärenbad Alpe.   Presently she shifted her
position, so that she could look up the long
valley towards the Mondscheinspitze, with the
Bärenkopf in the distance, and, towering
over all, the Tiernjoch, with its sinister
shadows.   Even on a summer's day, when the
other peaks gleamed white in the glory of the
afternoon sun, it looked dark and lowering.
Her mind went back to the stories Herr
Mensch had told them about it.   How, one
winter, sixty years ago, there had been a
fearful avalanche down its slopes, which had
partly buried a little hamlet that stood at the

foot of it, and how, when spring had brought the thaw and the snow had melted, the houses were so buried in rocks and earth that it had been well-nigh impossible to dig them out. There were other gruesome stories, too, of travellers who had been caught in the treacherous mist on its slopes and had never been seen again—or else had been found, a little heap of broken bones, at the bottom of the ravine which made one of its chief dangers. As she stood looking dreamily into the distance, she heard footsteps under the window, and then Wanda's precise English.

'Where is Grizel, Margia? I should like with her to speak.'

'Grizel's in a row,' replied Margia's voice. 'She vaselined the blackboards, and was awfully rude to Madame about it. So she's not to be with any of us till she says she's sorry.'

'Oh, I am so sorry!' said Wanda. 'Poor Grizel! How unhappy she must feel at having been rude! But how did she dare?'

'Goodness knows! She dares anything! She's going to climb that old Tiernjoch some day, she says,' floated up Margia's clear notes.

'Oh, but I do not think she can mean that!' replied the young Viennese. 'That is only talking, as Joey says.'

They moved on then, but the mischief had been done. Upstairs, in durance vile, the eavesdropper clenched her hands. So that was what they thought, was it? That it was

all talk on her part ?   Well, she would jolly
well show them !   She would show them that
very day !   No, the next day !   She would
get up early, and when they came to find her
she would be gone !   She'd show them all what
she dared to do and what she daren't !   She'd
make them sorry they'd treated her like this !

Miss Maynard entered at that moment to
tell her to get ready for a walk, and she had to
change her shoes and find her hat.   Throughout the hour and a half, during which they
went round the lower end of the lake to
Buchau, where they caught the steamer back
to Briesau, she remained obstinately dumb.
Miss Maynard made one or two remarks,
then, finding her efforts vain, lapsed into
thoughtfulness on her own part, leaving Grizel
to herself.

When they returned, the young lady was
taken back to her room, and Miss Maynard
brought her a couple of books and her embroidery before she withdrew, closing the door
quietly behind her.   There was no question
of locking her in; the door was merely shut.
Naughty as she had been, it never dawned on
Miss Bettany to think that the child would
abuse the trust reposed in her; and in her
normal frame of mind, Grizel would as soon
have thought of trying to fly as of betraying that trust.   But she was not normal at
present.   The one idea of 'showing them'
filled her mind to the exclusion of everything
else, and as she sat with *Henry Esmond* open

before her, Grizel was busily making plans for the morrow.

It would be an easy matter to get away. She must wake early—by four o'clock at latest. That would give her a start of four hours, since nobody was likely to come near her much before eight. By that time she hoped to be well on her way to the little Alpe or Alm half-way up the mountain, where herdsmen attended to the cattle who were grazed there in the summer. The question of food was rather a difficulty, for the one little shop the place boasted would not be open at that hour, and Grizel knew that bread and cheese was all she was likely to get from the herdsmen ; and the bread would most likely be reeking of garlic, which she detested. Finally, she decided that she must save all she could from her supper. She hoped they would bring her plenty.

Leaving *Henry Esmond* on the table, she strayed over to the window, and stood with her head thrown back gazing at the great gloomy mountain. Joey Bettany, passing beneath with Simone on her way to tennis, glanced up and saw her, though she did not see Joey. Her mind was full of her adventure to come—for that it would be an adventure she felt sure.

Half-past seven brought Marie and her supper. Grizel's spirits went up with a bound as she took in the bowl of soup, the rolls and butter, the large slice of *kuchen,* and the glass

of new milk. The soup and the milk would
do for the supper, and the rest she must put
away for the morning. Perhaps there would
be some apples in the kitchen. Things were
going well for her.

Later, she heard the others coming back
from cricket and tennis. Joey was talking.
'Look! Alpenglück!' she said, her words
carrying easily on the still air.

'Bother!' Juliet chimed in. 'No games
to-morrow, then, and it's Saturday!'

She heard no more, for just then the Head
came in to say 'good-night,' and see that
everything she needed was there.

Miss Bettany had meant to say something
to her, but the hard, defiant look Grizel
turned on her forbade anything of the kind.
She realised that, in the girl's present mood,
discussion would be worse than useless.

'Good-night, Grizel,' she said quietly.

'Good-night,' mumbled Grizel.

Then the door closed and she was alone.

CHAPTER XXII.

GRIZEL RUNS AWAY.

'SATURDAY morning! Thank goodness, no lessons!' And Margia heaved a sigh of relief.

'Lazy bones!' jeered Juliet from her cubicle, where she had been reading for the last half-hour.

'The hols. will be here soon anyhow,' said Joey Bettany. 'Let's hope it's decenter weather than this! A horrid grey day! I do hate them so!'

'There's mist on the mountains!' Margia had climbed out of bed, and was contemplating the Bärenbad, the Bärenkopf, and their fellows with pensive eyes. 'Can't see the top of old Mondy, and the Tiernjoch is lost!'

'It'll rain later,' observed Juliet, shutting her book with a sigh for her disturbed peace. 'We sha'n't even get a decent walk.'

'Frau Mensch asked Simone and Grizel and me to tea to-day,' observed Joey in rather muffled tones, since she was buried beneath her *plumeau*. 'I suppose we'll go, but it's rotten for Grizel. I wish she hadn't cheeked my sister!'

'It is quiet without Grizel,' observed Simone, who was sitting up in bed hugging her knees. ' And it will be not nice—I mean horreed ! ' as a groan from Joey reached her —' to have to say Grizel is being punished.'

' Don't you worry ! They 'll know all about it ! ' Joey assured her. ' I saw Frieda's eyes nearly jumping out of her head yesterday when she answered Mad—my sister ! Where 's my dressing-gown ? '

She scrambled out of bed, wriggled into her dressing-gown and bedroom slippers, and vanished in the direction of her sister's room.

' It 's rotten for Joey,' said Margia, who had gone back to bed again. ' Madame is her sister and Grizel is her chum. Whichever she sides with, it looks mean for the other ! I do think Grizel is an ass ! '

' I think so also,' remarked Simone, whose English was becoming much more fluent. ' And Grizel is not Joey's only chum, Margia.'

' That 's got nothing to do with it,' replied Margia. ' You 're simply silly about Jo Bettany, Simone ! '

' She is good to me ! ' Simone was much more self-controlled than she had been, but her voice sounded tearful now.

Juliet noticed it, and interposed tactfully. ' Jo Bettany is a splendid kid ! I wish we had heaps more like her ! '

' So do I,' said Amy, joining in the conversation for the first time. ' She tells the most gorgeousest stories I ever heard ! '

' Whose turn is it to go first to the bathroom to-day ? ' inquired Juliet, just forestalling Margia's remark that 'nobody ever says "gorgeousest" but babies.'

'It is me!' said Suzanne Mercier in her shy soft voice.

Both Suzanne and Yvette had very little to say at any time, and their voices were so seldom heard, that, as Grizel had once remarked, they might just as well never be there more than half the time. Now, Juliet nearly jumped.

'I always forget you two are there,' she said. 'If you're going, Suzanne, you'd better toddle along. I can hear Marie coming with Amy's water.'

She got up as she spoke, and fished out her bedroom slippers and rolled up her sleeves, preparatory to giving Amy her bath. That she should do it had become quite a recognised thing by now, and to Juliet it was a great thing that she could help even in so little, as some return for her Head's goodness to her. She could never help contrasting Miss Bettany's quiet acceptance of the state of things with the behaviour of her Anglo-Indian head-mistress under similar circumstances. That lady had been mainly concerned about the loss of her fees. Of Juliet's feelings she had thought not one jot. Juliet had not suddenly become an angel as a result of her present Head's treatment of her. She was a very human girl; but she was deeply grateful, and since she was thorough in whatever she did, she was making valiant efforts to become the

same sporting type of girl as that to which
her headmistress belonged. This bathing of
Amy, which had been a self-imposed task,
sometimes bored her very much, but Miss
Bettany's thanks had filled her with a determination to go on, and, as a result, she was
learning that a duty undertaken for love of a
person isn't half so tiresome as one which is
thrust on one.

As for Amy, she had quite overcome her fear
of Juliet, and chatted gaily as the elder girl
sponged her down and then rubbed her dry.

'There you are!' said Juliet finally, as she
finished drying between the little pink toes.
'Now buck up and get into your clothes!
Who's in the bathroom now?' she went on,
raising her voice slightly.

'Simone,' replied Joey, who had come back
from her sister. 'I'm next, an' then you.
Oh, an' Madame says go past Grizel's door
quietly, as she wants her to get a good sleep
'cos she seemed so tired last night.'

'All right,' said Juliet briefly. 'Stripped
your bed, Joey? I say, I don't think we'd
better put the *plumeaux* over the balcony
to-day. It looks as though there was going
to be a splash!'

''Twon't come yet,' said Joey the weather-
wise. 'Prob'ly not till this afternoon. It's
going to be a beastly day,' she added, shaking
her pillow vindictively. 'I jolly well wish it
was over!'

'Joey, I am returned! You had better

buck up!' said Simone's voice at this juncture, and Joey had, perforce, to seize her towels and hurry off.

Nobody seemed in a particularly happy mood this morning. The girls were subdued under the consciousness of Grizel's disgrace. The staff was worried for the same reason. In the kitchen, Marie was accusing her small brother Eigen, who came to help with odd jobs, of having helped himself to the apples she had left in a big dish overnight.

'Sixteen apples I leave,' she scolded, 'and now there are but ten! Where are the others, rascal? Thou hast eaten them! Thou hast stolen!'

Eigen, a stolid person of eleven, looked at his sister solemnly. '*Nein*, Marie,' was all he said in answer to her accusations.

'But I say thou hast! Who would take them if thou didst not, *junge Taugenichts*?'

'*Nein*, Marie,' said Eigen serenely. All he knew was that he hadn't touched the apples, whatever his sister might say, and he cared for nothing else.

Madge, hearing the disturbance in the kitchen, went to discover what it was all about.

'Why dost thou scold, Marie?' she inquired in fluent German.

'This rascal, Madame, he has stolen six apples—six.'

'Good gracious!' observed Jo, who had followed her sister. 'He'll be ill!'

'*Nein*, Marie,' observed Eigen, still as placidly as ever.

Marie turned to her mistress with outflung hands of helplessness. 'You hear him, Madame! That is all that he says! He who has stolen!'

'*Nein*, Marie!' was the parrot-like response of the accused youth.

'Wait, Marie,' said Miss Bettany, checking the flood of exclamations which she could see to be on Marie's tongue. 'He is a good boy. If he says he did not touch the apples, then I do not think he did. Eigen, hast thou seen the apples of which Marie speaks?'

Eigen looked at her hopefully. He had quite given up expecting any sense from his sister. She had made up her mind that he had taken the fruit, and no amount of argument would persuade her differently. But das Fräulein with the kind eyes and the pretty hair was another matter. She had often shown herself to be very understanding. So he said, 'Nein, gnädiges Fräulein.'

'Very well!' Miss Bettany turned to Marie. 'I am sure he speaks the truth, Marie, and one of the young ladies may have felt hungry during the night and taken them. I will inquire, and, meantime, say no more about it.'

'Bitte, mein Fräulein——' began Marie, but Miss Bettany's upraised hand stopped her, and she turned to go down to the cellar to fetch more apples, grumbling under her breath; while her young mistress left the kitchen, followed by Jo, who was wondering rather miserably how things would go that day.

'It's going to be simply horrid!' she decided, as she attacked her roll and honey with considerably less appetite than usual. 'Oh, I wish it was over!'

Inquiries about the apples did not solve the mystery. No one had touched them, and Juliet, who was a light sleeper, and who had, in any case, awakened early, was positive that no one had left the dormitory till the rising-bell had rung. 'Except Joey,' she added.

'Joey came to see me,' said Miss Bettany, 'so that's all right. Well, I'm sure that if Eigen says he hasn't touched the fruit, he hasn't. I imagine Marie didn't count very carefully when she put them out. That's more likely than that Eigen should have taken them when he says he didn't. Now, go and make your beds and then get ready for a good walk. It's going to rain later on, so you won't get games this afternoon, I'm afraid. Jo, you and Simone are going to Seespitz to the Mensches, so you'd better not go with the others. Get your practising and mending done this morning instead of going for the walk, and change before *Mittagessen*. Herr Mensch rang me up last night to say he was going to take you all for a motor ride up the Tiern Valley, and would be at the fence gate for you at two o'clock, so you must be ready. What he will do if it rains I can't tell you!'—thus

forestalling the question on Joey's lips. 'Now
run along, all of you, and get on. Please go
quietly.'

She had said grace previously, so they all
got up and went upstairs in subdued manner.
As she passed the door of Grizel's prison with
Simone close beside her, Joey heaved a little
sigh.

'What is it then, Joey?' demanded
Simone.

'I don't know. I feel as though something
horrid was going to happen,' returned her
friend. 'Sort of foretelling, you know!
Spooky and awful!' she added incoherently.

'I do not understand,' said Simone, who
might well be forgiven for not understanding.

'Oh, well, I can't explain!' replied Jo
impatiently. 'Come and make your bed!'

They were half-way through, when the
chink of china on a tray and the sound
of careful footsteps told them that breakfast
was going to Grizel.

'It's awfully jolly to have your breakfast
in bed,' grumbled Margia. 'I wish I had!
Worth being naughty for! I say! What's
that?' as a startled cry reached her ears.

Before anyone could answer her, there
came the sound of hurrying feet, and Miss
Bettany flung open the door of the dormitory.

'Girls! Which of you has seen Grizel
Cochrane this morning?'

A startled silence followed her question.
Finally Juliet answered.

' I don't think any of us have, Madame.
Isn't she in her room ? '

' No. The windows are wide open and her
clothes are gone ! Are you sure you haven't
seen her ? '

You could have heard a pin drop as they
digested this information.

' D' you mean you think she 's—run away ? '
ventured Margia at last.

' Of course she hasn't ! ' exploded Joey.
' She 's broken bounds, that 's all ! An' I
think she 's a beast ! '

' Hush, Joey ! ' said Miss Bettany. ' Of
course she hasn't run away, Margia ! For one
thing, she has no money, and for another, she
hasn't anywhere to run to. But it 's very
trying ! I did think I could trust you girls ! '

She turned and left the room as she spoke,
leaving a startled group behind her. They
did not quite know what to think. Up till
this moment they had felt a good deal of
sympathy for Grizel ; and her brilliant idea
of vaselining the blackboards had rather
captivated them. But this was quite another
thing. It was untrustworthy, and, as Margia
said later, ' not cricket.' With all her wilful-
ness, Grizel had never yet failed to play the
game, and the shock of discovering that she
could fail rather stunned them. Presently
Juliet went back to her task of bed-making,
and they all followed her example in a deathly
silence that said far more about their feelings
than any amount of speech could have done.

When they had finished, Joey and Simone
went to their practice, while the others got
ready for their walk with Miss Maynard.
Presently they set off, passing Madge and
Mademoiselle on the way, the one going over
to Buchau to make inquiries as to whether
Grizel had been seen about there, while the
other was going down to Spärtz by the mountain-path on the same quest.

For some forty minutes Joey worked away
steadily at her scales, her mind anywhere but
on what she was doing.   Suddenly she jumped
up.

'The Tiernjoch!' she gasped.   'That's
where she's gone!   Up the Tiernjoch!   Oh,
she was looking at it last night!   That's
what she was thinking of!   I must go and
fetch her back!'

With Jo the impulsive, to think was to act.
She dashed along to the cloakroom, tore
madly into her mac. and tammy, dashed into
Simone, who was struggling with one of
Gurlitt's *Kinderscenen*, and gasped, 'Simone,
Grizel's gone up the Tiernjoch!   I'm off to
fetch her back!   You must stay and tell
Madge when she comes!   Good-bye!'

Before the astounded Simone had taken in
half the sense of what she said, she had gone.
Thus it happened that a distracted and worn-
out Madge was met some hour and a half later
by a tearful Simone, who sobbed out that Joey
had gone up the wicked Tiernjoch to find
Grizel.

CHAPTER XXIII.

ON THE TIERNJOCH.

TO go back a few hours to the time when Grizel awoke in the early greyness of the morning is now necessary. When she had got into bed, she had banged her head on her pillow four times, saying solemnly 'Four o'clock!' as she did so. This is the best recipe I know for early waking, and Grizel knew it too. She woke up just as the old grandfather clock below chimed four times. For a minute she listened for the breathing of the others, then she remembered. She was by herself as a punishment, and she was going to climb the Tiernjoch that day. 'At last!' she thought, as she climbed cautiously out of bed, and, stealing across the room on tiptoe, opened the jalousies carefully. Luckily, every hinge in the house was kept well oiled, and they made no sound as she swung them slowly back. The dawn wind blew in chilly, and, if she had only realised it, bringing with it a foretaste of the mountain mists. In the sky a star or two still lingered, but soon they would have vanished, for the light was brightening with every minute. Shivering a little with cold and excitement, Grizel began to dress in the half light. She was soon ready, and then, picking up her electric torch, she stole down-stairs in her stockinged feet to the kitchen to see if Marie had, by chance, left any food about. She found the apples on the kitchen table and abstracted six, dropping five of them into her knapsack and beginning on the other. There was nothing else, however, and she dared not risk opening the cupboards in case any of the doors should creak. Still, six apples, two rolls of bread, and a slice of Marie's *kuchen* were not so bad, and she had a few hundred-*Kroner* notes, so she would be able to get cheese and milk from the herdsmen. She crept back upstairs, tucked the rest of her provender into her knapsack, and slung it across her shoulders.

The next thing was to get out. It would be madness to attempt to open the doors. What she decided on was almost as mad. The window of the room opened on to the balcony that ran all round the house. Grizel clambered over the railings, hung for a moment from the ledge of it, and then dropped. Mercifully, it was only ten feet above the ground, and she had learned how to fall easily, so beyond a bumped elbow she came to no harm. She picked herself up with a rueful face, and then proceeded to put on her shoes. Two minutes later she was flying up the path towards the valley at a rate that would have caused an experienced mountaineer to exclaim with horror.

When she reached the fence, the cows that

were pastured in the valley were coming along, led by the big cream-coloured bull who was lord of the herd. Grizel sat on the fence, the fresh morning air ruffling her curls, her face glowing with pleasure at the music made by the jingling bells. The boy who was herding them looked curiously at her, but made no comment. Probably he thought that she was waiting for the rest of a party. When they had passed, Grizel set off again, this time at a reasonable jog-trot pace, which she knew she could keep up for some time. By this time the stars had faded, and the light was rapidly streaking the sky. When she had reached the tiny hamlet of Lauterbach, the last remnants of the darkness had gone and it was broad daylight.

A man was chopping wood for the fires outside one châlet, and he was whistling a gay tune as he worked. Two or three goats, tethered nearby, bleated at the sound of her footsteps, and a baby kid came skipping alongside of her, its head cocked inquiringly on one side, its yellow eyes full of innocent inquiry which won her heart instantly.

' Oh, you darling ! ' she cried, trying to catch him in her arms. But Master Billy was as shy as he was curious. With a terrified ' Ma-a-a ! ' he made a side-dash away from her, and raced for home and mother.

Grizel threw back her head, laughing gaily at the sight. The peasant looked at her, and grunted ' Grüss' Gott ! ' She answered him,

and then went on.   All remembrance of the
fact that she was in disgrace and had no
business to be there had faded from her mind
in her enjoyment of the morning.   Even the
actual ascent of the great mountain that hung
so threateningly over the upper end of the
valley was forgotten.

Like a good many unimaginative people,
Grizel possessed the gift of living in the
immediate present.   Where Joey and Madge
would have been dreaming of the mountain
summits and the joy of the hard climb, she
was simply wild with delight in her present
surroundings.   As she swung along, she
began to sing one of the folk-songs she had
learnt in her English school, and the words
of ' High Germany ' rang through the quiet
valley :

' Oh, Polly love, oh, Polly, the rout is now begun,
And we must be a-marching at the beating of the
       drum.
Go, dress yourself all in your best, and come along
       with me ;
I 'll take you to the cruel wars in High Ger-
       many !'

'Oh, Harry love, oh, Harry, you hearken what
       I say,
My feet are all too tender ; I cannot march away.
Besides, my dearest Harry, though man and wife
       we be,
How am I fit for cruel wars in High Germany ?'

.   .   .   .

Oh, cursèd are the cruel wars that ever they should
    rise,
And out of Merrie England press many a lad
    likewise,
They pressed my Harry from me, as all my brothers
    three,
And sent them to the cruel wars in High Germany.

She finished up with a wild flourish of her stick,
and discovered herself at the foot of a narrow
path that wound up and up between bushes
and rocks. A tiny stream trickled down far
above her, looking like a silver thread in the
cold light.

Grizel stopped and debated with herself.
Should she eat her breakfast where she was,
or should she go on till she reached the Alm
where she would buy her milk ?

'I'll eat an apple,' she decided, 'then I'll
go on. Coo! What a scramble!'

She sat down on a convenient rock and bit
firmly into an apple. The sight of some
berries near at hand sent her flying across to
see if they were fit to eat. They were blue-
berries, but as yet they were more green than
blue, so she reluctantly left them alone and
returned to her stone and her apple.

'Jolly it is, early in the morning!' she
thought, as she flung the core into nearby
bushes. 'Well, I must pull up my socks and
get on with it!'

Accordingly, she shouldered her knapsack
once more, picked up her stick, and set off
gaily up the narrow path, whistling cheerily as

she went. Presently, however, the track left the bushes, and twisted about round boulders and over heaps of broken stones which she found tricky to negotiate. She had been right. It was a scramble! Up and up she clambered, unheeding of her legs and shoulders, which were beginning to ache with the unaccustomed exercise.

'The Sonnenscheinspitze was a circumstance to this,' she thought, as she toiled onwards, 'and as for the Mondscheinspitze, it was a baby's crawl! I hope it gets better farther on!'

Far from getting better, however, it got worse, and Grizel was forced to stop more than once to rest. 'Oof! This is some climb!' she sighed, as she sat down for the third time to mop her streaming face. 'However they get the cows up here is beyond me!'

As a matter of fact, the cows reached the Alm by a path which came over the shoulder of the mountain, and was much easier; but Grizel could not know that. Presently she set off again, and this time she succeeded in reaching the Alm. She nearly came to grief over the last few steps. The Alm itself overhung the path, and, in order to get on to it, she had to catch at a tree root and haul herself up. She was almost there when her hand slipped and she nearly fell. If she had gone, it would have meant a fall of twenty feet or more, for just here the rock had broken away. Luckily, she managed to scramble to safety somehow, and reached the short, sweet turf, where she lay with beating heart for the next few minutes.

Presently she got to her feet. With all her faults, Grizel was no coward. A weaker character might have given in at this point, but she simply set her teeth and went on. The Alm is a long one here, and the herdsmen's hut is built in a crevice in the rock, so it was a good ten minutes before she reached it. The men had long since gone to their day's work, and there was only a lad of sixteen or seventeen in the hut. He stared at her, but made no comment. When she asked for milk in her best German, he brought it to her in a big earthenware mug, and stood watching her while she drank it. Never had anything tasted so delicious to her as that draught of sweet milk, rich with yellow cream. When she had finished, the boy took the mug, saying in curiously hoarse, thick tones something of which she caught only the last words *ein Nebelstreif*. Grizel did not understand, but she was not going to let him know that if she could help it; so she looked as intelligent as she knew how, nodded her head, and said, ' Oh, ja-ja ! '

Again the boy spoke, this time saying something about *keine Aussicht*. This, Grizel knew, meant ' no view,' so she shook her head this time, saying, ' Nein, nein ! keine Aussicht ! ' which seemed to satisfy him, for,

with the usual ' Grüss' Gott ! ' he turned and
went back into the hut.

Grizel looked after him doubtfully before
she turned and went on her way. Walking
over the short, springy grass was a treat after
the hard, toilsome scramble over the rocks
and shale. She had got her second wind, and
went on joyously, munching an apple as she
went. It struck her that it was getting rather
misty, but she had no means of knowing the
time, as she was not wearing her watch, and
she supposed it to be the morning mists, which
would soon disappear. It was then about
eleven o'clock, as a matter of fact; and at the
foot of the mountain Joey Bettany was eyeing
the path up which her friend had come with
dubious eyes. Ten minutes took Grizel to the
far edge of the Alm, and once more the path
began to wind upwards. It was easy going
at first, but soon became more difficult. The
mist-clouds closed in round her, and presently
she found herself struggling upwards, surrounded by white walls of mountain fog,
which hid the path from her and deadened
all sounds save those of her own footsteps.
She was plucky enough, but the deadly
silence and the eeriness began to frighten her.
Some of the terrible stories Herr Mensch and
Herr Marani told them came back to torment
her now. She was worn out, and the climb
was becoming more and more difficult. Over
and over again she was obliged to sit down
and rest, and after each halt she felt herself

becoming stiffer and stiffer. Then suddenly
her foot struck a loosened stone and set it
rolling. She heard it go a little way, then
there was an awful silence, and at the same
moment the clouds lifted just sufficiently to
show her that she was standing on the edge
of a precipice !

As the realisation of the fact came to her,
Grizel felt the last remnant of her courage
oozing away, and clutched at it desperately.
If she had followed the inclination of the
moment, she would have flung herself down
on the ground and screamed. Luckily, she
did nothing of the kind. More, she even tried
to take a step or two forward. Then, as the
mists came swirling back once more, she gave
it up. She knew where she was, for Herr
Mensch had described the ascent to her more
than once. She had reached the worst bit of
all. Here, for one hundred and fifty yards,
the path, barely three feet wide in most
places, and even less in some, crawled along
the edge of a precipice which went sheer down
to the valley below. On the other side a wall
of stark rock rose, also sheerly, giving no hold
of any kind. This was the part where anyone
in the least degree nervous was roped, and it
was where the worst accidents always occurred.
What made things worse was the fact that
she had no idea how far along she had come.
With a pitiful attempt at self-control, she sat
down, slowly and carefully, curling herself up
against the rock-wall. Little shivers, partly

of cold, partly of terror, ran up and down her.
Lying there, with only a narrow shelf of rock
between her and instant death, Grizel prayed
as she had never prayed before. At first the
words would not come. Then gradually the
old familiar 'Our Father' rose to her lips.
That comforted her. 'Our Father, which art
in heaven,' she prayed aloud, the sound of
her own voice helping to steady her. 'Our
Father, oh, send someone! Please send
someone quickly. Our Father——'

'Grizel! Grizel!' The cry came faintly
through the mist.

She sat up. Joey! It was Joey's voice!
'Our Father,' she sobbed. Then, 'Joey!
Joey!'

'Hold on a tick! I'm coming! Where
are you?'

Grizel pulled herself together. 'Joey!
I'm on the precipice! I'm lying down!
Look out!'

Almost at once a figure loomed up out of
the mist, and then Joey, feeling her way carefully, was beside her. She was sitting down,
pulling her into her arms, holding her tightly,
saying, 'Grizel! Grizel!'

'Our Father,' began Grizel dully. 'Oh,
Joey, He sent you at last!'

Then darkness swept over her, and, to Joey's
utter dismay, she fainted. It was only for a
few moments, however. She struggled back
to consciousness, and with consciousness came
terror, complete and overwhelming. She

clung to the younger girl, shaking from head to foot, while Joey, with wide, straining eyes trying to see through the mists, held her tightly, murmuring words of comfort to her.

'Grizel! Darling! Don't cry! It's all right! Honest Injun, it is! There! Don't cry, Grizel! Joey's here! Joey's got you safely! It's all right!' Over and over again she repeated it, till finally the meaning of her words reached Grizel's brain, and she began to pull herself together.

'Joey!' she said presently. 'Oh, Joey! How did you know?'

'Where to come, d' you mean? I guessed! Grizel, are you better? Don't you think if we went on hands and knees you could get back to the rocks? We aren't awfully far along, I know. Two minutes would do it. Can't you try, Grizel?'

But Grizel dared not. The very suggestion set her whimpering piteously. 'Joey, I daren't! Oh, Joey, I know I should slip and fall! I daren't move! Don't you move either, Joey! If you do, we shall go over! Don't move, Joey! Please don't!'

'But, Grizel, old thing, it's so awfully cold, and you're wet through! Do let's have a shot at it! Honest Injun, it wouldn't take a minute!'

But Grizel's nerve was gone. She could only clutch her friend, crying piteously, and, mercifully for both of them, she made no attempt to move. Had she done so in her

present state of mind, there is little doubt but
that both of them must have gone over the
edge.   Finally, Joey gave up her coaxing, and
settled herself as comfortably as she could to
await the rescue she felt sure would come
soon.   Grizel, lying closely against her, had
ceased to cry.   Now she seemed drowsy and
dull.   With a sudden throb of fear, Joey
Bettany faced a new danger.   She had read
of the death sleep which continued cold
brings on, and she realised that already
Grizel was only semi-conscious.   At all costs
she must rouse her.

' Grizel ! ' she said imperatively.   ' Grizel !
Wake up !   You can't go to sleep ! '

Grizel muttered something drowsily, but
made no movement.   Joey slapped her face
smartly, and nearly brought disaster on them
both as the elder girl stirred.

' Grizel !   Grizel ! '

The fear in her tones reached Grizel's
drugged brain, and she half roused.

' Yes, Joey !   I 'm here ! '

' But you must stay here ! ' sobbed poor
Joey.   ' Oh, Grizel, don't go to sleep ! '

' I 'm not ; but I am so tired,' murmured
Grizel.

' I know, but oh, you mustn't !   Oh, I can't
bear it ! '

Her tears fell on Grizel's face, and did more
to wake her than anything else would have
done.   Joey crying was a wonder not to be
understood.

'Don't cry, Joey! It's all my fault, and I'm sorry now! Oh, if we both die it will be my fault, and Miss Bettany will never forgive me or look at me again!'

Joey began to gurgle hysterically at that. 'Don't be s—silly! If we both die we shall be d—— What's that?'

She sat with head upreared, listening for the sound her quick ears had caught. It came again—the long, melodious call of the mountaineer.

'Grizel!' she cried. 'We're found!' Then, with all her strength, she cooeed.

The yodel came again, nearer this time, and, as she answered it, Joey noticed that, at long last, the mists were thinning. Then came the sound of careful footsteps, and, finally, the dear familiar figure of Herr Mensch, looking more like a benevolent giant than ever. Behind him came the slighter form of Herr Marani, and behind him again two of the herdsmen, who had been pressed into service. To a skilled mountaineer like Herr Mensch the narrow path presented no difficulties. With one big stride he had stepped across the two girls, then, turning round, he bent down and picked up Grizel, while Herr Marani helped Joey to her feet. The next few minutes were dangerous enough, for Joey's cramped muscles would not work, and she nearly fell. Luckily, Herr Marani had her firmly, and twenty minutes later they were on the Alm, where Madge awaited them with white face

and eyes dark with the agony she had under-
gone.   If Herr Marani would have allowed
her, she would have carried Joey herself to the
herdsmen's hut, where a potent drink of hot
milk, mixed with brandy from Herr Mensch's
flask, was given to them before they made the
final descent to the valley.

Two hours later the sun appeared in full
glory, gilding all the peaks and driving away
the last rags of mist from the sinister mountain which had so nearly added two more to
the toll of its victims.   Madge, sitting by the
little bed in her own room where they had
placed Joey, caught the rays.

' You have come late,' she said, and turned
back once more to her watching.

CHAPTER XXIV.

CONSEQUENCES.

'MADAME! How is Joey?' Simone lifted tear-drenched eyes to Miss Bettany's face. It was the day after Grizel's grand escapade, which had so nearly ended in terrible disaster, and it was a day which none of the girls ever forgot. The sun shone gloriously the whole time, as if to make up for his behaviour of yesterday. The Tzigane band had come up the lake again, and was making music outside the Kron Prinz Karl. At this very moment they were playing the air of a popular song; many of the younger people who knew it had joined in the chorus, and the gay voices floated up to the Châlet through the clear summer air. But all this meant nothing to the school, for Grizel was ill with bronchitis, and Joey Bettany had never come out of the sleep into which she had fallen after they had laid her in Herr Mensch's car, which had been awaiting them at the foot of the mountain.

Herr Marani had gone hotfoot to Innsbrück to fetch the doctor, and he had said that the awful nerve strain through which the imaginative, highly strung child had gone might result in brain fever. That could only be

decided when she came out of the heavy
stupor in which she lay, and which might last
for two or three days yet. Grizel's case was
far simpler. It was a straightforward attack
of bronchitis, the natural result of having been
for hours in the clinging mists. It was, of
course, made worse by the fact that she had
gone all to pieces when she found herself in
her own bed; but with careful nursing—and
they could be sure of that—she would soon
be all right again. Joey's case was far more
doubtful. Then he left them, promising to
return the next day. Frau Mensch had
appeared in the morning and carried off Amy
and Margia, and Frau Rincini had sent Bette
over to fetch the little Merciers. She had
offered to have Simone as well, but Simone
had begged to stay, and Juliet had offered to
look after her, so they had given the child her
way.

Midday had brought Frau Marani with an
offer to nurse Grizel, and Madge herself had
never left Joey for a minute until the doctor
had arrived, and with one glance at her white
face had sternly ordered her out.

'It will make things worse if you are ill,'
he told her. 'Go and have some food, and
then a little walk. To-night you must sleep,
while the young lady—ah, Fräulein Maynard!
—watches. Nothing will occur for some hours
yet.' Then the anguish in her eyes touched his
compassion, and he added, 'She looks better
—seems more natural. Now go and rest.'

Madge did as he told her as far as going
out was concerned.   She had gone to the pine-
wood, and was wandering up and down, when
Simone had caught sight of her, and, breaking
away from Juliet, had rushed across the
meadow and caught her arm with hot little
hands.   Now, as she saw the child's face, all
puffed and swollen with crying, Miss Bettany
felt suddenly that she had been neglecting her
duty.   She slipped an arm round Simone, who
promptly began to sniff again.

' They can't say yet, dear.   The doctor says
nothing will happen for some hours yet, but
he thinks she looks more natural.   Don't cry,
Simone.'

Simone made a valiant attempt to check
her tears, and succeeded.   ' I do love Joey so
much !' she said quaveringly.   ' Oh, Madame,
if there is one little thing I can do you will
tell me ? '

' Yes,' said Madge.   ' I can tell you of one
little thing now.   You can stop crying and
try to be brave.   To-morrow there will be
school as usual.   Joey is far above the schoolrooms, and I know you will all be quiet.   We
shall break up on Tuesday or Wednesday,
instead of a week later as I had intended.   I
want you to be very brave, and work as
steadily as you can for the two days.   If the
others see you and Juliet '—she smiled at the
other girl, who had now come up with them—
' trying to go on as usual, they will try too,
and that will make things easier for us all.'

'I will try,' said Simone very soberly. 'I will try ver' hard.'

'I'll do my level best,' Juliet promised, 'and I will look after Simone, Madame.'

'Thank you, both of you,' said Madge. 'Now I must go back, as I may be needed. Juliet, take Simone to wash her face and hands, and both of you change your frocks. Good-bye.'

She turned and went back to the Châlet, feeling fresher for her little rest, and more able to cope with things. She found Joey lying as she had left her, with the doctor sitting by her side. He looked up as the girl entered, but made no other movement. Madge bent over the bed, looking at the dear, funny little face with a world of love in her eyes. Was it her imagination, or did Joey really look more like herself. She glanced up at the doctor inquiringly, and he nodded his head.

'Yes, it is really so. I begin to have hopes of her. We cannot yet say definitely, but the pulse is stronger, and the temperature has risen no further. Now go and change your clothes, and have a bath and wash your hair!'

Madge quite literally gaped at him, wondering if she had heard aright.

'Yes, I mean that,' he said, nodding his head again. 'Go to the hotel with this note and have your hair shampooed. There is more than time for it, and it is a better tonic than any I can mix for you in my dispensary.'

Sheer astonishment rendered her dumb and obedient. She had thought as she mounted the stairs that she could only leave the bedroom again when she knew that Joey was safe. Now, clutching his note, she made her way to the Kron Prinz Karl, where the Tzigane were playing a plaintive, haunting waltz, to which people were dancing on the grass at the side.

The Von Eschenaus were sitting at one of the little tables, and when Frau von Eschenau saw her, she came quickly over, taking her arm.

'Mein Fräulein, we are so grieved—Marie has cried herself sick for grief! Tell us, how is das Mädchen, and if there is anything we can do?'

'Thank you,' said Madge. 'There is really nothing. Joey is much the same, and I've come to get my hair shampooed—the doctor sent me.'

Frau von Eschenau stared. 'To get your hair shampooed?' she repeated doubtfully.

'Yes. I have a note for Herr Braun.'

'Then come this way, and we will find him. Doubtless he will be in the *Speisesaal*.'

The good-natured Viennese led her into the big dining-room, where Herr Braun was engaged in directing the laying of the tables for dinner. When he saw them, he hurried forward, exclaiming. Madge gave him the doctor's note, and he read it through with wonderment in his eyes. Then he nodded his head wisely.

'It is well, gnädiges Fräulein. If das Fräulein will come through here, it shall be done.'

He led her into the hairdressing-room, and forty minutes later Madge was going back to the Châlet feeling refreshed and ready for anything. Everything was as she had left it, save that Juliet and Simone were in fresh frocks. She peeped into Grizel's room, where good Frau Mensch sat knitting, one watchful eye on the bronchitis kettle. Grizel was sleeping, propped up with pillows to relieve the breathing. She looked flushed, but there was nothing alarming. The illness would take its natural course, and the doctor was not alarmed about her. So much Frau Mensch told the young headmistress, her busy fingers never ceasing their work.

'He will stay here for to-night,' she continued in her low, murmurous voice that made the guttural German sound soft and musical. 'I think he expects that little Jo will come to herself before the morning. Mademoiselle has come in, but she knows nothing about sick-nursing and would be useless. Frau Marani will come to-night and watch by das Mädchen, for Fräulein Maynard must sleep, and you will be with the little sister. *Na, mein Liebling*,' as Madge tried to thank her, ' it is nothing—we are glad to do what we can. You and she are very dear to us all, and we of the Tyrol do not show ingratitude. See! das Mädchen is waking —she opens her eyes.'

'What is it, dear?' said Madge. 'Do you want to know about Joey? She is still asleep. The doctor is staying here for a while.'

'Will—she—be—very—ill?' The words came slowly.

'She is very tired,' said Madge evasively, 'but she hasn't got bronchitis like you. Now you must rest, you naughty child. We want you to get well again as quickly as possible. The holidays are very near, you know.' She bent to kiss the child, and Grizel relaxed.

'I'm glad,' she said. 'It wouldn't have been—fair if Joey—had to be ill—for me.'

Madge left her after that, and went back to the other sick-room. The doctor looked at her keenly, but, beyond a grunt, he said nothing. Throughout the long night he sat there, watching the little white face on the pillow, Madge watching with him. Once only he left her, to go and see Grizel, and came back with the news that she was decidedly stronger. At ten o'clock Frau Marani appeared, and Frau Mensch went back to the hotel at Seespitz. Five o'clock in the morning brought Miss Maynard to insist that Madge should lie down on the couch and rest for a couple of hours, while she watched in her turn. At seven the doctor went to ring up his partner in Innsbrück and warn him that he should stay where he was for that day. Later, Marie came with hot coffee, rolls, and butter, of which the doctor insisted Madge should partake, and at five to nine she went downstairs to see to work for the day.

The girls came with grave faces, and kind messages and offers of help from their parents. The whole lake-side knew of poor Grizel's escapade, and a good many people had since learned of the dreadful possible result for Joey, so there were many inquiries.

Amy Stevens' first care was to grab Juliet and demand in an awestruck whisper, 'How is Joey? Has she come awake yet?'

'Not yet,' said Juliet, who looked white and heavy-eyed. 'Don't ask Madame any questions, Amy, will you? She's so fearfully worried.'

'Course I sha'n't!' returned Amy indignantly. 'I say, isn't the bell late?'

'There won't be any bell at all to-day,' explained Juliet. 'Just go straight in to prayers.'

'Juliet, will you come here one minute?' said Gisela. 'We want to know about Joey and Grizel too. How are they both?'

Grizel is getting on fairly well,' replied Juliet. 'Joey hasn't roused up yet. They can't say till she does what will happen. The doctor expects it will be to-day, and he is staying. He was here all last night too.'

'I love the Herr Doktor,' said Gisela. 'He is a great friend of Papa's, and a very clever doctor. That is why Papa brought him.'

Prayers were very solemn that morning,

and when they were over, there was a little stir among the girls. Madge looked at them.

'Joey is much the same,' she said. 'There is no change—yet.'

She left the actual schoolwork to Mademoiselle and Miss Maynard, flitting in and out at intervals.

The weary day wore on, and still there was no news from the room at the top of the house. The girls behaved like angels, as Miss Maynard said afterwards. There could be no music lessons, of course, and Mademoiselle had rung up Herr Anserl to tell him. The news brought him post-haste to the Châlet. Joey's musical gifts were negligible, but she had won his heart by her deep interest in his book on *The Lives of Famous Austrian Musicians*, which she had declared to be 'jolly decent!'

He went away only after he had extracted a promise from Mademoiselle that she would ring him up the instant there was any news, and then went home, where he proceeded to make his housekeeper's life a burden by wandering about the rooms and turning up in all sorts of places where he was not wanted.

The one bright spot during the day was the fact that Grizel, reassured by their repeated statements that Joey was asleep, and also by Madge's obvious forgiveness, was improving rapidly, temperature going down, breathing easier.

At about three o'clock, as Madge was wearily trying to help Amy Stevens dis-

entangle a glorious muddle of rivers and lakes
in her map of Asia, word came down that the
doctor would like to see her for a moment.
Literally flinging the map at the astonished
Amy, she fled up the stairs to her bedroom.
The doctor was standing by the bedside, one
hand on Joey's wrist. He looked up as her
sister entered.

'Ah, mein Fräulein, I have sent for you,
for I think she is beginning to arouse. Please
stand just there, where she can see you.'

Madge took up the position he pointed out,
and stood, her eyes fixed on Joey's face.
There was no doubt that she was coming out
of the stupor. Her lashes flickered more than
once, her lips were parted. The only question
was, Would she wake up the old Joey, or would
it be to the babbling delirium of fever ?

There was a silence in the room that could
be felt. The only sound to be heard was the
breathing of the four people—Frau Mensch
was by the window—and the ticking of the
doctor's watch. Then, slowly, slowly, the
long black lashes lifted, and Joey looked full
at her sister.

'Hullo !' she murmured. 'I 'm awfully
tired ! Hai-yah !' She finished with a little
yawn, turned slightly, snuggling down into the
pillow, and fell asleep.

'Gott sei dankt !' said the doctor quietly.
'She will do now ; there is no further danger.
Hush, *mein Kind,*' for Madge had begun to
cry. 'It is well now !'

'I know,' sobbed Madge. 'But oh, Herr Doktor, the relief!'

He signed to Frau Mensch, who led her down to the study, and let her cry away the last of the awful weight that had been hanging over her. When, finally, the tears were all dried, she found a dainty meal of soup, roll, and grapes awaiting her, and when she had finished, Frau Mensch suggested bed.

'I must tell the girls first,' said Madge. 'I will make myself tidy, and go and tell them.'

Ten minutes later Miss Bettany, who looked like herself once more, entered the room where they were all anxiously awaiting her news. She looked at them, but no words would come to her lips. It was Bernhilda the quiet who helped her out.

'Ah, Madame,' she said, 'there is no need to say anything. Joey will get well.'

Madge found her voice. 'Yes,' she said. 'She is sleeping now, and all is safe once more.'

And there were rejoicings in the Châlet School that afternoon.

CHAPTER XXV.

FRAU BERLIN AGAIN.

'OH, I say! Isn't this perfectly golloptious!'

'Joey! What an appalling expression! Where on earth did you get it?'

'What? "Golloptious"? I heard those schoolboys we ran into at Tiern See use it.'

'Well, I wish you wouldn't. It's all very well for schoolboys, but it isn't pretty for schoolgirls, so cut it out!'

Joey cocked her black head on one side consideringly. 'Getting a bit old-maidish, aren't you, old thing?' she said. 'Don't do it, Madgie Machree!'

'Joey, you little brute! I won't be called such awful names! And you might show a little more respect for your headmistress. You get worse and worse every day!'

'Poor old darling! Never mind! Wait till we get back to school again, and then you can be as crushing as you like. This is holiday-time, and there's no one to hear us for once. I think it was topping of the Maranis to take Grizel and Juliet away for the week and let us be on our own for a bit. And this really is a gorgeous place! I never imagined anything like it!'

Madge nodded as she glanced up at the
great peaks of the Rosengarten Gebirge which
towered above them. Their own limestone
crags in the North Tyrol were magnificent,
but they were not to be compared with these.
As far as they could see, lofty pinnacles of
rose-hued rock lifted magnificent heads to the
summer skies. To the eyes of the two
standing on the balcony looking at them, it
seemed as if some mighty sculptor had been
at work, and had hewn out of the living rock
weird and awful shapes. Here, an ogre's
castle frowned down at them; there, some
terrible beast of prehistoric ages crouched,
ready to spring; there, again, the huge
turrets of a king's palace, built in the morning
of the world, still kept watch and ward over
the flower-strewn valley beneath it. Every
here and there, cataracts flung themselves
downwards in silver ribbons which leaped
from rock to rock, all hurrying to join the
river which dashed past, making thunderous
music as it went, for the two previous days
had been very wet, and all the springs and
mountain streams were flooded.

Neither Madge nor Jo had been in the
South Tyrol before, though both knew the
North Tyrol very well, and when Frau
Marani had come with the suggestion that
Grizel and Juliet should go to Vienna with
them for a week while the two sisters had a
little holiday to themselves, it had been Joey's
idea that they should come here.

'We can't go too far,' she argued. 'For
one thing, we can't afford it. We've never
seen Meran, or Botzen, or Primeiro, or any of
those other places, and the Mensches say the
Dolomites are just gorgeous. It's warm
there, so it'll suit us both, and it's been
rather chilly here lately. So let's go there;
shall us?'

Madge had laughed and agreed. There was
nothing to keep them at Tiern See. Miss
Maynard was spending the holiday with her
family in the high Alps, and Mademoiselle
had gone home to her beloved Paris, taking
Simone and the two little Stevens with her.
The Maranis' kind invitation had settled
Juliet and Grizel, and so, seven days previously,
the two Bettanys had left Innsbrück, *en route*
for Botzen, by way of the magnificent
Kuntersweg Gorge. Botzen they had loved,
and Meran was a dream of delight. They
had left the little Roman town only that
morning to establish themselves in the tiny
village of Paneirimo, in the Rosengarten
Valley; and here, on the morrow, the other
two girls would join them. Joey now turned
and slipped an arm through her sister's.
'It's been jolly on our own! Madge, when
shall we be on our own again?'

Madge smiled down into her serious face.
'Christmas,' she replied. 'Miss Maynard is
going to take the others to Munich for
Christmas, and you and I will be by ourselves.'

'Topping! I love school all right, but it's

rather a bore sometimes to have to remember you 're Head, and I 've got to be proper to you. Even to-morrow I shall have to be careful ! '

' Which reminds me,' interrupted Madge, ' I told them at the Châlet to forward letters here. You might run and see if there are any, Jo. I forgot to ask.'

' Righto ! ' And Joey dashed off, to return in a very few minutes waving a whole budget. ' Here you are ! Dozens of them ! At least there are ten—eight for you and two for me. This is from Simone, and this looks like Marie von Eschenau. Madge ! You aren't paying any attention ! What on earth 's the matter ? Who 's your letter from ? Is there anything wrong ? What is it ? '

Madge pulled herself together with an effort and turned to her little sister. ' It 's rather dreadful news in one way, Joey. There has been a terrible motor accident in Rome, and Captain and Mrs Carrick were in it.'

' I say ! That 's rather rotten ! ' Joey looked serious. ' Are they awfully hurt ? '

' Mrs Carrick was killed at once,' said Madge, ' and Captain Carrick died two days ago. He has left me Juliet to bring up, as they have no relations.'

' I say ! Poor old Ju ! What beastly luck for her ! And yet, I don't know ! '

' Read your own letters, Joey, and don't say anything about it yet. I 'm going to our bedroom, so I 'll be there when you want me ! ' And Madge gathered up her letters and vanished.

Joey sat looking after her. ' Coo ! But it 's a horrid thing to have happened ! I 'm frantically sorry for Juliet ! ' She was silent for a minute, then she turned to her own letters. ' Let 's see what Simone 's got to say ! ' and she was soon buried fathoms deep in Simone's epistle.

Meanwhile, Madge Bettany sat in their bedroom re-reading the letter written by a doctor of the hospital where Captain Carrick had died. After describing generally his injuries, the writer had continued : ' Captain Carrick told me that his daughter was with you, and that you would be her guardian. He made a will before he died, leaving all he possessed, including some very valuable jewellery belonging to his wife and a sum of one hundred thousand lire, in trust to you for the girl. He asked me to say he hoped you had forgiven the trick he played on you, and would undertake the trust. The money, I gathered, he had won at the tables at Monte Carlo. He died three hours after he had made the will.'

The letter concluded with a request to know how the jewels and money were to be sent, and a suggestion that Madge should come to Rome to fetch them, when ' my wife will be delighted to welcome you to our home as our guest.'

When she had finished re-reading this startling communication, Madge sat thinking hard. In one way, this event settled the Juliet difficulty, but it by no means completely solved it. She had not much knowledge of what the lira was doing at the moment, but she decided that the hundred thousand would probably resolve itself into about a thousand pounds in English currency. 'And that,' she thought, 'won't be very much for her. Of course there's the jewellery.' Pondering over the problem seemed to bring her no nearer its solution, so she shelved the matter for the moment and turned her attention to her other letters. One was from Mrs Dene, who had written to make final arrangements for Rosalie, who was coming to the Châlet School next term. Another came from Mrs Stevens, thanking her for her care of Margia and Amy, and enclosing a very welcome cheque for the next term's fees. The third she took up was on very expensive paper, in a most illiterate hand, and bore the postmark of Bradford, which puzzled her extremely.

'Bradford!' she said aloud. 'Who on earth do I know in Bradford?'

'Open the letter, old thing, then you'll find out!' observed Joey's voice from the doorway.

Madge literally jumped. Joey happened to be wearing plimsolls, and her steps had been quite noiseless.

'Sorry!' she observed, as she dropped down beside her sister. 'I didn't mean to startle you. I'd finished my letters, so I thought I'd come to see what you were doing. I say! If Captain Carrick has left Juliet to you, how does he imagine you're going to manage for money?'

'There's money for her,' returned Madge. 'You needn't worry, Joey. But I'm rather afraid we shall have to go back to Tiern See to-morrow. They want me to go to Rome to see about Juliet's affairs.'

'Rome? Oh, Madge, take me! Do! I've never seen Rome yet!'

'Don't be silly, Joey! Where do you think the money is coming from for the fares?'

'Oh, goodness! I never thought of that! Jo looked conscience-stricken for a moment. Then she turned the subject. 'Let's see who your Bradford pal is.'

Madge opened the letter and glanced at the beginning. 'Honoured and respected Madam.' 'Good heavens! Who on earth can it be from?' She turned to the end, but found no enlightenment there. The signature, finished off with a flourish, was 'James H. Kettlewell.'

'James H. Kettlewell! Never heard of him!' began Joey.

'No; and yet it's vaguely familiar.' Madge thought hard for a minute. 'Joey! I've got it! Do you remember the man in

the Paris train who gave us gooseberries?
His name was Kettlewell, and he told us he
lived at Bradford!'

'So he did! Whatever can he be writing
about? Buck up and see!'

'He said he'd try to get me some pupils.
It's probably that,' said her sister.

'Can I look over?'

'Yes, if you want to. Or I'll read it
aloud; shall I? You read far more quickly
than I do.'

'Righto! Fire ahead! I'm all ears!'

'Ahem! "Honoured and respected
Madam,"' began Madge, '"I take my pen
in hand to inscribe this present epistle to
you."'

'Coo! What elegant English!' commented Joey.

'Be quiet! If you interrupt, I won't read
it to you at all!'

'Sorry! I'll be good! Do get on! I'm
dying to know what it's about!'

'Where was I? Oh, yes! "It is with the
greatest diffidence that I venture to approach
you on such a subject, knowing, as I do,
the delicacy with which it should be treated,
especially to a high-up lady like you——"
What on earth—— Is the man mad?'

'Oh, get on!' implored Joey impatiently.
'Don't be so aggravating!'

'All right! It's my letter, remember!
Let's see—"lady like you. Believe me,
honoured Madam, I should not have the—

the—oh—the temerity to approach you thus
were it not that I feel——" ' Her voice died
away as her eyes wandered down the page.
Then she suddenly sat bolt upright with
horror. ' Joey! It 's a very private letter!
I——'

' I s'pose you mean it 's a proposal! ' Joey
interrupted her. ' Oh, I knew what was
coming after the very first sentence! Oh, I
say! ' And she went off into fits of laughter.

Madge shook her slightly. ' Joey, behave
yourself! It 's not a thing to laugh at! If
I 'd known, I 'd never have read it to you.
I thought it was just an ordinary letter.
You must give me your word of honour never
to mention it to a soul! '

' What do you take me for? ' Joey was
righteously indignant. ' Of course I sha'n't.'

' Oh dear! This is dreadful! ' Madge had
turned over the page and was reading on.

' But of all the weird things to happen! '
Joey got up and strolled over to the window.
' I scarcely ever thought of him again. He
was awfully sweet and kind, of course; but
I must say it seems a mad thing to do when
he 'd only seen you once. Why, he couldn't
know if you were good-tempered, or a decent
housekeeper, or—or truthful, or anything! '

' Oh, Joey, be quiet! ' exclaimed the
exasperated Madge. ' You 'd talk the hind-
leg off a donkey! Oh dear! Why does
everything come at once? '

' It 's rotten luck, old thing! ' Joey's

teasing mood had suddenly vanished. 'You have had a time of it since we came to Austria! Let's hope next term is quieter than this has been! One thing, Grizel can't go off climbing mountains!'

Madge got up, folding her letter and putting it back into its envelope.

'Joey, I don't want you to think I'm always saying "don't," but I'd rather not talk about that affair just yet. It's too soon after!'

'Poor old thing! You had the worst of it, 'cos you had all the awful waiting! It was hard luck on you!' replied Joey, rubbing her head against her sister's shoulder rather like a big dog.

Madge cast a thought to those dreadful hours when it had been doubtful what was going to happen to the speaker, and suddenly hugged her. 'It was all very horrible. We won't talk about it at all, Joey. Let's see what the other letters are.'

There was nothing exciting in them. Two of them were from the aunts in England, one from an old school-friend of Madge's, and the last asked for a prospectus of the school.

'Which I haven't got none!' said its head-mistress, relapsing into schoolgirl language. 'We'd better draw one up some time; and now, let's go for a saunter by the river.'

They sallied out, and strolled along by the banks of the rushing stream.

'It's been a weird affair all round!' said Jo presently, as she stood throwing in pebbles,

trying to make them skim the surface of the
water.

'What has?' demanded her sister, turning
from a dreamy contemplation of the bastions
and battlements of the great mountain wall.

'Why, all this—coming to Austria, and
having the school, and Juliet, and—and James
H. Kettlewell's letter, and everything!'

'Yes; but I don't see why you call it a weird
affair!' Madge was deeply interested. Jo's
imagination often helped to throw new light
on matters, and she wondered what new light
was going to be thrown on the Châlet School.

'Why, it's this way. We come out to
Tiern See because we're frantically poor.
You decide to start a school, and it goes like—
like fun. We do heaps of things in one term,
and we grow from three to eighteen. Then,
when the school is just going like everything,
you get a chance to chuck it if you want to,
and get married. We're jolly lucky, I think!'

Madge nodded. 'Yes, that's quite true.
But oh, if we're going to have the same sort
of excitements each term that we've had this,
I shall want to give it up!'

'Still, they haven't been bad excitements,
'cept the last—not really bad! Madge! Did
you ever! There's Frau Berlin!'

'Frau Berlin? Where? Joey, don't
point! It's frightfully rude!'

'There! By that house! Well, I be
gumswizzled!'

'Joey!'

'Well, but did you ever! Glory! She's
coming along! Wonder if she'll know me?'

But she passed them without a look, while
Joey gazed at her with wide-open eyes.

'She'll recognise Grizel,' she said, when
the tartan-clad lady had finally waddled out
of hearing. 'Oh, Madge, if she does!'

'I'm not going to risk any more fusses,'
said Madge with determination. 'If there's
the slightest chance of that, back we go to-
morrow.'

'P'r'aps it would be best. I say, I'm
awfully hungry! Let's go back an' see if we
can get anything to eat. It must be nearly
dinner-time.'

As Madge was hungry too, she agreed, and
presently they were enjoying a substantial meal.
Just as they had reached the dessert stage the
door opened, and in rolled Frau Berlin!

'That settles it!' murmured Miss Bettany.
'You may pack up to-night, for as soon
as Grizel and Juliet arrive we go back to
Tiern See. I think I must go to Rome after
all, so that will be all right. It will just fit
in nicely.'

As soon as they could, they left the
Speisesaal and retired to their room.

'That's the finish!' said Jo, as she finally
rolled into bed at about half-past nine.
'There can't be anything more after this.'

However, Miss Josephine Bettany was no
prophetess, and the morrow was to bring
them just one surprise more.

CHAPTER XXVI.

A GRAND WIND-UP.

'WHAT do you think? An old pal of yours is here, Grizel—a very dear friend!'

Grizel, thus greeted by a wildly excited Joey on her arrival at Paneirimo, looked at her suspiciously. 'Is it a plant?' she demanded.

'Rather not! It's an honest fact! We met her yesterday, and she's staying in the hotel.'

'Who on earth is it?'

'Guess!'

'Can't! Can't think of a soul likely to be in Austria! Who is it, Joey?'

'Think, Griselda! Think of someone you met a short while ago!'

'But I haven't met anyone except people you have too. Why is it a pal of mine?'

Grizel was so thoroughly puzzled and bewildered that she passed the hated version of her name.

'Someone you had a fearful row with,' Joey prompted her, jumping tantalisingly up and down.

'I can't think—— Joey! You don't mean Frau Berlin? Oh, it is—it is!'

'Well done you! Yes, it is. Well, what do you think of it?'

'My dear! It's awful! Has she seen you yet? Does she know, d' you think?'

Joey shook her head till it resembled an O-Cedar mop. 'Don't think so! Anyway, we're not staying. Madge won't risk it. You know, you were awfully rude, Grizel.'

'I s'pose I was. Well, I couldn't help it—she was such a pig! But what d' you mean by not staying? Where are we going?'

'Home! Oh, you don't know yet, of course!' Joey cast a wary eye at Madge and Juliet, who were walking ahead. 'Come on down to the river. We aren't going till the afternoon train, and we're to spend the night at Innsbrück. It's rather awful in some ways, but, on the whole, I think it might be worse. My sister had a letter from Rome yesterday, and Juliet's father and mother are dead.'

Grizel gasped. 'Joey! Oh, how dreadful! Poor Juliet! What will she do?'

'Her father's asked Madge to look after her, and he's left her some money to do it with,' said Joey. 'That's one reason why we're going home. Madge has to go to Rome to get it. We're going back to Briesau, and Miss Maynard is coming to look after us. She was coming anyhow, so that's all right. What sort of a time did you have in Vienna?'

'Tophole!' And Grizel plunged straightway into an account of her adventures.

When, finally, they turned their steps towards
the hotel, they saw Madge coming to meet
them. She was by herself, and was walking
rather slowly.

'Have you told Juliet?' said Joey in
hushed tones as she reached them.

'Yes; I want you two to be very kind
to Juliet. She's been through a good deal
lately, and, naturally, she is very much upset.
I needn't tell you not to hang round her or
do anything silly like that, but just be as
nice as you can to her. We are going back
to Innsbrück this afternoon, and then to-
morrow we shall go up to Tiern See, and I
shall have to leave you there, as I must go
to Rome to settle up affairs for her. Miss
Maynard will be with you, and I want you
to give her as little trouble as possible. I'm
sorry I can't send for her to come here, but,
under the circumstances, I'm afraid it's
rather impossible.'

Grizel coloured furiously, although her
headmistress had not attempted to make the
last remark specially pointed. She knew well
enough, however, that her behaviour at the
Alte Post was mainly the cause of their
leaving Paneirimo that afternoon. She said
nothing, but followed Joey into the hotel with
unaccustomed meekness. Madge, herself, had
said nothing about what had occurred on that
Saturday when Grizel had followed her own
wilful way and tried to climb the Tiernjoch;
but Frau Marani had had no scruples, and she

had told the child very plainly of what they had feared for Joey during the two long days which had followed. Grizel had had a dreadful shock, and she was never again so thoughtless, even though the worst of the subduedness wore off after a time.

'Where is Juliet?' asked Joey, as they reached the foot of the stairs.

'Upstairs in our room,' replied Madge. 'Yes, go to her, you two. Take them both out and show them the place, Joey. There are one or two odds and ends of packing I want to finish up, and I'd rather not risk a fuss with that Frau Berlin, as you call her. So keep out of the way till luncheon. Our train goes at three, so you won't have much time here. Make the most of it.'

Upstairs in the big airy room with its twin beds they found Juliet standing at the window staring listlessly out at the mountains. She was not crying, as Joey had half feared, but she had a white, worn look, as though she had been ill, and her eyes were heavy and weary.

'Come an' see the mountains, old Ju!' said Joey, slipping her hand into the elder girl's. 'They're topping, though not a bit like ours at home, of course!'

'Yes, do come!' urged Grizel. 'And oh, Juliet, that awful old woman's here!'

'Which one?' asked Juliet, though with a complete lack of interest in her voice.

'Frau Berlin—the one who was such

a pig the day we went to Innsbrück to
get Madame's birthday gift. Don't you
remember ? '

' Oh, yes, I remember. All right, Joey,
I 'll come.'

But though she let them pull her downstairs and out into the sunshine, it seemed as
though she didn't really care much what she
did. The shock of hearing what Madge had
told her, even though the news had been
broken to her with great gentleness, had dazed
her for the time being. Through all the
chatter of the other two she was conscious
of just one thought—' If only I could have
felt they loved me ! '

However, the fresh air and sunshine did her
good, and when, finally, Miss Bettany came
to summon them to lunch, she looked better
than she had done.

No contretemps occurred with Frau Berlin,
for she did not appear. Nevertheless, Madge
felt very thankful when she found herself
safely in the Innsbrück train without having
had a scene. Juliet settled herself in a corner
with a book, but she did not appear to read
much. Most of the time she was gazing
unseeingly out of the window. The other
two had retired to the far end of the compartment, which they had to themselves, and
at Joey's bright suggestion embarked on a
game of Roadside Cribbage. Madge, sitting
with one eye on the silent girl opposite her
and the other on the *Wien Zeitung*, occasion-

ally heard exclamations of 'Three goats—
thirty!' 'Waterfall—five!' 'Mule—oh, bust
it! Back to the beginning!' but paid no
attention. She was not desperately interested
in her paper either. For the most part, her
thoughts were with the coming term. She
would have twenty-six girls this time, and
of these, twelve would be boarders. If the
school went on growing, she knew that she
must either build on to the present Châlet,
or else take another somewhere near. She
was not quite certain what to do. Herr
Marani and Herr Mensch were very good
friends to her, but she wished heartily that
Dick were at hand to advise her.

As she was thinking of this, she suddenly
became aware that the train was slackening
speed, and even as she looked up to see where
they were, it began to rock violently backwards and forwards with a sickening motion.
She had barely time to leap to her feet before,
with a mighty crash, the carriage gave a final
lurch and collapsed on its side. Above the
noise she heard the screams of the three girls,
mingling with shrieks from the other passengers. Mercifully, Joey had flung herself on
the floor, dragging Grizel with her; and, by
a positive miracle, neither Madge nor Juliet
had been badly hurt, though the former
was, like everyone else, slightly stunned, and
Juliet, as they found out after, was badly
bruised. Also, being thoroughly English,
they had had the window wide open, and so

had a means of exit. The door, when Miss Bettany tried it, was jammed.

'It's a good thing none of us are fat,' she said with a shaky laugh. 'Come along, you three; I'm going to push you through the window. Grizel first.'

Grizel had the sense to make no protests; besides, she was still rather dazed, so she allowed her headmistress to push and tug till she was through, and then, as the fresh air began to clear her stupefied brain, she reached down and helped to pull Juliet up. Joey was an easy matter, and she was soon standing on a heap of stones, looking very white and scared, while the two big girls dragged her sister out. They had just pulled her clear when, from the front of the train, came the dreaded cry of 'Fire!'

'Das Feuer! Das Feuer!' shrieked a fat woman, who was badly jammed in the window-frame of the next compartment.

If there had not been such appalling possibilities at hand, Madge could have burst out laughing. As it was, she flung a hasty 'Stay where you are! Don't dare to move!' at the terrified girls and dashed to the rescue. The scene was becoming ghastly. The big engine and three of the long carriages lay on their sides in a narrow gorge-like way. The foremost carriage was already wrapped in flames, and their roaring rose above the screams and cries of the people still imprisoned in the other carriages. The three remaining

on their wheels had disgorged all their
passengers, and already men were tearing
along, working madly to save those in such
deadly peril. Madge Bettany contrived to
take in all these things as she made that
frantic scramble on to the side of the carriage,
where a terrified fat woman, with grey hair
streaming wildly round her, was struggling
madly to get free of the window-frame, which
held her gripped as in a vice.

Through all the horror of it the English
girl contrived to keep her head.

' Steady ! ' she said, as she took the gripping
hands, and though the language was a foreign
one and a hated one, her voice brought self-
control to the maddened woman.

' I cannot get free,' she panted in German.
' Fräulein——'

' Keep still a moment ! Now ! Ready !
Then, as hard as you can ! '

Certainly Madge's slight form gave no
evidence of great strength. She said afterwards that she was possessed at the moment.
However that may be, there was a struggle, a
sound of rending and tearing, a sudden gasp,
and then the other woman suddenly shot out
over the wheels and on to the heap of stones,
her clothes in shreds, but otherwise safe.
Madge sprang down beside her, and then she
felt the world turning black, and she fainted.
When she came to herself she was lying on a
coat in a field. Joey was kneeling beside her,
crying vehemently, and a big fair man whom

she did not know was holding something to her lips. With an effort she pulled herself together and pushed it away.

' No, no,' she said.

' Oh, Madge ! ' sobbed Joey. ' O—ooh ! I thought you—you w—were dead ! '

' Hush ! ' said the man. ' She 'll be all right in a minute, kiddy. It 's only whisky-and-water I 'm giving you, Madam. Better take a little to buck you up ! '

' No ; I 'm all right ! ' With an effort she sat up, pushing the hair off her face. Joey promptly flung her arms round her, hugging her tightly. Juliet and Grizel seemed to have vanished.

' Oh, Madge darling ! Oh, I had such a fright ! Oh, Madge ! '

' There ! That 'll do,' said their benefactor. ' You 're not helping her, kid. Let her alone for a minute or two to come round. It 's quite all right—the other kids are safe enough, and—oh, you plucky girl ! It was one of the bravest things I 've ever seen ! '

' It was nothing,' returned Madge, who was rapidly coming to herself. ' Joey ! Don't strangle me, child ! Let me get up ! '

She contrived to get on to her feet, but was glad enough of the arm the stranger flung round her as she swayed for a moment.

' There ! ' he said rather roughly. ' Come over here and sit down a minute ! You can't do everything at once ! I 'll send the other kids along, and you 'll be all right in a minute.

No, there's nothing you can do. Everyone got clear but the driver. He fell on his head, poor chap! Even your fat rescue is recovered enough to fuss about having no skirt on——'

' Yes; and oh, Madge, who do you think it is ? ' interrupted Joey, with considerable lack of both manners and grammar. ' It 's Frau Berlin ! '

' Oh, goodness ! ' And Madge began to laugh weakly.

' Isn't it rum ? And we left Paneirimo because of her and Grizel, and then you save her life ! Yes, you did. The carriage got on fire just as you slithered down. If it hadn't been for you, she 'd have been burnt to death ! She was only bumped a bit, and she wanted to kiss you, only that man came and hiked you off into this field, and she suddenly found her clothes were all torn, so she wouldn't follow us ! Grizel and Juliet are over there. They aren't hurt, and nor am I. Do buck up, Madge ! '

Thus Joey, in a breathless, hurrying tumult of words.

' That man ' stood to one side, smiling, as the elder girl managed to take it all in. Then Grizel and Juliet appeared, and all the excitement began over again. At length he interfered.

' Now then, you kids, let 's go and see what we can do about getting on. I know this place, and we 're about ten miles from anywhere. Besides, Miss——? '

' Bettany,' supplied Madge. ' These are my sister Joey, and two of my pupils— Grizel Cochrane and Juliet Carrick.'

' Ah, thank you,' he replied. ' My name's Russell—James Russell, at your service. Well, as I was going to say, Miss Bettany, you had better get somewhere where you can lie down for a bit. There's a main road goes past here somewhere, and, with luck, we ought to get a lift in something. If you will take my arm, I think we can get there all right, and we can't do anything here.'

There was common sense in what he said, so they set off, Madge beginning to realise how very shaky she still felt. The girls were upset too, and it took them some time to make the high-road. Luckily, just as they reached it, a peasant came past with an empty hay-cart. Mr Russell quickly came to an arrangement with him, and a couple of hours later they were safely in the *Gasthaus* of a tiny village, Madge beginning to realise that the headache she was enduring was well on its way to beating anything of the kind she had ever suffered, while the three girls were stiff and aching. They stayed there all night, their new friend going on to Innsbrück after leaving his card with Joey and getting the Châlet address, so that he could wire to Miss Maynard not to expect them for another day. The morning found them all very tired and worn out, but Madge wanted to get back to Tiern See and home, so they set off, and finally arrived at the Châlet, where they were rapturously welcomed by an anxious Miss Maynard, who had been feeling very worried. Mr James Russell had been better than his word, for he had gone up to Tiern See and given her a full description of what had occurred.

'I'm thankful you've all arrived safely,' said the young mathematics mistress. 'I couldn't feel sure you wouldn't have another awful adventure.'

'I think I'd rather keep out of adventures for some time to come,' laughed Madge rather shakily. 'Teaching and school generally will be enough for me for the next three or four years, I can assure you.'

'Oh, I expect we'll have some more adventures presently,' said Joey.

And so they did. But that, as Mr Kipling says, is another story.

THE END.

Books by MAY BALDWIN.

A RIPPING GIRL.	6/- net
A CITY SCHOOLGIRL	5/- net
A SCHOOLGIRL OF MOSCOW	5/- net
A SCHOOLGIRL OF THE BLUE	5/- net
MRS MANNING'S WARDS	5/- net
ONLY PAT: A NAIROBI SCHOOLGIRL	5/- net
PEG'S ADVENTURES IN PARIS	5/- net
THREE PICKLES IN AND OUT OF SCHOOL	5/- net
A POPULAR GIRL	4/- net
A RIOTOUS TERM AT ST NORBERT'S	4/- net
MISS PETER	4/- net
SPOILT CYNTHIA AT SCHOOL	4/- net
THE BRILLIANT GIRLS OF THE SCHOOL	4/- net
THE GIRLS' ETON	4/- net
A PLUCKY GIRL.	3/6 net
A SCHOOLGIRL'S DIARY	3/6 net
CORAH'S SCHOOL CHUMS	3/6 net
DORA: A HIGH SCHOOL GIRL	3/6 net
GIRLS OF ST GABRIELS	3/6 net
HIGH-JINKS AT PRIORY SCHOOL	3/6 net
HILDA'S EXPERIENCES.	3/6 net
HOLLY HOUSE AND RIDGE'S ROW	3/6 net
KENYA KIDDIES	3/6 net
MURIEL AND HER AUNT LU	3/6 net
ROONI	3/6 net
SARAH'S SCHOOL FRIEND	3/6 net
SUNSET ROCK	3/6 net
THE SCHOOL IN THE WILDS	3/6 net
THE TWINS MAKE GOOD	3/6 net
GOLDEN SQUARE HIGH SCHOOL	3/- net
MOLL MEREDYTH, MADCAP	3/- net
BARBARA BELLAMY	2/6 net
IRENE TO THE RESCUE	2/6 net
PHYLLIS M'PHILEMY	2/6 net
SIBYL; or, OLD SCHOOL FRIENDS	2/6 net
JEAN AND THE BOYS	2/6 net
TEDDY AND LILY'S ADVENTURES	2/6 net
THAT LITTLE LIMB.	2/- net

W. & R. CHAMBERS, Ltd., London and Edinburgh.